HEART
QUEST.

Romance the way it's meant to be

HeartQuest brings you romantic fiction
with a foundation of biblical truth.
Adventure, mystery, intrigue, and suspense
mingle in these heartwarming stories of
men and women of faith striving to build
a love that will last a lifetime.

May HeartQuest books sweep you
into the arms of God, who longs for you
and pursues you always.

catching
katie

ROBIN LEE
HATCHER

HEART
QUEST.

Romance fiction from
Tyndale House Publishers, Inc., Wheaton, Illinois

www.heartquest.com

Visit Tyndale's exciting Web site at www.tyndale.com

Check out the latest about HeartQuest Books at www.heartquest.com

HeartQuest is a registered trademark of Tyndale House Publishers, Inc.

Edited by Traci L. DePree

Designed by Jenny Swanson

Scripture quotations are taken from the *Holy Bible,* King James Version.

Scripture quotation in the epigraph is taken from the *Holy Bible,* New Living Translation,
copyright © 1996. Used by permission of Tyndale House Publishers, Inc., Wheaton, Illinois 60189.
All rights reserved.

Library of Congress Cataloging-in-Publication Data

Hatcher, Robin Lee.
   Catching Katie / Robin Lee Hatcher.
      p. cm. — (HeartQuest)
ISBN 0-8423-6099-9
1. Suffragists—Fiction. 2. Idaho—Fiction. I. Title. II. Series.
PS3558.A73574 C38 2004
813'.54—dc21   2003013281

Printed in the United States of America

09 08 07 06 05 04
9 8 7 6 5 4 3 2 1

In memory of my grandmother,
Madge Ruth Ashmore Johnson,
1880-1963.

A masterful storyteller,
A farmer's wife,
A mother to four daughters—
my wonderful mom among them—
A woman who loved Jesus Christ and God's Word,
And a candidate for public office in Idaho so long ago.

There is no longer Jew or Gentile, slave or free, male or female. For you are all Christians—you are one in Christ Jesus.

GALATIANS 3:28

All my life I have been devoted to the advancement of women in education and opportunity.
I firmly believe God has a work for them to do as evangelists, as bearers of Christ's message to the ungospeled, to the prayer meeting, to the church generally and to the world at large, such as most people have not dreamed.

FRANCES WILLARD,
FOUNDER OF THE WOMEN'S CHRISTIAN TEMPERANCE UNION

ONE

The Homestead Weekly Herald
Homestead, Idaho
Friday Morning
May 19, 1916

Local Woman Returns to Homestead

The Homestead Herald has recently learned that Miss Katherine L. Jones, daughter of Mr. and Mrs. Yancy Jones of the Lazy L Ranch, is returning to Homestead next week after residing in the East for several years. Miss Jones was born and raised in Long Bow Valley and is a 1913 graduate of Vassar College in Poughkeepsie, New York.

A welcome-home potluck is being planned for Friday, May 26, at the Homestead Community Church. Everyone is invited.

The wind tugged at Katie's hat, and mud splattered her duster as the motorcar bumped and rocked its way toward Homestead. Katie had driven on more than a few bad roads in recent weeks, but none so deplorable as this one between Idaho's capital city and Katie's hometown.

Not that she hadn't been warned.

"You ain't meanin' t' take that 'mobile up thataway, are you?" the old man at the Boise hotel had asked her last night. "That road's not fit for those confounded contraptions. If'n you had a lick o' sense, you'd wait and take the train, young lady."

It certainly would have been easier to heed the man's advice, but she hadn't wanted to wait until Friday. The Susan B, as Katie fondly called the intrepid—and often cantankerous—Model T Ford, had come too far, had climbed too many hills in reverse, to be left behind now. The motorcar wasn't about to be undone by a few more deep ruts or other adverse road conditions.

Nor was Katie herself.

She thought of her father as she tightened her grip on the steering wheel. Yancy Jones wasn't going to be any too pleased when he learned that his daughter had motored, unaccompanied by an escort, across the country in her own automobile. Her father was old-fashioned in many ways. Although she knew he loved her and tried to be tolerant of his freethinking daughter, he didn't care for many of Katie's newfangled notions.

That's why she hadn't told her parents in her most recent letter, which informed them of her upcoming visit to Homestead, that for the past several weeks she'd been a participant in the Suffrage Special, as it was known in the newspapers. Touring the West by motorcar, the gifted speakers and leaders of the suffrage movement were calling upon women voters to help form a new political party dedicated to the passage of a national woman's suffrage amendment. Katie had felt privileged to be a part of the entourage, for she was an impassioned supporter of the movement.

Suffrage would give women full rights of citizenship. It would give them access to better educational opportunities. It would open doors to their ability to serve in professions such as medicine and the law. It would help women campaign for social purity and for adequate housing. It would help win the fight against permissive work laws. Suffrage would offer protection for women who were abused or abandoned. It would give them more autonomy in matters related to property rights and child custody.

Katie couldn't understand why there was any resistance at

all, especially among Christian women, to the passage of suffrage. Evangelical Christianity, which had spread with the Second Great Awakening in America, emphasized the moral and religious autonomy of women and established women's moral authority in the priesthood of all believers. Many of the leaders in both the National American Woman Suffrage Association and in the Woman's Christian Temperance Union were women of strong faith as well as strong convictions.

The front tire hit a large hole, sending the Susan B jouncing toward the edge of the road and the sharp drop-off to the river below. Katie felt her hair slipping free of its pins as her hat slid sideways on her head. The end of her scarf flew up into her face, blinding her. Quickly she braked, bringing the motorcar to an abrupt halt. She let out an exasperated sigh as she tried to right her touring hat, but all she succeeded in doing was loosening the remainder of her hairpins, causing her hair to tumble into her face.

"Oh, bother," she muttered in frustration. She removed the straw bonnet and shoved back the mass of hair. "I've a good mind to cut it all off." Men wore their hair short so they didn't have to be concerned with such nonsense. Maybe she *would* cut it once she got to Homestead. Nothing like a fast hairstyle to get folks talking.

With a quick twist and the jab of a few hairpins, Katie secured her hair atop her head once more, then set her hat back in place. A glance at the sun hovering above the canyon rim told her she'd best hurry if she wanted to reach town before dark. Although the Susan B was equipped with headlamps, it would be hazardous to negotiate this winding river canyon after nightfall. Katie certainly didn't warm to the idea of spending the night on the road, sleeping in the motorcar.

Besides, she was excited about getting home. It had been three years since her parents had come back East for her graduation from Vassar College, and she hadn't seen her brothers, Sammy and Ricky, in seven years. They were young men now instead of the boys of ten and nine she'd left behind.

Then there was Ben Rafferty. Dearest, best, beloved Benjie. It would be grand to see him again. He was the only one who hadn't tried to dissuade her from remaining in the East, working for the NAWSA. His letters while she was at school and then in Washington had been filled with encouragement. He'd always told her to pursue her calling, no matter what stood in the way.

That was exactly what she'd done.

She'd had dreams for Ben, too, and she wondered why he'd returned to Homestead after his graduation from college. He could have had a marvelous career in any number of cities around the country. He could have made a name for himself, become a famous man of letters. Instead he'd gone to work for the *Homestead Herald* and then purchased the newspaper when Mr. Bonnell, the owner, died.

But wasn't it lucky for me that he did?

Katie accelerated, her mind churning as fast as the tires on the bumpy road. She had much to accomplish now that she was coming home.

Home. She was surprised how good the word made her feel. Of course, it wouldn't be the same town she'd left behind. So much must have changed. Some of the older folks had died. Some of the younger people had moved away. Most of her schoolmates were married and had children.

What will they think of me?

She knew the answer to that question. They would think her as strange as they always had.

"Too headstrong for your own good," her father had told her more than once.

"Just like me," her mother had countered every time. "I knew what I wanted and went after it. That's how I got your father to marry me."

Katie grinned at the memory. Yes, it was good to be coming home. Until recently she hadn't realized how much she was needed in Idaho. Not until Inez Milholland, the spirited suffragette lawyer, had explained to Katie the good she could do.

"Miss Jones," Inez had said a few months ago, "you come from one of the few enfranchised states in our Union. But are the women of Idaho exercising their right to participate in their government? I fear not in the numbers they should. We must find a way to see they do so, for all our sakes. It is women for women now and shall be until the fight is won. We shall stand shoulder to shoulder for the greatest principle the world has known, the right of self-government. Victory is in sight, Miss Jones. We must not let it slip away for lack of attention."

Katie felt a shiver of excitement roll up her spine as she recalled Milholland's words. She must not fail the women who were working so tirelessly in support of a federal suffrage amendment. She must do her part. She *would* do her part.

Her attention returned to the road as the mountains suddenly parted and she beheld her first glimpse in seven years of Long Bow Valley and, in the distance, Homestead.

Katie was home.

———— ✦ ————

Ben frowned as he read over his editorial for the third time. It was boring. The words were as dry as dust, pure and simple. With a sigh, he dropped the papers onto his desk, then leaned back in his swivel chair and rubbed his eyes with his knuckles. He wondered if he was ever going to get it right.

Staring at the ceiling, he allowed his thoughts to drift once again to Katie. Only three more days and she would be here. And it was about time, too. When he'd left Homestead to go to school eleven years before, he'd never dreamed it would be so long before he saw his dearest friend again. He hadn't expected her to go off to college four years later and then choose not to return. His mother feared Katie had been gone so long they wouldn't recognize her, but Ben knew that was impossible.

He remembered the little girl with the thick black braids reaching to her waist and the enormous brown eyes that had seemed too big for her face. He remembered the tomboy, often dressed in shirt and trousers, scabs on her knees, scrapes on her hands. He remembered the girl who could swing a baseball bat as hard as any boy in Homestead and who was absolutely fearless as she raced her horse alongside the train. He remembered his childhood pal in a hundred different ways, and all of them made him smile.

Katie Jones was unforgettable.

She was certainly different from Charlotte Orson, the young woman Ben had been keeping company with of late. Charlotte, the daughter of a minister, was quiet and unassuming. Not in his wildest dreams could he imagine Charlotte in trousers or swinging a baseball bat or riding a horse astride. No, Charlotte was much more conventional than the irrepressible Katie.

Ben closed his eyes and rubbed his forehead with the fingertips of one hand.

There were many in Homestead who'd already decided Ben and Charlotte were perfect together. A few figured they'd be married before year's end. But Ben wasn't convinced. Not yet anyway. He was fond of Charlotte, of course, and he hoped his feelings would deepen with time. The Bible said, "Whoso findeth a wife findeth a good thing, and obtaineth favour of the Lord." He believed that to be true. He wanted a home and a wife and children. But how did a man know when he'd found the right woman to be his wife? Was fondness enough? He didn't know. He just didn't know.

With a shake of his head, Ben opened his eyes and looked at the partially written editorial on his desk. It hadn't changed itself in the last few minutes while he'd been daydreaming. It was still boring, boring, boring. He picked up his pen, promising himself that he would finish it, even if he had to sit there until the wee hours of the morning.

Maybe if he added a paragraph right here, and then—

"You're working late, Mr. Rafferty."

He glanced up, surprised that someone had entered without his hearing the door open.

The woman smiled. "Haven't you a welcome for an old friend?"

Ben stood. "Katie?"

"Have I changed so much?"

Had Katie changed? *Yes!* When had she become a woman? A beautiful woman? And despite the flecks of mud on her cheeks and clothes, she *was* beautiful. She hadn't been beautiful before, had she? Ben didn't think so. She'd just been Katie.

A frown replaced her smile. "Well, for pity's sake, say something."

He moved from behind his desk, stepping toward her, studying her face for some sign of the gawky schoolgirl he remembered. Her eyes were the same luminous dark brown, but they no longer seemed too big for her face. Her complexion was smooth, her skin the color of honey. She was still tiny, a good foot shorter than he was, but she was noticeably more curvaceous than the girl he'd left behind. The braids were gone, he suspected, but he couldn't be certain because of the broad-brimmed hat and scarf she wore.

"Have I *really* changed so much?" she repeated.

"I can't believe it's you."

Her dazzling smile returned. "It's me all right, Benjie." Then, without warning, she threw herself into his arms and kissed him on the cheek as she hugged him tightly. Her laughter warmed the office like a fresh ray of sunshine. "Oh, Benjie, it's so good to see you."

Suddenly he laughed with her, all else forgotten. "It's good to see you, too." He set her back from him, his hands still on her upper arms. "How did you get here? You're not expected until Friday."

"I arrived in Boise City yesterday and decided to drive up. My motorcar is out front."

"You *drove*?"

"All the way from Washington, D.C. I've been following the Suffrage Special on its tour of the West in the Susan B."

"The Susan B?"

Katie took hold of his hand and drew him toward the door. "She's my Ford touring car. I named her for Susan B. Anthony. Come take a look at her."

This was Katie all right. Leave it to her to be the first valley resident to own an automobile. Leave it to her to motor clear across the country regardless of conventions that said a woman shouldn't do such things.

"There she is." Katie waved an arm toward the Model T Ford parked in front of the *Homestead Herald* office. "Isn't she scrumptious?" She squeezed his fingers as she turned toward him. "Will you drive out with me to the Lazy L? I'm sure Papa will loan you a horse to get back to town, and I'd love to talk with you awhile. It's been so long since we've seen each other, and I want to catch up on all the news."

"Don't want to face your father alone, huh?"

She lifted her chin defiantly. "That's not it at all."

"No?"

"No."

"No?"

Katie pursed her lips for a moment, then broke into a

smile. "All right. Maybe that is it. A little. But *just* a little." She stepped closer, and he caught a whiff of rose water. "Honestly, Benjie, I do want to talk with you."

When Ben was twelve and Katie just shy of eleven, she had told him she wouldn't ever marry. She'd wanted to accomplish something special. Even then, Katie had been a girl with big dreams and a desire to change the world for the better. Now, seeing that she was no longer the girl of his memories, he wondered if there was a special man in her life, someone who might change her ideas about marriage and settling down.

"Say you will, Benjie. Please?"

Memories of Katie saying those same words rushed over him—*Say you will, Benjie. Please?*—and he knew it was useless to argue. She would get her way before she was through. It had always been so between them.

He nodded. "Let me get my hat and lock up."

━━◆━━

While Ben was still inside, Katie let her gaze wander the length and breadth of Main Street. She was surprised by the emotions she felt at the sight of her hometown. She hadn't thought she wanted to return to Homestead, to leave her friends and the intense activities of Washington for the quiet sameness of Idaho. Yet now that she was here, she was glad. It was here, right down the street in the Homestead Community Church, where she'd first felt God tugging on her heart, placing in her a desire to make a difference for good in the lives of others. Coming home again had stirred up so many memories, memories that had already strengthened her resolve to complete the work God had set before her.

She heard the door close. She glanced at Ben as he stepped up beside her.

Homestead might not have changed much, but the same couldn't be said for Ben Rafferty. He'd grown tall, and his shoulders were amazingly broad beneath the cut of his suit coat. The angles of his face had sharpened, matured. The boyish good looks had more than fulfilled their promise in the man he'd become. The color of his hair—which brushed his collar and begged to be trimmed—had darkened to a rich shade of gold. She thought it a shame when he placed his hat on his head, hiding it from view.

"Ready?" he asked, glancing down and meeting her gaze.

She felt a sudden embarrassment, as if she'd been caught doing something inappropriate.

"Katie?"

She saw a teasing good humor in his dark blue eyes, and her embarrassment vanished. This was Benjie. This was her dearest friend in the world.

"I'm ready," she answered.

Ben took hold of her arm and guided her toward the passenger door. "Mind if I do the driving?"

She cast a dubious look in his direction.

"I *know* how to drive, Katie. I went to college, too."

It was on the tip of her tongue to tell him she never allowed anyone else to drive her motorcar, but his next words caused her to swallow the argument unspoken.

"You wouldn't withhold the pleasure from me, would you?" He ran his fingers along the side of the door. "It's been a long time since I've had the opportunity."

"Of course you may drive her, Benjie. Anytime you wish."

Grinning like a schoolboy, Ben reached inside the automobile and pulled the latch, then opened the door with a flourish and assisted Katie onto the running board and into the Susan B. When she was settled and the door once again closed, he went around to the opposite door, reached in, and set the levers. He whistled a tuneless melody as he walked to the front of the motorcar and gave the engine crank a hefty turn. Without a trace of her sometimes temperamental behavior, the Susan B sprang to life.

Straightening, Ben shot Katie a look of pure joy before returning to the driver's side, where he vaulted over the stationary door and settled onto the seat behind the wheel. A few minutes later, the two of them were well on their way to the Lazy L Ranch.

Ben had forgotten how much he enjoyed driving an automobile. Homestead had a way of making one forget there was a whole other world beyond this valley and the surrounding mountains. Maybe it was good to remind himself of that fact every so often.

Overhead, dusk splashed the smattering of clouds with shades of pink, announcing the coming of night.

"The headlamps are electric," Katie said softly.

Her voice drew Ben's gaze in her direction. She was holding her hat on with one hand while the fingers of her other hand fiddled with a button on her duster.

"It hasn't changed much, has it?" he asked.

"Homestead?" She shook her head. "No. Not much."

"Surprised?"

"Not really." She smiled. "Tell me about the newspaper."

"Nothing much to tell. It's still a weekly. I do everything but the typesetting. Harvey Trent does that. Harv's the best typesetter west of the Mississippi. He used to work for the *Idaho Daily Statesman* down in Boise, but I lured him away." He chuckled, remembering how hard it had been to convince the man to move to Homestead.

"Do you write all the articles and columns?"

"Yes."

"It must be a great deal of work. Week after week. Maybe you should hire a columnist to help you."

"A columnist?"

Katie met his gaze and flashed him another smile. "Don't you think a woman's column would be of interest to your readers? Of *course* it would be of interest. Women read your newspaper, too. Don't you think they would enjoy a column from a woman's perspective?"

"And who would write this column?"

She twisted on the car seat, then leaned forward, touching his arm. "Oh, Benjie, there is so much they need to hear. Do you know how fortunate the women of Idaho are, to be able to vote? But so many waste that right. It's a right that should be exercised, but they throw it away, leaving it up to men to decide what happens in our country. If only we could make them see—"

"*We?*" He allowed the automobile to roll to a stop.

Katie's eyes danced with excitement. "Yes. *We*. Don't you see how much good we could do? You own the newspaper, and I have so much to share about the world beyond this valley. Wonderful things are happening that could make life better for women and children. I've met some of the most distinguished and gifted women in the country. Even now they're calling upon women voters of the enfranchised states to—"

"Hold up a minute, Katie."

Her expression sobered.

Ben searched his mind for the right words. It wasn't that he didn't support suffrage for women. He did. A woman's vote was as valid as any man's, just as a woman's life was as valuable in God's eyes as any man's. He believed changes in the law were needed—and were surely coming—that would protect the rights of women. But he believed slow and easy was the better way. He wasn't convinced that Homestead—or the rest of Idaho, for that matter—was ready for Katie Jones, suffragette. Katie never did anything halfway. She would stir up a hornet's nest in no time.

And there he'd be, smack-dab in the middle of it.

Her fingers tightened on his arm. "Benjie, you mustn't disappoint me." Her voice was low and earnest. Her gaze never wavered from his. "I need your help."

He looked away, staring off toward Tin Horn Pass and the darkening skyline. A woman's column. Perhaps it wasn't a bad idea. Hadn't he just been thinking that the *Homestead Herald* lacked sparkle? An article or two from Katie would no doubt give it that.

"You know I wouldn't ask if this weren't important to me, Benjie. I'm certain God made me for such a time as this. Everything in my past has led me back here for this moment. To help people."

"I don't know. A column—"

"I received very high marks in composition while at Vassar College, Mr. Rafferty, and I'll be happy to provide references related to my work experience and performance, should you require them."

He glanced at her, but the light had grown too dim to tell if she was teasing him or not.

"Benjie, I need someone to support me in this."

He sighed. That was it, then. There was no point resisting any longer. "Do you have a title for this proposed column of yours?"

Katie leaned toward him and kissed his cheek. "As a matter of fact, I do. I plan to call it 'Unshackled.' "

" 'Unshackled'?"

"Isn't it wonderful? Penny—you remember me writing you all about Penelope Rudyard?—she thought of it. Penny said women must be unshackled from the restraints that have bound them for centuries, but before they can break free they must first realize they're in bondage. That's what my column will do. Help women see the truth that God has a plan for them just as He does for men. Do you like it? Don't you think it will catch women's attention?"

Yes, he thought it would catch women's attention. And the attention of a few men about town, too. "I'll have to give it some thought, Katie."

⊷ ⊨♦⊨ ⊶

Katie's heart raced as the Susan B puttered slowly toward the Lazy L, the way lighted by the automobile's electric head-lamps. The ranch house stood at the end of the road, a black silhouette against a backdrop of mountains. Golden light spilled through the windows, looking warm and inviting.

Katie felt a tumble of nerves as the house came into view. Odd. This was her home, yet she felt like a stranger. She'd left this place a girl and now was coming back a woman. Would everything at the ranch be as changed as she was? But Homestead was still the same. Could the Lazy L be so different?

As if he'd read her mind, Ben said, "Everyone's missed you, Katie. They'll all be glad to have you home."

She swallowed hard as she saw two male figures run into the light from the house. They were joined a moment later by a third man. Once again Katie leaned forward, straining to see more clearly. Could Sammy and Ricky have grown so tall, or were those some of the ranch hands? Were they men she would know, or had her papa hired new cowboys to work the place? Was one of them Papa himself? Then a woman—it had to be her mother—stepped onto the porch, and Katie's heart skipped a beat in anticipation.

As the motorcar rolled into the yard, Katie heard a shout. "It's Katie!"

The car stopped, and everyone rushed forward.

The next few minutes were a blur of hugs and kisses and exclamations. Her brothers had, indeed, grown tall—so tall, her feet left the ground when they hugged her. Her mother smelled of lemon verbena, as always. And her father . . .

Yancy cupped the side of her face with one work-roughened palm. "I reckon I'm as pleased as a flea in a doghouse t' have you home, Katie Lark. 'Bout time, too." Then he hugged her tightly.

I love you, Papa. Her throat was too tight to say the words aloud.

"Where'd you get the automobile, Ben?" Rick asked.

"It belongs to Katie."

She felt her father stiffen as he stepped back. "Yours?"

She nodded, holding herself as straight and tall as possible. "Yes." She drew a deep breath, then added, "I drove up from Boise City this morning."

Rick whistled. "You *drove* up? All by yourself?"

She never let her gaze waver from her father's. "It's not such an amazing thing. Driving an automobile is quite simple. Even for a woman."

An all-too-familiar expression settled on Yancy's face, and Katie knew now was not the time to tell him she'd motored all the way from Washington, D.C., in that very same automobile.

Her mother placed an arm around Katie's back. "Let's not stand in the night air any longer." Lark drew her daughter toward the house. "Katie has had a long trip and a tiring day. Ben, would you like some coffee?"

"No, thank you, Mrs. Jones. If I can borrow a horse, I'll be getting back to town. I've still got some work to do at the newspaper."

Katie stopped and glanced over her shoulder. "Thank you for driving me out, Benjie."

"I was glad to do it." He winked at her, then added softly, "It's good to have you home."

She felt a warm glow of happiness. "Thanks, Benjie."

"Stop in at the newspaper when you're settled."

"I will."

Yancy set off toward the barn. "Come on, Ben. I'll get you that horse."

Katie watched as Ben followed her father across the yard, disappearing into the shadows of night. She'd missed him. All these years, no matter what she'd been doing or where she'd been living or who her other friends were, she'd always missed Benjie. He'd been her rock throughout childhood. No matter who else had criticized her, Benjie had been there to restore her faith in God, in herself, and in her dreams. Ben had never seemed disappointed by anything she'd said or done. He'd never seemed to think her odd or peculiar as so many others had.

She wondered if she would have had the courage to return if Ben hadn't been here, too.

Her mother's arm tightened around her shoulders. "Come inside, dear. It's turning cold."

Katie's niggling doubts dissipated. "It's good to be home, Mother," she whispered. "So very good to be home."

TWO

Katie awakened to the song of a robin outside her open window. Smiling contentedly, she snuggled deeper beneath the warm quilt, reluctant to get up just yet. Slowly she became aware of other sounds besides those of the bird.

The bark of a dog—Josie was her name, or so her brothers had told her last night. Just a year old and as yet without manners or the good sense not to bark so early in the morning.

Men's voices. Laughter, good-humored and low. The sort of laughter peculiar to men when they thought there was no woman within hearing distance.

The snort and stomping of horses as they milled in the corral.

The strident bawling of a calf, probably lost from its mother.

A screen door slamming closed.

The creak of a loose board on the front porch.

Katie opened one eye. Morning sunlight slipped between

the curtain and the window casing, bright and promising, a reminder that she was wasting time abed.

With a sigh of resignation, she pushed aside the sheet and quilt and sat up, then drew her knees to her chest as she gazed about. This had been her bedroom for most of her life, and trappings of girlhood were everywhere. Dolls, never played with, lined a shelf along one wall. Dresses that were now too youthful in style filled the wardrobe. A jump rope, frayed at one end. A black satin pouch, filled with her favorite marbles. A baseball and bat.

For some reason, these things were both familiar and foreign. It seemed to Katie that the girl who had lived in this room years ago had been someone other than herself.

A light rapping sounded. "Katie?"

"Grandma?" She hopped out of bed, hurried across the room, and yanked open the door. There stood Addie Rider, Katie's maternal grandmother. Addie opened her arms, and Katie moved into them. "Oh, Grandma, it's so good to see you."

After a tight hug, Addie held Katie at arm's length and inspected her with that schoolteacher's gaze of hers. Finally she gave an approving nod. "It's mighty good to see you, too, my darling girl."

Katie took her grandmother by the hand and pulled her into the bedroom. "Come and sit. You look absolutely scrumptious, Grandma. I've missed you so much. It's been weeks since I got your last letter. How's Grandpa Will?"

"Your grandpa's fine. His back is still bothering him more than he cares to admit, but Will's always been the stubborn sort." Her faded green eyes twinkled, and Katie could tell her grandmother was looking back through time. Then Addie gave her head a shake. "But it's not your grandpa I've come to talk about. Let me have another look at you."

Obediently Katie stepped back and turned slowly, her arms extended at her sides.

Her grandmother clucked her tongue. "I do declare, Katherine Jones. You became a beautiful woman while you were away." She sat on the edge of the bed, then patted the mattress. "Now, sit and let's talk. I've missed our chats."

"So have I. More than you know."

"I hear you've brought an automobile with you."

"Yes, and Papa wasn't any too pleased about it."

"No, Yancy wouldn't be. You know how protective he is."

"*Over*protective, you mean."

Addie chuckled. "It's only because he loves you."

"I know."

And Katie *did* know her father loved her. If only he could agree with the choices she made. *That* she was certain he did not do. Her father would like her to settle in Homestead, marry, and give him grandchildren. He wanted to know that she was safe and secure—and in his mind that meant marriage.

"I suppose all the men in this family tend to be overprotective," her grandmother continued. "Perhaps it's one of the things that attracts us to them, even when it makes us crazy at the same time. Your grandpa always was trying to take care of me, as if I didn't have a mind of my own. It was the same with your mother and father, although in a different way." She paused thoughtfully, then added, "It'll be interesting to see what sort of man you choose to marry, Katie Lark."

"But I don't plan to marry."

Her grandmother raised an eyebrow.

"Truly, I don't. It isn't that I have anything against marriage, Grandma. I only have to look at my own parents or at you and Grandpa to know it can be wonderful. But not all women are as fortunate. For centuries, many women have been subject to the whims and demands and mistreatment of men. We are on the verge of gaining the right to vote throughout this country, but the work won't stop there. There is so much ignorance, so much poverty, but so few workers. Women must be willing to sacrifice for the cause of freedom for all, just as Miss Anthony did. She never married because it left her free to go where God called her. That's what I need to do as well."

"My!" Addie placed the palm of one hand on her chest, as if shocked by Katie's emphatic and impassioned declaration.

Katie leaned forward. "You of all people should understand, Grandma. You came here all by yourself, a schoolteacher facing a brand-new challenge. You lived in your own small cabin, and you earned your own way. You didn't marry because it was expected of you."

"No, Katie, I didn't. I married your grandpa because I fell in love with him."

"Love should be the *only* reason for women to marry. But all too often they're forced to marry for economic reasons, because they have no other choice. I've dedicated myself to changing that. I won't ever marry."

"What if *you* fall in love?"

"I don't intend to let that happen."

"Were it only that easy," her grandmother said softly.

"Speaking of marriage, Ben has been keeping steady company with Reverend Orson's daughter. Reverend Orson is the pastor at King of Glory."

Katie felt an odd twinge in her chest.

"Well, everyone seems to expect he'll ask Miss Orson to marry him before the summer's out. Not that Ben has said anything to that effect, mind you. But you know how folks will talk."

"Benjie married . . ." She let the words drift into silence, disquieted by the sense of loneliness that swept over her. It shouldn't surprise her, shouldn't matter to her. But for some reason, it did.

"What are your plans, dear, now that you're back? Besides never to fall in love and get married."

Katie straightened and met her grandmother's gaze. "You won't believe it. I'm going to write a column for the *Herald.*" Excitement returned. "I talked to Benjie about it yesterday, and he agreed that I could. Well, that isn't quite true. He said he would think about it. But I know he'll agree. It will be a column for women. Not about how to make an apple pie or starch a shirt properly or any of those old things. My column's going to be about woman's suffrage and how politics are as important to us as to men."

Addie chuckled as she gave her head a slow shake. "Oh, dear. Does your father know about this?"

"Not yet, and you mustn't tell him. Promise me, Grandma, that you won't say a word. I want him to be surprised, to read it with an open mind."

"I hope you know what you're doing."

"I do, Grandma."

Addie leaned forward and kissed Katie's cheek. "You're as stubborn as any of the men in this family, and then some."

＊　≡◊≡　＊

Ben stood against the awning support in front of the hardware store. "Headed for the dress shop again?" he asked his sister as she and her fiancé came toward him on the sidewalk. "Matthew, are you certain you can afford such a wife? Sophia's likely to drive you to the poorhouse."

Sophia gave him a dark glance, but Matthew Jacobs merely agreed in good humor. "It's true. My income from the Book Shoppe is meager." He patted Sophia's hand where it rested in the crook of his arm, turning a doting gaze upon her. "But every bride should have new dresses with which to begin her married life, and we're thankful your father has been so generous. I'll have little enough means with which to spoil Sophia after we're married. I guess I should have had greater ambitions than to be a small-town shopkeeper."

"I'll have everything I desire, Matthew, as long as I have you."

Ben rolled his eyes at his sister's sugary comment, but he kept silent. It was useless to tease these two lovebirds. They would go on billing and cooing as they'd been doing for months. Thank goodness the wedding was a mere two weeks away. He wasn't certain how much more he could take. Still, there were moments when he envied them, when he wondered what it might be like to be so in love that one forgot all else.

A passing carriage horse reared in its traces, and its shrill whinny split the air. As the horse bolted, the driver, Norman Henderson, shouted a curse that caused Sophia to blush bright red. Ben turned to see what had caused the commotion, and there came the Susan B down Main Street—puttering, popping, and choking—and drawing the attention of all.

He should have known it was Katie causing the furor.

"My stars," Sophia whispered. "Is that *Katie?*"

Ben grinned. "It is indeed."

"She's driving an automobile," Matthew said.

Ben's smile broadened. "That she is."

Katie brought the Model T to a stop in front of the three of them. "Hello." Her face was aglow, her expression only moderately sheepish. "It seems I've upset Mr. Henderson's horse."

"*And* Mr. Henderson." Ben stepped off the sidewalk and offered his hand to help her from the motorcar.

Katie's dark brown eyes twinkled as she slid across the seat toward him. "I suppose I should apologize to him," she whispered without the slightest note of remorse.

Years ago, Ben and Katie, with the encouragement of the three Henderson sons, had set off firecrackers underneath Norman Henderson's porch in the middle of the night. The farmer had raced out of the house in his striped nightshirt and nightcap, waving his shotgun and cussing a blue streak. Luckily for them all, he'd never found out who was to blame. Otherwise they'd have all faced a tanning they wouldn't have forgotten.

As Katie placed her hand in Ben's and disembarked from the motorcar, Ben wondered if she remembered that episode, too. But the memory was quickly forgotten when he saw what she was wearing—bright pink cycling bloomers!

Katie released his hand and stepped onto the sidewalk, obviously unmindful of everyone's stares.

And Ben, for one, couldn't stop staring. The Turkish-style trousers extended to just below her knees, and the white stockings she wore did little to hide her shapely calves from view. He could be wrong, but he thought they were probably the first pair of adult female legs ever purposely revealed on Homestead's Main Street.

Katie gave Sophia an enthusiastic hug. "It's so good to see you. I heard you're getting married." She turned toward Matthew. "May I offer my congratulations. You're getting a wonderful bride."

Matthew Jacobs mumbled a greeting while Sophia stared in wide-eyed silence. With a curtness bordering on rude, Matthew nodded, bade both Katie and Ben good day, then led his intended down the sidewalk.

After the couple disappeared into Madeline's Dress Shop, Katie looked at Ben. "I've written my first column. I hope you like it." She held out several sheets of paper that were covered in neat script.

"I wasn't expecting anything this soon." He took the papers from her.

"No point in dallying, Mr. Rafferty. I take my obligation to the newspaper and to the people of this valley quite seriously."

He lifted one eyebrow. "Ever think of writing a fashion column?"

Katie laughed as she glanced down at her attire. "Do you suppose your sister is ordering an identical outfit this very moment? I noticed she couldn't seem to take her eyes off mine. And Matthew was obviously overwhelmed."

"Katie, you're the limit."

"So I've been told. Quite often, in fact."

Ben loved the way her brown eyes sparkled when she laughed. He loved the gentle bow of her mouth when she smiled. He'd always thought women looked ridiculous in cycling bloomers, and the color would have been unsuitable on most. But Katie looked wonderful, bloomers and all. Her hair was tied back at the nape with a pink satin ribbon. Wisps had pulled free to curl around her face, giving her a wild, abandoned look. Had she always had such an adorable, heart-shaped face and turned-up nose and—

"Well? Are you going to read it?"

"Read what?"

"My column." She frowned, tilting her head to one side. "Benjie, are you all right?"

To be honest, he wasn't sure. He was feeling mighty peculiar at the moment. As if the lunch he'd eaten at Zoe's Restaurant wasn't sitting too well.

Katie leaned forward, still frowning. "Benjie?" Her black hair smelled of rose water and gleamed with blue highlights in the midday sun.

He blinked and gave his head a quick shake. "I'm all right." Then he held up the papers between then. "I'll go and read these right now." He took a step backward, but the faint scent of roses lingered in his nostrils and the odd feeling remained in his midsection.

He muttered a sudden farewell, then turned and strode

quickly along the sidewalk toward the office of the *Homestead Herald*.

Maybe he wasn't all right. Maybe the roast beef was bad. Or perhaps it was due to too little sleep last night. Or maybe it was Katie's bright pink bloomers.

Didn't she have *any* common sense? Didn't she know how folks in Homestead would react? An automobile *and* bloomers! Why, she would be lucky if she weren't drummed right out of town.

Hearing the Susan B come to life, Ben glanced behind him in time to see Katie slide across the seat of the automobile. Then she backed it into the middle of the street and drove away.

He didn't want others looking down their noses at Katie. He wanted them to see her as he did—free and wild, full of life and laughter. He supposed it would be up to him to save her from herself.

He smiled ruefully. Come to think of it, he'd rather missed saving Katie from herself. He'd certainly had no greater challenge. Not even owning the newspaper provided the same sorts of tests and trials Katie did.

⇥ ⊠ ⟻

Madeline Percy stared out the window of her dress shop, her wrinkled face flushed with indignation. "Well, I never. When Reverend Percy hears of this . . ." She shook her head, then turned toward her customers. "Matthew, I expect your father and my husband shall both have a few words to say from their pulpits about the devil's work come Sunday."

"I should think so."

Sophia wanted to protest. As a young girl, Katie had been different from other girls but never bad. She was simply . . . not ordinary. Naturally Sophia couldn't approve of Katie's choice of apparel, but she couldn't help being fascinated by it, either. Katie seemed so uninhibited . . . so free. Sophia envied her. Still, she kept her thoughts to herself. She didn't want to disagree with Matthew.

Madeline stepped behind the counter and reached toward a large box on the shelf. "Her father should lock her in a room until she learns some modest behavior. But I suppose we shouldn't any of us be surprised. That girl was always a strange one. Going off to attend college has only made it worse. If you ask me, women have no business in college. They can get all the education they need at home. That's where they belong until they find a husband." She clucked her tongue. "Thank heaven for levelheaded young men such as you, Matthew. You would never allow your wife to wear such inappropriate clothing."

"No, indeed I wouldn't."

Sophia felt a flash of irritation but again she kept silent. She and Matthew never disagreed on anything. They never argued. Not ever.

"Now here is what a respectable young woman wears in public." The dressmaker pushed aside the tissue paper and lifted a dress from the box.

Sophia hated the unadorned white gown upon sight, despite the fact that it was in the height of fashion this season.

"Step into the back, dear, and try it on," Madeline said.

Sophia thought of Katie in her pink bloomers and suddenly wished she had the courage to wear them.

As she walked into the back room and closed the curtain, she wondered what it must have been like for Katie to go to college, then live and work in Washington, D.C. Sophia had visited her grandparents in San Francisco a few times through the years, but she could scarcely imagine living in such a metropolis. The idea both frightened and intrigued her.

"I needn't worry about my Sophia being anything other than an obedient wife," she heard Matthew say. "The Raffertys have brought her up properly."

Sophia paused to stare at her reflection in the cheval glass. *Matthew's obedient wife.* Was that who she saw before her? The description left her feeling strangely uneasy. *His obedient wife.* Wasn't that what she was supposed to be? what she wanted to be? Wasn't that what was expected of all women when they married? Of course it was.

Then why did Matthew's words make her think of a faithful hunting dog doing its master's bidding? Why did she suddenly want to toss this dress in his face and order a pair of cycling bloomers?

She gave her head a swift shake, driving off the unsettling thoughts. With her wedding only two weeks away, she wasn't about to let anything spoil her happiness. Not even her own unexpected misgivings.

⊷ ⊷ ⊷

Nestled in a grove of trees to the west of town, the Rafferty residence stood tall and stately, the most elegant house in all of Homestead, as befitted the town's wealthiest family. But it was also a home filled with love and warmth, and Katie had many fond memories tied to it.

"We've missed you, Katherine," Rose Rafferty said as she refilled Katie's coffee cup.

"I've missed all of you, too, Mrs. Rafferty. I suppose Benjie hasn't gotten into nearly as much mischief since I've been away."

Rose chuckled as she settled onto the chair across from Katie. "No, he hasn't. In fact, he's become quite the serious businessman." Her smile faded. "Actually, I think his work consumes him far too much. He lives in his office. I realize the newspaper means a great deal to him, but still . . ." Rose's words drifted into silence.

"I expected he would work for one of the large newspapers in the East after college."

She remembered the times Ben had read stories to her about places like Chicago and Boston and New York City, or even Paris and London and Rome. It had seemed that it was Ben who was destined to see and write about other places. With his intelligence and golden good looks, she'd been certain he would make a name for himself in the newspaper world.

"I'm glad he chose to return." Rose leaned forward and patted Katie's hand. "I've seen how hard it's been on your mother, having you so far from home. When the time comes for my children to marry and start their families, I want them to be close to me."

"Do you expect Ben to marry soon?" There was that curious feeling in Katie's chest again.

"I don't know. For several months he's been keeping rather steady company with Miss Orson, but he hasn't said a word to me about his feelings for her. He can be quite closemouthed, you know."

"What's she like?"

Rose nodded. "I'd forgotten you haven't had time to meet her yet. Charlotte and her father moved here nearly four years ago. She's a lovely young woman. I'm sure you'll like her when you meet her."

For some inexplicable reason, Katie was sure she *wouldn't* like Miss Orson.

Unexpectedly Rose wagged her finger at Katie. "I suppose you know you spoiled your mother's surprise by arriving the way you did."

"Yes, I know. Sammy said Mother arranged for the town band to greet me at the depot. I don't know whether to be disappointed or not. Does Mr. Leonhardt still play the tuba?" She could almost hear the off-key *oompah-pah,* could almost see his red, puffed-out cheeks.

Ben's mother smiled. "He does, and you'll still have the pleasure of listening to him. The ladies of the Morning Glory Circle are going ahead with our potluck supper in your honor, surprise or no, and the band is going to be there."

Katie let out an exaggerated groan and covered her ears with the palms of her hands.

Rose laughed. "Fanny McLeod promised to make some of her wonderful huckleberry pies."

"Mmm." Katie lowered her hands and rolled her eyes in ecstasy. "My favorite dessert."

"No one makes them like Fanny."

"No indeed." She grinned. "I guess I can stand Mr. Leonhardt's tuba in exchange for huckleberry pie."

"I thought you'd say that, Katherine. Some things never change."

THREE

The next afternoon, Ben drove out to see Katie. As his buggy horse trotted along the road, Ben rested his forearms on his thighs, the reins looped through his fingers. His gaze swept the gently rolling valley toward the mountains in the east. He couldn't see the house or outbuildings belonging to Yancy Jones, but he could see plenty of Lazy L cattle. He'd always liked the sight of the sluggish bovines grazing in pastures of knee-high grasses. It was just one of many things he'd missed when he'd been away from Homestead.

Ben had discovered, during his school years back East, that this was where he belonged. Things were changing fast everywhere else. Even now many European countries were at war, and Ben suspected the United States wouldn't be able to avoid participation much longer. But here in Long Bow Valley, life continued as it had for decades.

He grinned, remembering Katie as he'd seen her yesterday, standing beside her automobile in her pink bloomers. Maybe everything wasn't the same as it had always been, and maybe some change wasn't bad.

He glanced at the folder on the seat beside him. In it was Katie's column. He was pleasantly surprised by what she'd written. It wasn't a firebrand diatribe on the national suffrage situation, as he'd expected. It was a story about pursuing one's dreams, and it was warm, witty, and well crafted. He'd had to do little editing, which he knew would please Katie.

Ben's horse and buggy crested a small rise, and the Lazy L came into view. The two-story, white clapboard house had been added on to several times over the years as the Jones family grew and their fortunes increased. The additions had given the home an odd shape, but it appealed to Ben. Perhaps it was because it wasn't fancy or pretentious. It had a lived-in look that somehow defined the word *home*.

As if she'd been expecting him, Katie stepped onto the front porch. She lifted her arm and waved, then hurried down the steps into the sunshine. She wore a black-and-white shirt-waist, an attractive dress that accentuated her feminine curves. Her head was uncovered; her black hair—long and lush and gleaming with bluish highlights in the sun—was captured by a ribbon at the nape.

Ben found himself wondering once again at the changes time had wrought in Katie. He also wondered at the way those changes made him feel.

"You must have known I was thinking about you," she called as he entered the yard.

"Were you?" He drew his horse to a halt.

She smiled. "You know I was. And you know why."

He grinned in return. "I guess I do at that."

"Well?"

"Well . . . " He hopped down.

She walked to the side of the buggy and touched his arm. "Tell me. What did you think?"

"It's good, Katie. You've got a real talent."

She beamed. "Do you really think so?"

"Yes."

"Oh, Benjie, you can't know how much your opinion means to me. You've always been so wonderful with words."

Had he? Then why was he feeling at such a loss for them at the moment? He couldn't seem to focus on anything except Katie's fingers on his sleeve, warming the skin beneath, leaving him strangely disoriented.

"Come inside. Mother made lemonade before she went over to Grandma and Grandpa's."

Get ahold of yourself, Rafferty. "Thanks. I could use something cool to drink. It's a bit warm for this time of year."

"I'm ready for summer." Katie led the way toward the house, talking all the while. "It was a harsh winter in Washington. The building where I work is terribly drafty, and the house Penny and I share is sometimes even worse. Then, of course, there was the trip out here. Most of the time, I love the Susan B, but when it's cold—" She ended her sentence with a laugh.

Following after her, Ben tried his best to concentrate on what she was saying rather than noticing the way her skirts caressed her ankles as she walked.

He suddenly found himself comparing Katie to Charlotte. Where Katie Jones was petite and shapely, Charlotte Orson was tall and willowy. Where Katie's coloring was dark, Charlotte's was pale. Where Katie's personality was outgoing and vibrant, Charlotte's was quiet and contained. Katie's energy sometimes created a drain on those around her; Charlotte's presence brought peace. Katie seemed to pull against society at every turn; Charlotte lived easily within the boundaries of her world. Katie and Charlotte . . . as different as night from day. And it was Katie who—

"I haven't told anyone except Grandma Addie about my column," Katie said. "Will it be in tomorrow's paper?" She stopped and glanced over her shoulder.

Katie who what? Where had his thoughts been taking him? He couldn't be sure.

"Do you think Papa will be pleased, Benjie?"

"With the article?" His throat felt dry. "Sure. I don't see why not."

"He hates the Susan B."

"You've always been too sensitive when it comes to your dad." Ben reached out and touched her sleeve. "The automobile is new to him. He'll get used to it. And to your column."

"You've always understood me better than anyone, Benjie. You've never made me feel . . . different."

But you are *different, Katie. Maybe that's what I love about you most.*

Love? The notion caught him by surprise, almost stopped his heart.

But why should it? He *did* love her. He always had. And

she loved him. In her letters, she called him her "beloved Benjie." *Love* was only one of the words that described his friendship with Katie. There were so many more: *trust, laughter, camaraderie, loyalty.* She was closer to him than his own sister was, understood him better than anyone else he knew.

Katie smiled. "Sit down, Benjie, and let me get you your lemonade. Then you can tell me how truly wonderful and exceptional my first column for the *Herald* is."

Ben's tension eased. It wasn't so strange that he should love Katie. Who wouldn't?

⊷ ≡◆≡ ⊶

Blanche Coleson kept a close eye on her pupils as they filed out of the schoolhouse at the end of each day. Personal experience had taught her that to lower her guard was to leave herself open to all kinds of practical jokes. Especially from the older boys.

Miserable heathens that they were.

She ran her fingertips over her hair, checking for any truant strands. There weren't any. She hadn't expected there to be. Blanche allowed no disorder in her very orderly life.

When the door closed behind the last departing student, Blanche let out a long sigh, then rose from her chair and set about cleaning the blackboards. Afterward she wrote the next day's math problems on the side blackboard and the next day's language questions on the blackboard behind her desk. When all was in readiness, she claimed her handbag and lunch pail, put her straw hat on her head, and left the school.

The town of Homestead provided its schoolteacher with two rooms above Yardley's Drugstore as part of her wages, and that was where Blanche went at the close of each school day. Her walk home took her past Berchtwald's Watch Shop, Long Bow Billiards Saloon, and Carson's Barbershop. Occasionally she would stop in at Berchtwald's and allow the old German to verify the accuracy of her watch, but never did she so much as turn her head in the direction of the billiards saloon. Such a place was suitable only for the lowest forms of humanity. Which meant, of course, that it was a suitable place for men.

Vile, drunken, sweaty creatures—men—with few exceptions. Blanche had only to remember her father for proof of that. Zebulon Coleson had been too lazy to work, and his family would have starved if not for Blanche's mother. But how much money could a woman earn when a new baby arrived every year or two? Having babies and taking care of her worthless husband had killed Victoria Coleson as surely as if Blanche's father had put a gun to her head and pulled the trigger.

Fifteen years after he'd gone to his just reward, his memory still made Blanche seethe with hatred.

Several men loitered outside the hardware store, making Blanche thankful that her lodgings were on the other side of the street. There was little she hated as much as having to walk past a group of idle males and feel their gazes on her. It positively made her skin crawl.

Vincent Michaels, the town's lawyer, drew his buggy to a halt outside the sheriff's office. Blanche wondered on whose behalf he was making his call, then thought with some disgust that if the sheriff and lawyer were doing their jobs properly, she wouldn't have to be concerned about men who loitered outside the hardware store.

She had nearly reached the outside staircase leading to her two-room apartment when Rose Rafferty came out of the drugstore, stopping her progress.

"Good afternoon, Miss Coleson," Rose greeted her. "Is school out so soon?"

Blanche checked the watch pinned to her bodice. "The same time as always. Precisely four o'clock."

Rose chuckled, acting as if Blanche had said something amusing. Then she shook her head. "I swear the days get shorter every year. Don't you find it so?"

"Twenty-four hours have always been twenty-four hours, Mrs. Rafferty. Now, if you'll excuse me . . . " Blanche turned toward the side stairway once again.

"We will see you tomorrow evening at the potluck supper for Katie, won't we?"

She paused and glanced over her shoulder. "I'll be there, Mrs. Rafferty. I've been looking forward to making Miss Jones's acquaintance for quite some time."

Rose bade her farewell then, and Blanche was at last able to retreat to the privacy of her rooms. As she removed her hat and set it on the small table near the door, she found herself thinking about Katie Jones. It was no exaggeration to say she was looking forward to meeting her. She'd heard the young woman had been working for the National American Woman Suffrage Association in the nation's capital for some time. It was even said Miss Jones personally knew such women as Inez Milholland, Lucy Burns, and Alice Paul. Blanche would give almost anything to be able to say the same about herself. Of course, if she'd been born to a privileged family, she too might have attended Vassar and traveled the country and met such dignitaries from the suffrage movement instead of being stuck in some backwater Idaho village like Homestead, teaching school to a group of ungrateful brats.

But then, life often wasn't fair to women—Blanche Coleson had always found it so. And she despised all men because of it.

⊶ ⊱◈⊰ ⊷

The day took on a special glow for Katie as she sat in the kitchen, reminiscing with Ben. She found herself thinking again how much he'd changed. He was taller and even more handsome than the teenager she remembered. But he was the same, too. His dark blue eyes revealed his enthusiasm and intelligence. His smile came slowly but was real and honest.

And he could still spin a story like no one else Katie knew. She was soon wrapped up in the lives of the people of Homestead, some old friends and some strangers to her. The one name that didn't come up was Charlotte Orson. Katie was curiously glad of that.

It caught her by surprise when her father and brothers traipsed into the kitchen, after brushing off the dust of a day's labors. Somehow an entire afternoon had slipped away, and she hadn't begun to prepare supper as she'd promised her mother.

"It's my fault, Mr. Jones," Ben volunteered in a valiant attempt to shoulder the blame. "I've been monopolizing Katie's time." He rose from his chair. "I've hired her to write a column for the newspaper."

"A column?" Yancy's glance shifted from Ben to Katie. She nodded.

Her father shook his head slowly. "I sure hope you know what you're doing, kitten."

"I do, Papa."

"Sure seems things were simpler when I was your age," Yancy added.

"Listen," Ben interjected, "since it's my fault your supper isn't ready, why don't we all go into town to eat? My treat."

"All right!" Sam and Rick exclaimed in unison.

"I don't reckon that's necessary," Yancy said.

"I insist, Mr. Jones."

"Come on, Pa," Rick urged.

"It'd be a nice treat for Ma," Sam added. "She's been workin' mighty hard on tomorrow night's doin's for Katie's homecomin'."

Yancy looked from one young person to the next, then admitted his defeat. "Looks like I'm outnumbered. Guess we'll accept your invitation, Ben. Soon as Lark gets home, we'll come into town."

Rick let out a whoop. "Can we ride in Katie's motorcar?"

"No." The single word brooked no argument. "We'll take the surrey, as usual."

Katie wanted to kick her brother for mentioning her automobile.

"Katie," Ben said, "I'd like you to come back to town with me. I'll show you around my office and introduce you to Harvey Trent. We can meet your family at the restaurant later."

"I'd like that, Benjie." She glanced at her father. "Do you mind, Papa?"

"No. Go on ahead."

Katie turned toward the kitchen door. "I'll get my hat." Then she hurried from the room.

A short while later, she was seated in Ben's buggy, the horse pulling them away from the Lazy L. Katie stared ahead with unseeing eyes, lost in thought. She was remembering all those times, as a little girl, when she'd sat on her papa's lap and he'd hugged her and told her how special she was. She didn't want to disappoint him in anything she did, and yet she knew she had to be true to herself. More importantly, she had to be true to God.

It was Ben who broke the lengthy silence. "Your father's going to like your column when he reads it."

"Do you think so?"

"Yes."

"I'm not going to change, Benjie."

"No one's asking you to."

"I think Papa is."

"And I think you're wrong. Give it some time. You've only been home a couple of days."

She let out a long sigh. "I can't be what he wants me to be."

"What do you think that is?"

She gave a helpless shrug. "Something I'm not. Something I don't even want to be."

FOUR

The Homestead Weekly Herald
Homestead, Idaho
Friday Morning
May 26, 1916

Katie Jones to Pen Weekly Column for Women; "Katie's Corner" Debuts on Page 3 of This Week's Herald

The Homestead Herald is pleased to announce the debut of a new column of interest to our women readers. The column will be written by Miss Katherine L. Jones, daughter of Yancy and Lark Jones of the Lazy L Ranch. Miss Jones, a graduate of Vassar College, has recently returned to Homestead after several years in the East, where she was active in the work for passage of a national woman's suffrage amendment.

In addition, articles of specific interest to our women readers will now be found in the "Women's News Department" on page 3 of every edition of the Herald.

The door to the *Homestead Herald* flew open, crashing against the wall. Ben jumped up from his chair, but not before Katie entered the office, waving a copy of the newspaper in her right hand.

" 'Katie's Corner'?" she spat out the words as if they were poison. "You called my column 'Katie's Corner'?" She slammed the door closed, then marched toward him, fury in every step.

He grinned. He wasn't surprised to see her. In truth, he'd

wondered what was taking her so long to get there. "I thought it had a nice ring."

"How could you do it, Ben Rafferty?" She dropped the paper onto his desk. Her eyes flashed with anger as she rested her fists on her hips. "It sounds like a column about canning peaches or quilt making or something. Exactly what it *won't* be, and you know it."

He considered letting her fuss and fume a little longer. He enjoyed the way she looked, her cheeks infused with indignant color, her mouth set in a stubborn line. It reminded him of the time she'd punched Elmer Henderson for shoving Esther Leon-hardt into a mud puddle. Katie, about eight years old at the time, hadn't thought twice about attacking the much larger boy.

Come to think of it, she looked mad enough to start punching again. Only Ben would be the target this time.

"Think about it a moment, Katie. You'll catch more flies with honey than with vinegar."

She raised her eyebrows skeptically.

"If you put a heading like 'Unshackled' on your column, you'll lose some of the very readers you want. They'll think it too radical. Some husbands might refuse to allow their wives to read it."

"What right has any man to refuse his wife to read anything she wants to read?"

Ben leaned forward, placing his knuckles on his desktop. "None, but a lot of them would do it anyway."

"All the same—"

"All the same, you know I'm right."

She dropped her gaze to the newspaper on his desk. Her

shoulders slumped as her anger dissipated. "But 'Katie's Corner'? It's so . . . so *bland.*"

"But the column won't be bland, and that's what matters."

Katie considered his comment in silence.

"What did your father think of it?"

"He said it was very good." A gentle smile curved the corners of her mouth. "I think he was proud of me."

Ben felt an odd tightness in his chest. *I'm proud of you, too, Katie.*

"You should have been a politician, Mr. Rafferty. You maneuvered me quite expertly." Her eyes sparkled with mischief. "You won't manage me so easily in the future, I promise you."

For some unknown reason, Ben once again recalled the time he'd kissed her up at Tin Horn Pass.

Katie took hold of his hand. "I was planning to saddle one of the horses and ride up to the pass today. Come with me."

Had she read his mind?

"You can spare an afternoon, Benjie."

He couldn't refuse. He didn't want to. But before he could voice his acquiescence, the door opened again, this time slowly, accompanied by its usual squeak.

And there, in the opening, stood Charlotte.

Her gaze flicked from Ben to Katie to Ben again. Uncertainty filled her pale blue eyes.

Ben pulled his hand from Katie's and stepped around his desk, then crossed to the door. "Come in, Miss Orson. There's someone I'd like you to meet." He took hold of her elbow and drew her into the office. "Miss Orson, this is Katie Jones. Katie, Charlotte Orson."

Charlotte's smile was as gentle and sweet as her voice. "I'm so pleased to meet you, Miss Jones. I've been hearing stories about you ever since I arrived in Homestead. Ben's always telling my father and me about what trouble the two of you got into as children."

Katie held out her hand. "I'm sure none of those stories have painted me in a flattering light, Miss Orson. I hope they won't influence you adversely."

"On the contrary, I am predisposed to like you very much." Charlotte's smile remained even after the handshake ended. "Your column in today's paper was wonderful. That's what I came to tell Mr. Rafferty."

"Thank you."

"I know everyone will be talking about it at the potluck tonight." Charlotte turned to look at Ben. "I would never have the courage to write for a newspaper. I'm much too shy."

Ben could think of nothing to do except nod in agreement.

"Well, I didn't mean to disturb you. You two were probably discussing Miss Jones's next column, and here I am intruding on your business."

Business? No. What Charlotte had intruded upon was an opportunity for fun, to slip away with Katie, forget the newspaper for a few hours, and ride up to the pass. Only how could Ben say that to Charlotte? They might not have an understanding, but neither did he wish to hurt her.

Katie must have seen his indecision, for she said, "Not at

all, Miss Orson. I was just leaving." She glanced at Ben. "I'll
see you tonight at the potluck." Then she was gone.

Ben walked to the large window that looked out onto Main
Street and watched Katie start the Susan B with a quick crank,
then hike up her skirts and climb into the motorcar. As she
drove away, his thoughts drifted to a day eleven years before.

⊹

The August sun beat down unmercifully upon the platform of
the Homestead train depot. Ben, age fourteen, felt the sweat
trickling down his spine, but he didn't know if it was from
the heat or from nerves.

"You're certain you have everything?" his mother asked.

"I'm sure."

"You didn't forget to pack your—"

"Rose," Ben's father interrupted, "stop fussing over the
boy." Michael Rafferty placed his hand on Ben's shoulder.
"You'll do fine."

Ben wished he thought so. He'd been waiting for this day
for an eternity. Now that it was here, he wasn't so sure he
wanted to leave Homestead. Higher education didn't seem as
appealing when it meant leaving everything he knew.

Katie took hold of Ben's hand and drew him away from
the two families—the Raffertys and the Joneses. When they
arrived at the corner of the depot, she stopped and reached
into the pocket of her dress, something she usually wore only
to church and to school. "I want you to have this." She held
out her favorite marble. "Maybe it'll bring you luck."

"You don't have to do that, Katie."

"I want to." Her dark eyes filled with tears. "I'm gonna miss you, Benjie."

He gave one of her long braids a quick tug. "I'm going to miss you, too. But I won't be gone so long. You'll see."

"It's not fair, you going off to school and me being stuck here. I want to go with you."

"Reddington Academy is just for boys. And after that I'll be at Harvard. Girls aren't allowed there either."

She stuck out her chin. "That's not fair."

Ben didn't know what to say to make Katie feel better. How could he make her understand this was just the way things were?

"What if you don't ever come back?" she asked softly.

"Ah, I'll be back, Katie. Don't you worry about that. I gotta come back to see you, don't I?"

━◆═◆━

Charlotte touched Ben's forearm. "She seems very nice."

He blinked and looked at the woman beside him. *What's the matter with me?*

Charlotte smiled her sweet smile. "I'll see you at six?"

"Six? Oh, yes. The potluck. I'll be at your home at six o'clock."

"Good day, Mr. . . . Good day, Benjamin." Then she walked from his office with quick, silent footsteps.

Ben was left once again thinking how different Charlotte and Katie were—and uncertain about why it mattered to him.

Katie's column was the subject of conversation in many kitchens and places of work that day. Everyone seemed to be surprised that the irrepressible Miss Jones had written such a warm and gentle piece, although there were many who were relieved that it hadn't been as extreme as some of her views.

"I'd say your brother put her in her proper place," Matthew Jacobs told Sophia when they met for lunch at the hotel's restaurant.

Sophia felt a stab of disappointment. "Do you think so?"

"Of course. Ben couldn't let her write anything fanatical for the *Herald*. The men of Homestead wouldn't stand for it."

"The men of Homestead," she repeated beneath her breath.

"What that young woman needs is someone to take her in hand. A husband. Although who in his right mind would want to marry Katie, I can't imagine."

"Matthew, what an unkind thing to say."

"It's nothing but the truth. Katie isn't exactly wifely material."

Sophia stiffened. *And I am, no doubt!*

"Who knows what sort of disreputable behavior she's practiced while in the East?"

"A college education is not a sin, Matthew Jacobs." She tapped her fork against the edge of her plate, trying to swallow her irritation.

He looked surprised at her response. "I didn't say it was."

"No, but you implied as much."

"Did I?" He shook his head. "You must have misunderstood me, my dear. It isn't a sin, although I do believe it to be a waste of time and money. What will Katie do with all that learning once she's married?"

"What if she doesn't marry? You just said no man in his right mind would want to be her husband."

"No indeed, but it would be better for her if she would marry. She needs someone to remind her of her proper place." He touched the back of her hand, stilling her fork tapping. "I'm glad you've had better sense than to befriend her as your brother has. And I'm more than a little surprised he's continued that friendship."

Sophia pulled her hand from beneath his. "They've been close since they were babies in the nursery. Why shouldn't Ben be friends with Katie?"

"Isn't it obvious?"

"No, Matthew, it isn't. Please explain it to me."

He sighed. "Your brother has an important standing in this community. The Raffertys are the town's most influential family, and Ben owns the newspaper. He has the ear of many. His opinions are known far beyond this valley. Continued friendship with that woman is a betrayal of his responsibility to the community."

"Katie isn't bad, Matthew. She's merely high-spirited."

"Be that as it may, I want you to keep away from her. I won't have your reputation tarnished by her crazy antics."

"Am I allowed to speak to her at the potluck supper tonight?"

Matthew didn't seem to notice her sarcasm. "Well, of course, my dear. We needn't be rude."

Had he always spoken to her like this? Sophia wondered as she stared at her fiancé across the table. Had he always treated her like a dense child?

She felt more than a little unsettled by those questions.

＊＊ ≡◇≡ ＊＊

It had been years since Katie donned a pair of boy's trousers, sat astride a horse, and galloped across open fields as if racing the wind itself. She'd forgotten how good it felt.

Katie had enjoyed many sorts of freedoms while in Washington, but riding like this hadn't been one of them. There'd been little time to pursue personal pleasures. The intensity of their work had been all-consuming for the women of NAWSA.

As she reached the top of the pass, she reined in her mount, then twisted in the saddle to look at the scene below. Freshly turned earth and spring green pastures checkerboarded the land. Pony Creek, like a blue ribbon, wriggled and wound its way toward the mouth of the mountains at the opposite end of the bow-shaped valley. In the center was Homestead, small and neat, a safe community, tucked away from the hurry and bustle of the rest of the world.

She could almost hear Ben saying, "This is where I belong, Katie."

She wished she could say she belonged here, too, but she couldn't. She didn't know where God would have her settle. Maybe He wouldn't. Maybe her place would forever change, going where the cause needed her most. Perhaps she would be a vagabond for the Lord. Wasn't that why she'd returned to Homestead? To do the work He'd called her to.

Katie dismounted and walked along the ridge, leading the small bay mare by the reins.

Her first column for the *Herald* was a success, judging by her father's reaction as well as Miss Charlotte Orson's. She had tried to prove that women could have whatever they wanted if they would but pursue it. She'd wanted to let them see that dreams could come true if only one knew what to dream. It wasn't that she believed there was anything wrong with being a wife and mother, though there were some in the suffrage movement who did. No, Katie believed what was important was for each woman to find what God wanted for her and then pursue it wholeheartedly. But before they could begin to dream big dreams—whether that meant marriage or going to medical school or serving on a mission field in Africa—most women needed to stop seeing themselves as second-rate citizens.

Her next column would need to be more specific. It had to have more punch, more grit, more reality than hope. But Ben was right about catching more flies with honey than with vinegar. She must learn to be subtle.

Subtlety had never been one of her virtues.

Charlotte Orson is probably subtlety personified.

Katie's thought brought her to an abrupt halt. "Who wants to be subtle?" She looked at her horse, as if expecting an answer.

The mare stared at her in unblinking silence.

"Do you suppose he's going to marry her?"

More silence.

"Well—" she turned and began walking once again—
"I shouldn't be surprised if he does."

She pictured Ben and Charlotte as they'd looked standing
side by side in the newspaper office, both of them blond
haired—his the shade of a gold piece, hers as pale as wheat at
harvesttime—and both of them blue eyed. They would no
doubt produce beautiful, fair-haired children.

She kicked a rock out of her path, feeling suddenly irritated with Ben Rafferty—and not because he'd named her
column "Katie's Corner." No, she was angry for something
even she couldn't define.

And she had the feeling it would be best if she didn't try.

◆ ⟭◆⟬ ◆

The ladies of the Morning Glory Circle had done themselves
proud. The Homestead Community Church had never looked
as festive as it did for the potluck supper that night. Dried-
flower arrangements decorated each of the tables, thanks to
the talents of Miss Maud Leonhardt. Lacy tablecloths, cour-
tesy of Leslie Blake, covered the rough wood tables. Rose
Rafferty had provided her silver tea service and elegant china
for the occasion.

Nearly the entire population of Homestead and the
surrounding valley turned out to welcome Katie home. The
hall buzzed with voices as men grouped together to discuss
farming and politics, and women busied themselves laying
out the dishes of food while keeping an eye on their respective offspring.

Ben was standing with Reverend Orson; Albert Tobias, Homestead's mayor; and the three Henderson brothers—Isaac, Elmer, and Andrew—when the Jones family arrived. He saw Katie pause inside the doorway. Her gaze swept the room, not stopping until she found him.

Ben smiled.

She smiled back.

"My daughter was quite right," Obadiah Orson said. "Miss Jones is an attractive young woman. Not at all what I'd expected after the tales I've heard."

Charlotte appeared at Ben's side as if summoned by her father's comment. After sharing a glance, she moved past the small gathering of men, smiling warmly as she walked toward Katie.

"Hello again, Miss Jones. Everyone's been awaiting your arrival. Good evening, Mr. and Mrs. Jones." Then, as naturally as if it were her father's church and Katie her close friend, Charlotte took on the role of hostess, drawing Katie into the hall and introducing her to one and all.

Charlotte's warmth and her kindness to others were just two of the traits that had drawn Ben to her. She was patient with old folks and children alike. She never uttered a cross word. She was the picture of serenity.

So different from Katie.

As his gaze shifted to tonight's honored guest, he remembered the way Katie had stormed into his office this morning, her eyes sparking with fury, her cheeks flushed. Katie did everything with passion. Was she ever serene?

Isaac Henderson let out a low whistle. "I never thought

she'd grow up t' be so pretty." He elbowed Andrew in the ribs. "Did you?"

"You kiddin'?" the youngest Henderson brother answered. "I can't hardly remember her wearin' a dress, let alone cleanin' up so nice."

Elmer chuckled. "And t'think she gave me a shiner. Come on, boys. Let's get reacquainted."

The urge to pass out a few shiners himself almost overwhelmed Ben.

He stared at Katie in her dark blue tubular skirt wrapped with filmy scarves, and again he remembered the rough-and-tumble tomboy with unruly black hair.

Why hadn't he expected Katie to grow up? Why was he so surprised by the changes in her? And why was he so bothered by them?

Albert Tobias shook his head and grinned. "Haven't seen those Henderson brothers so excited since their pa brought home that prize bull last year. You wait and see. There's going to be a lot of traffic goin' back and forth to the Jones place this summer."

"I do believe you're right, Albert," Reverend Orson answered. "I do believe you're right."

Ben was prone to agree, and the idea left him feeling more irritated by the second.

━━◄◆►━━

Katie couldn't remember enjoying herself as much as she did tonight. Being welcomed home. Feeling awash with acceptance. Hearing that she'd been missed by so many people. She'd forgotten what it was like to be known so well by so many. Here in Homestead she wasn't lost in the masses. She was one of the community.

Over the course of the evening she stuffed herself on the good home cooking provided by the ladies of the Morning Glory Circle—which Katie was invited to join as soon as she was more settled. She cooed over babies and marveled at the handsome toddlers of her former class-mates. She listened to Homestead's band play and managed not to wince when Mr. Leonhardt's tuba hit its usual sour notes.

And she observed Ben with Charlotte.

She wondered why he'd never written to her about Charlotte. He'd never so much as mentioned her name, even though, according to others, they'd been keeping company for some time now. Katie had thought Ben shared every-thing with her in his letters, yet it was clear she'd been wrong. There were some things he'd chosen not to share.

Katie wanted to dislike the woman. Perhaps because the minister's daughter was everything Yancy Jones wanted Katie to be—sweet and pliable and agreeable and eager for marriage rather than a career or serving a cause.

Apparently Charlotte was everything Ben wanted, too. Throughout the evening they were nearly always together. They sat beside each other as they ate supper. Charlotte's hand was often within the crook of Ben's arm as they visited with people of the community. There was a rightness about the look of them as a couple. And she was kindness itself to Katie.

Yes, Katie wanted to dislike Charlotte, but it seemed it was impossible *not* to like her.

Especially if she made Ben happy.

FIVE

Katie chewed on the end of the pencil while glaring at the white sheet of paper on the desk. Her second column was not going well. She kept thinking about Ben's advice. How on earth could she couch the unpleasant truth about the helpless and hopeless conditions of countless women in honeyed terms?

She dropped the pencil onto the desk, then rose from her chair and began pacing her bedroom, hands clasped behind her back. The voices of so many women crying out for freedom, for basic human rights, rang in her head, those softer voices of the National American Woman Suffrage Association and the more strident tones of the Congressional Union for Woman Suffrage. How could she make those words palatable to the readers of the *Homestead Herald*?

She stopped abruptly. Palatable? Was that her job? To make the truth *palatable* to the readers of her column or to any of the men and women of Long Bow Valley?

Most assuredly not!

Wasn't it Jesus Himself who had modeled a radical example of empowerment for all believers, women included? He'd made women coheirs of His grace. He'd included them in ways unheard of in the culture of His day. Women had followed Jesus during His earthly ministry, not as stragglers but as disciples, as adherents, as believers who were a vital part of His work. When He gave His commission to go into all the world, He commissioned women along with the men. And when the Holy Ghost came at Pentecost, the women in that upper room were filled with the Spirit, too. Nowhere in Katie's studies of the Scriptures could she find an example where Christ treated a woman as an inferior to any man. From the woman at the well to the woman caught in adultery to Mary the sister of Martha to Mary Magdalene, Jesus had modeled something new.

Women were neither less than nor more than men. They were simply equal. They were made in the image of God, and He had a plan for each of their lives. It was that truth that formed the foundation for Katie's passion for woman's suffrage. And God had called her to share that truth—share it, not make it pleasant or palatable.

She returned to her desk and began to write with new enthusiasm. She lost all track of time as her pencil skimmed across the paper. The words seemed inspired, flowing onto the pages with little effort.

"Katie? I'm sorry to bother you, dear. Do you have a moment?"

The sudden interruption caused the rest of an unfinished

sentence to vanish into thin air. With a sigh, Katie dropped the pencil onto the desk and turned to look at her mother.

"You have a caller."

"Who is it?"

Her mother motioned toward the stairway. "It's Sophia Rafferty."

"Sophia?" Katie glanced dolefully at the paper on her desk. Just when she was getting the words right, too.

But curiosity overruled the temptation to send back her regrets. She and Sophia were nearly the same age, and they'd gone through school together. But the two had never been close friends. Katie had been far too much of a tomboy for that.

Subduing another sigh, Katie rose and followed her mother downstairs.

"Here she is, Sophia," Lark announced as they entered the front parlor.

Sophia turned from the window.

"Hello, Sophia," Katie said. "This is a pleasant surprise."

"Hello, Katie. I hope I'm not intruding."

"Not at all."

Sophia had the same smile as Ben. It came slowly, moving from the corners of her mouth up to the pretty blue of her eyes.

"Why don't the two of you sit down and get reacquainted," Lark suggested, "while I make some tea. It won't take me but a minute or two."

Sophia settled on the sofa, her hands folded in her lap. "The potluck last night was lovely."

"Yes." Katie sat on a nearby chair.

"There was such a crowd, I didn't have a chance to really talk with you."

"No, it was difficult to spend much time with anyone."

"Katie . . ." Sophia let the word drift into silence, then drew a deep breath and began again. "Katie, I'd like to ask you about your work."

"My work?"

Sophia nodded.

"I'm not quite sure—"

"Matthew says an education for a woman is a waste of time and money. That it will do her no good once she's married."

Anger flared, hot and instant, in Katie's chest. "Oh, he does, does he? Thank goodness I have no intentions of marrying. I would hate for those years at Vassar to be squandered."

Sophia twisted a handkerchief in her hands. "I've never wanted to go to college. I've never wanted to be anything other than Matthew's wife and a mother to the children we'll have, God willing. But . . . but I'd like to understand more about why you're doing . . . why you want to risk so much criticism for . . . I mean, women in Idaho already have the vote."

Excitement flared inside Katie. She leaned forward and touched the back of Sophia's hand. "I'd love to tell you about it. It's so important."

⋅—⊨◆⊨—⋅

Sophia Rafferty hadn't been gone from the Lazy L more than fifteen minutes when more visitors arrived. This time it was

Katie's Aunt Naomi—Lark's sister—and her nine-month-old son, Donald.

"I'm dying to hear all about your experiences, Katie. Nothing very exciting happens around here." Naomi grinned. "Except for the mischief three children can make, that is." She glanced down at her youngest child, watching as he crawled toward Katie. "Especially Donnie there. He never stops."

"I can't believe I've got three cousins." Katie smiled at the baby.

"It'll be four come December."

"Naomi!" Lark cried, jumping up from her chair and rushing to hug her sister. "Why didn't you tell me?"

"I didn't know for sure until I saw Dr. Tom this morning. Frank and I are thrilled."

Katie lifted Donnie into her arms and nuzzled his neck beneath his ear, whispering, "Enjoy being the baby of the family while you can, little cousin."

He laughed gleefully, as if she'd told him a joke.

Katie felt a poignant tug in her chest as she wondered what it might be like to hold in her arms a baby that had grown inside her own body for nine months. It was a totally new and unexpected feeling, and she wasn't the least bit sure it was one she welcomed.

✦

Ben enjoyed coming into the newspaper office on Saturdays. It was Harvey Trent's day off, and the building was completely silent. Ben could work without interruption, catching up on reading other newspapers, seeing what more he could do to improve the *Herald*. This was a time when he came up with ideas for new articles or better layouts or innovative ways to advertise. He could usually get lots done on a Saturday.

But this afternoon he found himself unable to concentrate. His thoughts kept drifting.

Mostly to Katie.

Last night at the potluck supper, she'd looked as pretty as anything he'd ever seen. She'd been surrounded by the young men of the valley, particularly the three Henderson boys. Only they weren't boys; they were men, and they hadn't looked at Katie as though she was just one of the gang, either.

Not that it should matter to him. Katie was her own woman. Besides, she was smart enough to steer clear of the Hendersons. Oh, not that they were a bad lot. Actually he rather liked the three brothers. But they wouldn't be right for Katie. No indeed. They wouldn't be right at all.

He gave his head a shake. What was he worried about? Katie had no intention of marrying. She'd told him so herself. She wasn't interested in marriage or a husband. She had her cause to fight for.

But what if she changed her mind? What if one of the Hendersons was able to woo her, win her? What then?

It would be disastrous—that's what!

Maybe someone should warn the Henderson boys. Maybe *he* should warn them—for Katie's sake.

Restless, Ben rose from his desk chair and walked to the window. Across the street, Leslie Blake swept the newly paved sidewalk in front of the mercantile. At the corner of Barber and Main, Frank Murray, Homestead's sheriff, talked to his wife, Naomi. Dr. Tom McLeod drove his buggy past the newspaper office, probably on his way to make a call on a patient out in the valley. Several children raced down Barber Street, Sigmund Leonhardt's ugly yellow dog following them.

A typical day in Homestead, the kind of day Ben liked best.

He wondered what Katie was doing right now.

As if in answer, he saw the Susan B roll into town, accompanied by its usual coughing and putting, breaking the silence of the peaceful day.

Ben grinned.

Katie must have seen him standing at the window. She steered the motorcar toward the newspaper office and braked, smiled and waved, then got out. A moment later she entered his office.

"Are you working on a Saturday, Mr. Rafferty? Shame on you. On a beautiful, sunshiny day like today? Even a newspaperman needs to have fun."

He remembered Charlotte saying much the same thing to him not long ago. He'd paid her no heed when she'd tried to tempt him from his work.

Katie's words had a different effect on him.

"We had visitors all morning at home, and I needed some time away," she continued. "I decided to go for a drive. Why don't you come along?"

"Well, I . . ."

Her eyes sparkled. "It's as hot as midsummer. I thought I might go for a swim."

When they were kids, they'd spent many a summer day at

the swimming hole at the north end of the valley. Ben had hung a rope to the limb of a tall tree, and they'd swung over the pond and dropped into the clear, cold, backed-up waters of Pony Creek.

"I've got work to do," he answered out of habit.

"Oh, come on, Benjie. I've got my bathing costume in the Susan B, and we can stop and get yours on our way out of town. It will be fun. No one else will be there. The water's too cold for most folks."

He imagined Katie in a neck-to-knee bathing costume, her hair tucked beneath a cap, droplets of water glistening on her skin. He found the image more inviting than he thought he should. "Too cold for me these days. I'm not a young boy anymore."

She laughed. "What's that got to do with it?"

Everything, he wanted to tell her. *It's got everything to do with it.* Especially when he looked at her and saw anything but his childhood friend and swimming buddy. Especially when she watched him with those luminous, guileless eyes of hers. Especially when he should be thinking about Charlotte instead. Charlotte wanted what Ben wanted—home and family. Charlotte would be a wonderful wife for any man. Katie would always be special to him, but she wanted something different for her life than to be a wife.

"Come on, Benjie. We've scarcely had a moment alone since I got back. You can spare me a few hours."

Guilt warred with temptation. It was Charlotte he ought to spend his Saturdays with. Charlotte was the young woman everyone expected him to marry.

But is Charlotte who I want to marry? He didn't know. He felt all confused.

"Benjie?"

"All right. I'll go." But he was going to be sorry. He knew it as surely as he knew his own name.

※◆※

Two hours later they lay on a blanket, warming themselves in the sun. Katie couldn't remember a more perfect afternoon than this one. It was like being a child again. She and Ben had swung on the old rope and plunged into the icy pool below. Shouting and laughing, they'd splashed each other in a water war. They'd raced each other to one end of the pond and back again. And finally, shivering, their lips blue, they'd dropped onto the blanket and waited for the sun to drive away the chill from their bones.

Perfect. A perfect day.

Katie rolled onto her side, her head supported by the heel of her hand, her elbow resting on the ground. Ben's eyes were closed, his face turned toward the sun.

His mother had told her Ben worked too hard, and Katie believed it. She'd noticed the tightness that appeared on his face occasionally, but it was gone for the moment.

"It's good to see you relax, Benjie."

He opened his eyes, and Katie felt a strange drop in her stomach, like when she'd let go of the rope and fallen into the icy water. Her insides went all aquiver.

She sat up and stared at the pond, not understanding the

wave of emotions rushing through her. A moment later Ben did the same.

"Why did you come back to Homestead, Benjie?"

"I never wanted to live anywhere but here."

"But I thought—"

"Your dreams always took you away from here, Katie. Mine always brought me back." He tossed a pebble into the water. "I like the quiet sameness of each day. I like knowing by name everyone who walks into my office. I like being part of a place where people care about one another, where they care about the ordinary, everyday kinds of things."

"But you could have been famous. You could have—"

"That sort of success wasn't worth what I would've had to give up, Katie. I want to put down roots here in Homestead, same as my parents did. I want a home, a wife, children. All the normal things, I guess. I suppose that doesn't sound like much to you, but it does to me."

Silence fell around them, as if anticipating Katie's next question.

"Are you going to marry Charlotte?" Her chest felt tight. She didn't dare look at Ben, but she wasn't sure why. She didn't understand much of anything at the moment.

"She's a lovely woman."

"Yes, she is."

"Charlotte told me she likes you."

"I get the feeling she likes everyone." *Saint Charlotte,* Katie thought sarcastically, then was instantly ashamed of herself.

"What about you, Katie? Is there anyone special, anyone—"

"I've already told you I don't intend to get married." She rose from the blanket and walked to the water's edge.

"That could change if you met the right man."

She turned to look at him. "I don't *want* to meet a man. My work is too important to me. This is what I believe I was born to do. St. Paul said it was good not to marry if singleness is one's calling." Her throat felt tight as she added, "I don't want to change, Benjie. This is who I am."

As Ben rose from the blanket, she watched, keenly aware that he was no longer the boy she used to swim with, cognizant of how tall he'd become, of the breadth of his wide shoulders, the cut of his strong jaw, the set of his fine mouth. He drew near to her, and her awareness of the changes in him intensified.

It wasn't until he'd gathered her in his arms and pulled her head against his chest that she realized she was crying.

"It's okay, Katie. Nobody's asking you to change. Especially not me."

But he was. In some strange, indefinable way, Ben Rafferty had silently asked her to be someone and something different from who and what she was. She'd felt it in her heart, seen it in his eyes. She wasn't sure what it meant or why it hurt so much. She only knew their friendship had been altered.

Katie rarely felt fear, but at this moment she *was* afraid. She felt as if she were standing on a precipice, ready to topple over the edge, and the bottom was too far away to see.

Ben's hand gently stroked her head. "I think it's time we started back to town. I . . . I'm having supper tonight at Charlotte's. I need to clean up."

Katie fought a new wave of tears, hot and burning in her throat, but she swallowed them back as she slowly withdrew from his embrace. "Of course." She wiped her eyes with the backs of her hands. "I didn't realize it had grown so late."

"You go on and change. I'll wait by the Susan B."

Her throat was too thick to speak, so she simply nodded, then went to gather her clothes so she could dress and then drive Ben back to town. . . .

Back to Charlotte.

SIX

A shiver of excitement traced Katie's spine as she entered the Homestead Community Church the following Tuesday evening. She'd been asked to speak to the women of the Morning Glory Circle about her experiences in Washington, D.C. This was her first—and, perhaps, most important—opportunity to share the significance of the suffrage movement with the women of Homestead.

For three days now she'd been wrestling with a strange malaise, a feeling that nothing was going to go right, a disquiet of her heart. But now she was herself again. Her sense of purpose and direction had returned with a new and greater assurance.

After opening with a brief word of prayer, Katie smiled at the group of women seated before her. "Thank you all for coming tonight and for asking me to be here with you." Her gaze scanned the crowd.

In the first row were Katie's mother and grandmother. Their eyes shone with pride, love, and support. Beside them were Sophia and Rose Rafferty and Charlotte Orson. Sophia leaned slightly forward on her chair, as if afraid she might miss some word of importance. Charlotte's demeanor was much more reserved. The schoolmarm, Blanche Coleson—dressed all in black, not so much as a hair out of place—sat in the second row next to the three Barber sisters: Leslie Blake, Annalee Leonhardt, and Rachel Henderson. Fanny McLeod, the doctor's wife, sat behind Blanche in the third row. Even Madeline Percy, a member of First Church since becoming that minister's wife, had come to hear Katie speak. There were others, many more than Katie had dared hope for.

"I must tell you before I begin that I'm rather nervous. I have not done a great deal of public speaking."

"You'll do just fine," Priscilla Jacobs stated with a nod of encouragement.

Katie drew a deep breath and began. "As most of you know, I've been living and working in Washington, D.C., since my graduation from Vassar College. During the past three years, I've had the rare opportunity to meet many dedicated people who are working hard so that all women have equal opportunities in this great country of ours."

Images of the women she'd worked with flashed in her mind, each of them smiling, as if to say, *You're doing fine, Katie.*

"For centuries, women have been at the center of the home. We have believed in the sanctity of marriage. We have raised our children to be moral and upright citizens. We have sought to help others through our Christian work. In such organizations as the Woman's Christian Temperance Union, women have sought to broaden the sense of social responsibility in men, not only in the home but in the larger community."

"That's true," Leslie Blake whispered to her two sisters, but loud enough for everyone to hear. "Mother worked with the WCTU before we came to Homestead."

"Much has been accomplished in the past fifty years since the end of the Civil War," Katie went on. "Improvements have been realized in laws that govern property rights for married and single women, legal guardianship of minor children, and rights of contract. But we have a long way to go to reach true equality. We do not yet have the same rights under the law as men. We are still often at the mercy of unfair practices and we lack equal educational and employment opportunities, solely because of our gender."

Katie had their full attention, and knowing it made her pulse race with excitement.

"Even now, the Suffrage Special is finishing its tour of the enfranchised states. Suffrage leaders are calling upon women voters to meet in Chicago on June fifth to form a new party. Those of us currently entrusted with the right to vote must continue to use every means at our disposal until that same right is granted to all women."

Katie noticed a few furtive glances, but she ignored them.

"The current Democratic administration refuses to support woman's suffrage, and our strategy must continue to be that of holding responsible the party in power. It is up to those of us who have the right to vote to see that the Democrats are not reelected to office at any level."

This time there was some noticeable shifting on chairs. Katie could feel members of her audience pulling back from her. Her tone strengthened with new urgency. She couldn't let them slip away. She had to convince them of the truth in what she said.

"Tonight I am asking that you exercise your right to vote in the coming elections. I ask you to consider your votes carefully, both in the primaries and in November. I ask that you do not reelect Governor Alexander, because of his party affiliation if for no other reason. I ask that you speak to your husbands and encourage them to do likewise. We must refuse to uphold any party that has ignored the claims of women."

Madeline Percy rose from her chair. "I cannot believe we have been invited to this church—to this place of worship—to listen to such rubbish. Miss Jones, the glory of womanhood has been her purity, her superiority to men in the possession of a higher moral sense and standard. Would you have us risk this precious certainty for a doubtful good?"

"Mrs. Percy, my Bible tells me that all—men and women alike—have sinned and fallen short of the glory of God. I cannot believe that women innately have a higher moral sense than men anymore than I can believe we are inferior and more prone to deception as the daughters of Eve."

"You are no minister. You have no authority to teach what the Bible says."

Losing patience, Katie inquired, "Is it your wish, Mrs. Percy, to be dominated by ignorance or selfishness or by both?"

"Well, I never!" Madeline's pointed chin thrust upward, and her eyes flashed with indignation. She whirled, pushing her way past Sarah Wesley as she marched out of the church.

Katie swept her gaze over the remaining women in the room. Their expressions were varied, from horrified to confused to exultant. Hoping to soothe those who had been affronted, Katie softened her tone, "Susan B. Anthony once wrote that sometimes those women who oppose their own freedom have been so thoroughly trained to let men do all the thinking, they have really come to believe it is unwomanly to think and express an opinion themselves concerning a public question. They conscientiously and earnestly believe it is somehow more creditable to beg a man to vote than it is to show one's appreciation of the dignity of a vote by using the ballot oneself. They forget, too, but for the suffrage movement, they would not have the privilege of coming before men in public to criticize and to ask that we, those of us who fight for suffrage for all, not be given the things for which we pray."

A frown creased Lark's forehead, but Grandma Addie continue to smile, as if delighted by every word Katie uttered. Sophia looked, at turns, both confused and inspired. Blanche's face was flushed, and she was nodding in agreement. Charlotte remained serene, her expression revealing none of her thoughts.

Katie drew another deep breath. "The politicians in Washington are currently consumed by the problem of neutrality toward the European war. They say they cannot allow anything such as suffrage for women to interfere with these concerns. These politicians—all men, I might remind you—believe it is their business to keep the United States of America out of the carnage in Europe. But when, I ask you, have men shown themselves adept at keeping nations out of war? Woman's suffrage is not unimportant, nor should it be shuffled aside. Women must pursue this right, no matter what other issues arise. We have voices. We must raise them."

Blanche Coleson jumped to her feet and began to applaud. "Bravo, Miss Jones! Bravo!"

Others, however, quickly gathered their belongings and slipped from the room, no doubt wishing they had followed Madeline Percy when she'd first stormed out. But the majority remained. They came forward to congratulate Katie, to tell her they had enjoyed her speech, to say she'd done an admirable job, and to ask questions about the association. By this time the nervousness she'd felt earlier had disappeared. She didn't mind that some of her audience had rejected what she said. She'd known better than to expect all to embrace the cause.

She could scarcely wait to send a letter to Penelope Rudyard, detailing tonight's triumph. Her friend would be proud of her, as would all the others in NAWSA's offices. There was still much to be done, as Katie had told the women here tonight, but she'd made a start.

It wasn't until she and her mother, having watched Grandma Addie ride away with Grandpa Will, were climbing into the Susan B for the drive home that Katie realized Charlotte had not remained to talk after her speech.

As Ben reached for his suit coat, a knock rattled the window in the newspaper office's door. He turned and was surprised to find Charlotte standing on the other side.

He hurried to let her in. "I was just on my way over to the church. Why didn't you wait for me there?"

"I did wait for a while. But when you didn't arrive, I thought I would come here." There was a quaver in her voice.

Ben glanced at the clock on the wall.

"The meeting didn't last as long as we'd expected," she said in answer to his unspoken question.

He put his hands on her upper arms. "Charlotte, is something wrong?"

She shook her head without meeting his gaze.

"Charlotte?"

She looked up. "I'm afraid Miss Jones has made herself rather unpopular with certain members of our community. Oh, Benjamin, you must tell her to be more circumspect."

"What's happened?"

"She has no idea how outrageous she sounds, spouting those progressive ideologies. She can only cause trouble, making women unhappy with their lot in life."

So Katie was being Katie. Ben smiled, imagining what she must have said, how her eyes must have sparkled with enthusiasm.

"Benjamin, are you listening to me?"

He focused his gaze on the woman before him. "Of course."

"Miss Jones is your friend. You must caution her before she gets hurt. There are some who can be cruel under the guise of righteous indignation. You know whom I mean. They will make things very unpleasant for her."

How like Charlotte to disagree with Katie but want to protect her at the same time. He should love her for that alone.

But I haven't fallen in love with her yet. Why is that? Am I expecting love to feel different than it really is? Do I want something that doesn't exist?

He thought of Katie in her bathing costume, her dark hair stringing down her back. He pictured her swinging on the old rope over the pond, letting go, falling with a shriek and a great splash. It was as though that splash rippled through him, this time carrying a startling realization with it.

I'm in love with Katie.

Perhaps he'd known it that day by the water, that day when she'd told him she would never marry, that day when he'd held her against him and she'd cried. Or perhaps he'd known it the day he'd called on her at the Lazy L, the day he'd convinced himself everyone was as fond of Katie as he was. Or perhaps he'd known it the very moment she'd arrived back in Homestead, when she'd stood before him, a woman instead of a tomboy in pigtails.

But he hadn't wanted to face it then, and he didn't want to face it now. Because nothing else had changed. Katie had no intention of sharing her life with a man, of marrying and settling down and having a family. That wasn't what Katie wanted.

And what did *he* want? The very things Katie didn't want—marriage, children, a home, and family.

"Benjamin?" Charlotte's fingers alighted on his forearm. "You *will* talk to Miss Jones, won't you? You will caution her about the things she says?"

"Yes," he answered absentmindedly, "I'll talk to Katie."

"Thank you. I knew I could count on you."

He nodded, still distracted.

Suddenly, Charlotte took his face between her hands, pulled his head toward her, and kissed him. Not a chaste kiss on the cheek, but one on the lips. It was tender, sweet, and brief. Too brief, perhaps, to cause the reaction she must have wanted him to feel. The reaction he *didn't* feel.

"Benjamin," she whispered as she drew back from him. "I . . . I don't know what came over me. I'm sorry." Her cheeks were flushed, and he knew she was embarrassed by her own impulsive action.

Why didn't he feel for Charlotte what she obviously felt for him? He should. It made perfect sense. At least it did to most of the folks in town. If he just gave himself a little more time, time to spend with Charlotte, to get to know her in a deeper way, surely feelings of love would follow. As for Katie, time would take care of her, too. The two of them had been friends all their lives. They would go on being friends. This . . . *feeling* he had for her would pass, and what would remain in its wake would be the affection of old friends.

"Charlotte," he said, offering his arm to her, "allow me to see you home."

The large plate-glass window of the newspaper office, combined with the golden glow of lamplight, provided an easy view of the kissing couple for anyone who happened along Main Street. Certainly both Katie and her mother saw them as the motorcar rolled past the *Homestead Herald* on their way out of town.

"Well, it shouldn't be long now," Lark commented.

"What shouldn't be long?"

"Before we hear the announcement of their engagement— Ben and Charlotte's. Not that we all haven't been expecting it. They've always seemed so well suited."

"Have they?"

Katie was glad for the shelter of night. She didn't know what she was feeling at the moment, but she didn't want her mother to see whatever was written on her face.

"You should be happy for Ben," Lark chastised gently.

"I am."

"Katie . . ." Her mother paused a moment, then continued, "did you and Ben have a quarrel?"

"No, we haven't quarreled."

An unwelcome memory flooded her mind. The memory of Ben's arms around her, his hand stroking her head. The clean, manly scent of him lingered in her nostrils. The gentle tone of his voice echoed in her ears.

Ben would marry Charlotte before long. Everyone expected it. Tonight Katie had seen evidence that confirmed the expectations of one and all. She should be glad for Ben.

She should be glad for Charlotte. They were perfect for each other. Ben wanted to be married, and Charlotte would make him a wonderful wife. It was as clear as anything that this was the right choice for Katie's dear, dear friend.

Then why didn't she feel happy for him?

Katie wasn't so naive that she didn't recognize envy when she felt it. But *why* was she envious? She didn't *want* to marry. She'd made that decision long ago. It wasn't that she didn't believe in the institution of marriage. She had grown up surrounded by good examples of what marriage could and should be like. But . . .

Lark's fingers alighted on Katie's arm. "What's troubling you, dear?"

"I don't know. Maybe I just realized Benjie and I aren't children any longer."

"No." Her mother chuckled. "Indeed you're not."

"Will she really make him happy?" Sadness pierced Katie's heart as she asked the question, not certain what she wanted the answer to be.

"Yes, Katie, I believe Charlotte will make him happy."

She released a shallow sigh. "Then I'm glad for them both. Honest and truly, I am."

SEVEN

Ben was on his way to the office the following morning when he noticed a small group of men standing in front of Childers Livery.

"Well, I'll be hanged if I'll have my wife listenin' to such claptrap," Norman Henderson shouted. "Yancy ought t'have enough backbone to make that gal of his stay at home and mind her tongue. Her and her fast ways."

So, it's begun already. Ben walked across the dusty street to join the others.

Seeing his approach, Norman pointed an accusing finger in his direction. "Ben Rafferty, you're as much at fault as that father of hers."

"At fault for what, Norm?"

"What possessed you t'let her write for your newspaper?"

"Because Miss Jones has the necessary skills and education to do it and do it well. And because—as owner, editor, and publisher—I thought the paper ought to have such a column."

"We don't need her puttin' her highfalutin Eastern ideas in your paper for our women to read. Gives 'em notions to want things they weren't meant to have."

Ben raised an eyebrow. "Are you afraid of what *your* wife might learn? Are you afraid she'll start thinking for herself?"

The farmer's cheeks turned red, and his eyes bulged.

"Listen, Ben," Leroy Smith, the town's banker, interrupted before Norman could explode. "I'm not saying women shouldn't have the right to vote. They've had it in Idaho for the last twenty years, and it hasn't done this state any harm." He adjusted his glasses on the bridge of his nose. "But when Miss Jones begins telling folks to vote the governor out of office because his party isn't supporting something she wants . . ."

Oh, Katie, you are stirring up a hornet's nest, aren't you?

Matthew's father, the Reverend Simon Jacobs, cleared his throat. "Seems to me she's done nothing except speak her mind regarding a public official. That's done in every election. Public debate is a time-honored tradition. It's the American way."

"What else could you say, Reverend?" Norman asked gruffly. "She was invited to speak in *your* church last night. And I still want to hear what Rafferty means to do about that column of hers."

Ben skewered the farmer with an intense gaze but held his anger in check. "I don't intend to do anything except publish it. Miss Jones hasn't abused her position with the *Herald*, nor has she jeopardized the integrity of the paper by what she's written. As a citizen of this town and of this state, she has a right to express her opinions."

"What she needs is a good thrashin'."

One quick stride brought Ben nose to nose with Norman Henderson. When he spoke, he measured his words with care. "I think not."

"Gentlemen, please." Reverend Jacobs placed his arms between Ben and Norman and eased them apart. "We accomplish nothing by fighting among ourselves."

"We don't need her kind of thinkin' round here."

Ben itched to punch Norman square between the eyes.

"Let's all be about our work now," the reverend encouraged before Ben could follow through on his impulse.

For a moment no one moved. The air, totally motionless, seemed thick. Then the men began to disperse, heading to their places of business or to their farms and homes. Finally only Ben and Reverend Jacobs remained.

Ben let out a long breath of air. "Sorry, Reverend."

"Quite all right, young man. I must confess I, too, was losing my temper." Reverend Jacobs tapped his chin with his index finger, his expression thoughtful. "You might warn Katie about the attitude of these men."

That was the second time in less than twenty-four hours Ben had been asked to talk to Katie, but he didn't particularly want to oblige either Charlotte or the reverend. He wasn't prepared to face Katie just yet, not while the realization of his feelings for her was still so fresh in his mind.

And in his heart.

The reverend gave his head a slow shake. "My wife doesn't

agree. She was quite taken by what Katie had to say last night, and I suspect others were, too. Although her opinions are anything but traditional, I find no scriptural error in them." He chuckled softly. "I don't believe Norman or my son or any of the others realize what they're up against when it comes to Katie."

"No, they don't."

"I daresay Homestead is going to be changed by the return of Miss Jones."

Yes, Homestead would be changed by her return, and Ben's whole world was changing right with it.

"Well, I must be on my way. I promised to make a call out at the Evans farm this morning. Mr. Childers should have my buggy ready to go. Good day to you, Benjamin." With that, the reverend turned and disappeared through the open doorway of the livery.

***

Wednesday, May 31, 1916

My dear Penny,

Last night I spoke to the women of the Morning Glory Circle, explaining the importance of woman's suffrage and how much their votes are needed in this year's elections. My speech met with some resistance, but overall, I would say it was a success.

Mrs. Percy, wife of the minister at First Church, walked out in the middle of my presentation. There was an exchange of words between us, and my attitude, I'm ashamed to say, was not very Christian. But everyone else remained to hear me through, despite my lapse in judgment. Although some were obviously affronted by the notion of women thinking and acting for themselves independently of their husbands or fathers, most were at least willing to listen and consider what I had to say and not reject everything straightaway.

Upon my return to Homestead, my dear friend Benjamin Rafferty agreed to allow me to write a column for the newspaper. He's given it a highly objectionable heading too adorable to be stomached. (Your title, dear Penny, was by far superior.) My first column appeared in last week's edition of the Herald. It was a pleasant little piece, written with great care in order to appeal to one and all. I must have succeeded because my father liked it exceedingly well.

Since I was much too excited after my speaking engagement to sleep, I finished my second column early this morning, long before the rising of the sun. I was not as restrained as I was with my first endeavor. I suppose I must prepare myself for even more objections than those that my speech aroused. But when haven't we encountered resistance and objections to the truth we share with others?

I realize, dearest Penny, that this letter shall be posted and arrive in Washington before you return from the convention in Chicago. I am quite envious of you and the thousands of women who will be there, and I sometimes wonder at my decision to return to Homestead before rather than after such a momentous and historic event. However, my work is begun, and I cannot leave it, so I will be content with my choice.

I must close now and deliver my column to my editor. I wouldn't want Mr. Rafferty to be upset with his new columnist.

Give my regards to one and all.

Your devoted friend,
Katherine Lark Jones

Postscript. It appears my dear Benjie will be getting married soon.

Sophia's hands paused above the bread dough. "Mother?"

"Hmmm."

She glanced over her shoulder toward the table where Rose Rafferty was rolling piecrusts. "Has Father ever made you feel that . . . that you hadn't the right to think for yourself?"

"What a question!"

"I know you and Father love each other, and you think he's just about perfect in every way. But do you ever wish . . ." She let her voice trail into silence, uncertain what it was she wanted to ask.

Rose wiped her hands of flour and walked to her daughter's side. A frown knit her dark brows. "Has this something to do with Katie's talk last night?"

"Not really." Sophia shook her head, then sighed. "It has more to do with Matthew."

Her mother touched her shoulder in gentle encouragement but said nothing. She simply waited until Sophia was ready to continue.

Tears welled in Sophia's eyes as she stared down at the lump of bread dough before her. "I'm not sure I can be the sort of wife he expects me to be."

"And what is that?"

"Subservient." She sighed again. "Unable to think for myself."

Her mother placed her arm around Sophia's back.

"Sometimes it seems he doesn't listen to me or care what I think or feel. As if . . . as if whatever I have to say couldn't possibly be of any importance because—" she paused to take a quick breath, then finished— "because I'm a woman."

"I see."

Sophia moved away from her mother's protective arm. "I was so happy when Matthew proposed." She walked to the sink, where she washed away the traces of dough and flour from her hands. Then, restlessly, she began to pace the circumference of the kitchen. "Truly, I was happy. But what if I was wrong about marrying him? What if I don't . . . love him enough?" *What if I don't love him at all?*

"Sophia, come and sit down."

She paused in her pacing to glance at her mother.

Rose pointed at a chair near the table. "Sit down, dear. We need to talk."

With her shoulders suddenly slumped, Sophia did as her mother instructed.

Once they were both seated, Rose leaned forward, reaching across the table with both arms, and took hold of her daughter's hands, giving them a light squeeze. "Sophia, marriage isn't easy under the best of circumstances. Even when two people are in love and want only the best for each other, it's difficult. It takes listening and compromise and understanding and patience." She smiled gently. "Goodness knows, it's a miracle when the right people find each other. I know it was a miracle I found your father. I tried hard enough to run away from my feelings for him."

For as long as she could remember, Sophia had witnessed that tender expression steal across her mother's face whenever she talked about Michael Rafferty. It had been Sophia's dream to marry and have children and to talk about her husband with that same sort of rapt countenance. But lately it seemed all she felt for Matthew was irritation.

Her mother's grip tightened. "I wonder if I haven't given you the impression things have been perfect for your parents. If so, I can assure you that isn't true. Your father and I have had disagreements—plenty of them—throughout our marriage. But our love and respect for each other as individuals helped us solve our differences. Your father sees me as an equal, both personally and spiritually. He doesn't dominate. He leads with love." Her eyes narrowed. "Have you told Matthew what you're feeling? Have you tried talking to him?"

Sophia shook her head.

"Well then, you must do so at once." Rose released her daughter's hands and sat back on her chair. "Your wedding is less than a week away."

"But I don't know what to say."

"You'll think of something."

"What if . . . what if nothing changes after we've talked? Or what if I'm wrong, and then he decides not to marry me and I lose him?"

"Better to find out now before you're married, rather than after, when it's too late to change things."

Sophia knew her mother was right, but fear made it difficult to follow the advice. Not a fear that nothing would change. Fear that *everything* would change.

She'd had a crush on Matthew since she was a girl in braids and short skirts. She'd decided he was the man she wanted to marry when she was sixteen and he was twenty-three. She'd nearly given up hope of his proposing as one year after another slipped away. She'd begun to believe she was destined to be an old maid.

Then, last winter, the day a gently falling snow had turned the valley into a wonderland of white, he'd appeared on her front porch and made all her dreams come true with three little words: *Sophia, marry me.*

Was she prepared to risk the future she'd dreamed of by causing an argument now? They'd never disagreed on anything before Katie's return to Homestead. What if he was right about Katie? What if Katie's views were nonsense and Sophia was being led astray by them? What if she was merely feeling prewedding jitters and nothing more?

As if in answer to her unspoken questions, she recalled something Katie had said to her. *"The problem with too many marriages is that the wife throws away every plan and purpose for her own life—including the ones God has called her to—in order to conform to the plan and purpose of the husband's life. Men seem to want wives with intelligence, and then, after they are married, they want to make these same women into reflections of themselves. Only when men begin to recognize their wives as equals, only when wives stop selling their birthright for a beggarly portion, shall all women benefit. As Christians we are called to be meek but never cowardly, never timid."*

Sophia lifted her gaze. "You're right, Mother. I must speak to him."

"Yes, dear. You must." Rose offered a smile of encouragement. "It will be all right. You'll see."

"I hope so. I do hope so."

❈

Katie sat on the running board of the Susan B, her chin cupped in her hands, elbows resting on her thighs, while steam rose from the automobile's radiator. Of all the times for the flivver to overheat, this was not the best. Her column was due this afternoon.

Why, oh why, had she waited until the last minute to get it finished? She'd started it last Saturday. Why had she allowed other things to interfere with its completion until last night?

"We must not allow other demands on our lives to

98

impede our work," Alice Paul had told her once. "We must remain focused on our goal at all times, even when the demands of families—be they parents or husbands or children—would draw us away."

The rattle of harness and clip-clop of a horse's hooves intruded on Katie's memory. She straightened and looked down the road. Coming toward her in his buggy was Ben.

She felt an odd shortness of breath, as if she were as overheated as the Model T.

"Problems?" Ben called to her as he drew closer.

He was expected to marry Charlotte, she reminded herself. Everyone thought so. Even Katie.

She stood. "The Susan B overheated. I'll be able to get her started again in a little bit."

He stopped the buggy, then looped the reins and climbed out. "Does this happen often?"

He gave her that dazzling smile. It was easy to see why Charlotte would love Ben, would want to marry him, if for no other reason than he was the most handsome man in all of Long Bow Valley.

Katie watched as he stepped to the front of the motorcar and lifted the hood.

He bent over and stared at the machinery. "You're sure you don't have some other problem?"

Her heart twisted. "Like what?"

"With the engine." He glanced up, meeting her gaze. "Not that I'd know. I'm no mechanic."

He was going to marry Charlotte, and he was going to be very happy. Katie was going to be thrilled for him. When his children were born, they would call her Auntie Katie, and perhaps she would take care of them on occasion. She would hold them as she had her aunt Naomi's baby, and they would giggle and coo, and she would love them. When they were older, she would tell them stories about their father when he was a boy.

"Katie?"

She blinked. "What? Oh . . . no, there's nothing wrong with the engine. The Susan B just likes to overheat every now and again. It's part of her charm." She turned and reached into the car. "I was bringing you my column."

"And I was on my way out to see you." Ben closed the hood.

Her heart thudded. "You were?"

"Yes. Charlotte asked me to speak to you."

Oh, Benjie, I do so want you to be happy. Really I do.

"Your talk last night has upset some folk."

Katie nodded, reminded suddenly of her mission in Homestead. She held out the carefully penned article. "If so, then this shall no doubt upset them further."

"Are you sure this is what you want to do, Katie?" He took it from her.

"I'm sure."

His voice softened. "Are you?"

She wanted to be angry. She wanted to upbraid him for speaking to her as if she were a schoolgirl, questioning her actions. But it wasn't anger she felt. It was confusion.

He drew a step closer as he perused the column she'd finished this morning. The sun glinted off his golden hair, casting a broad-shouldered shadow on the dusty road near her feet.

"Katie?"

Looking up, she felt a shortness of breath. "Don't worry about me, Benjie." She forced a smile. "I know what I'm doing."

But at the moment, she wondered if she spoke the truth.

 The Homestead Weekly Herald
Homestead, Idaho
Friday Morning
June 2, 1916

Katie's Corner: Current Law Says Women's Judgment Unsound

In 1896, when I was but four years old, the govern-ing body of the state of Idaho saw fit to enfran-chise women. Ever since, the vote has belonged to each of us as a right of our citizenship in this state. Yet many-dare I saw most-women of Idaho do not exercise that right of citizenship.

Why not? I must ask.

What a glorious thing it is to vote! Susan B. Anthony once said the law granting such a right implies that your judgment is sound and your opinion worthy to be counted. Yet in most of the country the law says that women's judgment is unsound and their opinions unworthy.

Without the right to vote, the blessings of liberty are forever withheld from women and their female posterity. The time is now for Idaho women in all walks of life-married and single, old and young-to step forward and be counted in support of the national suffrage amendment. . . .

That Friday's edition of the *Homestead Herald* incited more arguments than any edition since the paper was founded.

At the Lazy L Ranch, Yancy found himself in hot water with Lark when he suggested their daughter might want to give up writing for the newspaper. How, for the love of Pete, he inquired, was she going to get some fella's spurs all in a tangle if she kept on actin' like she didn't have enough sense to teach a hen to cluck? His wife responded by saying maybe their daughter wanted more out of life than to tangle some idiot's spurs. At which point each quit speaking to the other—Yancy riding out to check fences and Lark yanking weeds from her garden with more than her usual resolve.

At the Henderson farm, Norman made it clear he would not tolerate his wife—and the mother of his three grown sons—attending any future meetings of the Morning Glory Circle where Katie might be speaking. Nor was he to see her reading the propaganda included in *that woman's* column. Rachel agreed, but he found his next meal charred beyond recognition.

When George Blake commented that Katie's progressive notions wouldn't hold with the womenfolk of Long Bow Valley—since they knew their proper place—Leslie Blake wanted to know if he thought her vote was wasted because she was female. His reply regarding women and the ballot box, spoken with a laugh and meant as a joke, guaranteed he would be sleeping on the sofa for at least the next week.

While eating his breakfast at Zoe's Restaurant that morning, Phillip Carson made a ribald comment about fast young women who didn't know their place was to be either wives or schoolteachers, whereupon Blanche Coleson, who was seated at the next table, rose from her chair and dumped her meal of fried eggs and sausage over the top of his head.

After a fistfight broke out behind Childers Livery between Sam Jones and Andrew Henderson, the mayor and the sheriff paid a joint call on the editor of the *Homestead Herald*.

"Listen, Benjamin," Albert Tobias, the mayor, pleaded, "I'm asking you to stop publishing that column. For the sake of the community."

Sheriff Frank Murray rested his knuckles on the top of Ben's desk. "No one knows better than I do how pigheaded that niece of mine can be. The whole lot of Rider women are headstrong and opinionated." He rapped the desk four times, in rhythm with his words. "But by sugar, Ben, this is letting things go too far. You're the one who hired Katie, and you've got to fire her. Cancel that tripe before we've got every wife in the valley knocking her husband over the head with an iron skillet."

Ben couldn't help it—he laughed.

The mayor puffed up like a bantam rooster. "This is *not* a laughing matter."

Ben rubbed his hand over his face, fighting for control. He knew it wasn't funny. The suffrage issue had divided many people down through the years, and his quiet little hometown wasn't likely to be any different. But as editor he also knew the matter to be newsworthy. He didn't ask everyone to agree with what was in the newspaper, only that they read and consider it.

For that matter, he wasn't sure *he* agreed with everything

Katie had written. But he did believe in the freedom of speech, and he wasn't about to allow anyone to silence Katie just because they didn't want to hear an opinion that differed from their own.

Ben rose from his chair. "Gentlemen, I know this isn't a joking matter, and I apologize for my laughter. I also regret that anything printed in the *Herald* has caused fights among our citizens." He gave each of them a pointed look. "But the readers of my newspaper *will* be kept apprised of matters of interest in our country and our world. The passage of a national woman's suffrage amendment is just such a matter. And there is no one in Long Bow Valley more qualified to write about it than our own Miss Jones."

Frank took a step backward. "I'll be hanged if you don't believe that nonsense, too."

What Ben really believed was that he cared about Katie. Cared about her too much to let folks stop her from doing whatever would make her happy, whatever she cared about so passionately.

He wanted to shield her, too, from the anger her words had stirred up, but she wouldn't let him. Although she hadn't said it aloud, she'd made it clear, the day he'd come upon her and the overheated Susan B, that she wouldn't have him protecting her. She was determined to do this, to convince the people of this valley and probably the entire state to use their ballots to help all women get the vote.

Come to think of it, didn't all women *deserve* that right?

He met Frank's inquisitive gaze. "Yes, I guess I do believe that nonsense."

Katie was horrified when her brother Sam walked into the kitchen, sporting a black eye, a swollen nose, and various other cuts and bruises.

"This ain't nothin'." He gingerly washed the dried blood from the corner of his nose. "Wait 'til you hear what the schoolmarm did to old Mr. Carson at the restaurant."

Despite Sam's jocular way of telling a story, Katie's horror didn't lessen when she heard the details of both his fight with the youngest Henderson brother and the altercation between Blanche Coleson and the barber.

"Oh, dear . . ." She covered her face with her hands. "Benjie warned me. I knew some folks would disagree with what I had to say, but I never thought it would come to fisti-cuffs." She looked at Sam through parted fingers, needing reassurance that he wasn't badly hurt.

"You needed someone to stand up for you." He fingered the swollen corner of his mouth. "I couldn't have Andrew sayin' things about my own sister. Not the sorts o' things he was sayin'."

Her voice dropped to a whisper as she lowered her hands. "Like what?"

"Ain't important."

"Like what, Sam?"

Her brother shook his head, a stubborn look turning his face to stone. It was that same look all the Jones men got when they were through talking and nothing anyone did could drag another word out of them.

But she didn't need him to say more. She could guess what Andrew had said. She'd heard enough insults slung at the women who participated in suffrage parades or who spoke at assemblies and conventions. Her imagination was fertile enough to fill in her brother's silence with any number of comments that might have incited Sam to feel obligated to fight on her behalf.

She rose from her chair and crossed the kitchen. Even though Sam was seven years younger, he stood ten inches taller, and Katie had to reach high to touch his cheek with her fingertips.

"Thank you for defending my honor, Sammy. I should have realized what my work would do to all of you. I'm sorry. Truly sorry."

"Ahh, it's all right, sis. I don't reckon I minded. I never have cared much for Andy anyhow." He tried to smile, but the swollen left corner of his mouth wouldn't oblige.

Katie felt like hitting somebody herself. It shouldn't have to be like this. Why couldn't they all see that? Why were the hopes and dreams and desires of women thought to be unimportant, secondary—even to the women themselves?

Her pulse quickened. This was not the time to pull back and apologize, she realized with sudden clarity. This was the time to organize, to take action.

Katie turned from her brother and hurried across the kitchen.

"Where're you off to?" Sam asked.

"To town. I need to pay a few calls."

It took Katie only a matter of minutes to gather her handbag, a pencil and notebook, and her hat. Then she was down the stairs and out the front door, hurrying toward the Susan B.

"No acting up today," she told the automobile as she set the spark and throttle levers. "We have important work to do." She walked to the front of the motorcar, where she seized the crank with her right hand and slipped her left forefinger through the choke wire.

Katie was small, but she was strong. Starting the Susan B for the past year had seen to that. It took only two revolutions of the crank before the engine roared to life. Quickly she jumped onto the running board and adjusted the levers again. The Susan B coughed, sputtered, then settled into her normal putting and chugging noises.

"Attagirl." Katie slid across the imitation-leather seat and took hold of the steering wheel. She unblocked the hand brake and pressed down on the first-gear pedal, and they were off, Katie's thoughts moving even faster than the Model T's twenty-two miles per hour.

She would pay a visit to Sophia first. Sophia was well liked in Homestead. Unlike Katie, who had always been viewed as a bit strange, Sophia was a model of Homestead society's vision of proper young womanhood. If Sophia continued to show interest in woman's suffrage, it would strengthen the cause in Long Bow Valley.

Then, Katie decided, as soon as school let out she would stop in to see Blanche Coleson. Katie wasn't sure how she felt about the unmarried schoolmarm. Something in Blanche's manner made her nervous. However, Blanche was a staunch supporter of the cause, and that was what Katie needed now.

Finally she supposed she should drop by the paper. She didn't have to be told there were people pressuring Ben to cancel her column; she just knew. She also knew he wouldn't do it. Ben had too much integrity, was too good a news-paperman, to give in to such demands. Still, this was what he'd expected to happen. This was what he'd hoped to protect her from. She had to let him know she was holding up under fire.

I wonder what Charlotte thinks about it.

She frowned, and her hands tightened on the steering wheel. She should make a special effort to win Miss Orson's support. Did she want her own dear Benjie married to a mealymouthed woman who was afraid of her own shadow, too timid for words?

Her frown deepened. That wasn't fair. She didn't know that Charlotte was mealymouthed or timid. In fact, she liked her. Despite herself, she'd liked her.

And who wouldn't? Ben certainly liked her.

She recalled the way the two of them had looked, stand-ing near the plate-glass window of the newspaper office, lamplight spilling over them as they kissed.

Katie had never been kissed like that, with a man's arms wound around her, her head bent back, her body close to his. Of course, she'd had only a few gentlemen callers and so hadn't had many opportunities. Nonetheless, those kisses she'd received had been hurried and furtive and had left her uninterested in pursuing more of them.

But maybe, if she'd been kissed the way Ben had kissed Charlotte . . .

The small chimes above the Book Shoppe's doorway jingled as Sophia entered.

"Be right with you," Matthew said from somewhere deep in the store.

Sophia waited nervously for him to appear. It had taken her two full days to work up her courage, and it was all she could do to stand her ground.

As he stepped from behind the bookshelves and saw her, Matthew's face lit with a smile. "Sophia. What a pleasant surprise." He strode forward and placed a kiss on her cheek. "I assumed you'd be much too involved with last-minute plans for the wedding to come see me today. Only four days more and you'll be mine."

You'll be mine. . . . Why should those words bother her so much? Wasn't being his what she wanted?

"I . . . I needed to . . . to see you," she stammered. She drew a deep breath, trying to steady her nerves. "Matthew, we need to talk."

His fingers closed gently around her upper arms. "Is something wrong?"

"No." She shook her head. "No. I mean, I don't *think* anything's wrong. But we . . . I think we need to talk, Matthew."

"All right."

Cupping her right elbow in the palm of his left hand, he guided her toward a bench beneath the west side window. She settled onto it, smoothing her skirts as she did so. Then her fiancé sat beside her. Words whirled in her head as she sought the right ones with which to begin. But none seemed right.

"What is it?" Matthew prompted after a lengthy silence, a hint of impatience in his tone.

"Did you read Katie's column this morning?" She almost hoped he hadn't.

His expression hardened. "I did, and I'm of the firm opinion that your brother needs to put an end to it."

"Why do you think that?"

"Because it's nonsense, that's why. Katie always has been a peculiar one, but she's infecting the whole town with her odd views now. You've no idea how angry folks are."

"Why is it nonsense? *I* voted in the last election. Did you think that was nonsense? Was it wrong of me?"

"Of course it wasn't wrong, my dear girl. As you'll recall, we discussed each of the candidates, and I explained why you should vote as you did."

Sophia clenched her hands in her lap. "Are you so certain I voted as you wished?"

He looked confused.

"You really don't believe I'm intelligent enough to judge a candidate for myself, do you? You don't think I could cast a vote without asking you first."

"Sophia, you've changed the subject. But if it's politics you wish to discuss, I can only say women shouldn't concern themselves with it. It's a man's business. It always has been, and that's how it should remain."

She felt coiled as tight as a spring. "And what is a *woman's* business, Matthew?" Her voice was barely above a whisper. "Can you tell me that?"

"Why, the home, of course, and the children when they come." He looked so genuinely bemused by her questions that it might have been funny. It might have been. . . .

But it wasn't.

Sophia rose from the bench and stepped away. She heard Matthew rise as well, but she didn't look behind her. "I'm going to help Katie with her suffrage work, if she'll let me. I think you should know that."

"Help her! Great Scott, Sophia! Have you lost your senses?"

"No, I haven't. I may have just found them."

He took a quick step forward, stopping behind her, placing his hands on her shoulders. "My dear, you're going to be far too busy making our home comfortable to be gadding about with Katie."

Anger flared with a suddenness that shook her. "Not if I choose to give time to her work instead." She stared at the shop door, wishing he wasn't holding her shoulders, wishing she could leave now before anything worse happened.

"Think what it is you're saying, Sophia. You'll be ostracized. Half the town is already angry with Katie. Do you want them angry with you, too?"

"It's mostly the men who are angry, isn't it?"

"Does it matter?"

She turned to face him. "Not to me, it doesn't. I'm going to do it whether they're angry or not."

"Sophia, I *forbid* it."

114

She'd feared it would come to this. Deep down in her heart, she'd *known* it would come to this. And it was deep down in her heart where she hurt, now that it had happened.

She drew a breath and let it out on a sigh. "You can't forbid me, Matthew. I can do what I please."

"As your husband—"

"Don't say it." She took a step backward.

"I will not have my wife—"

"Matthew—" her voice quavered slightly— "I've loved you for a long, long time." She drew another quick breath, and her voice steadied, strengthened. "But I'm not a little girl with fairy-tale dreams. I'm a woman. I have a brain. I can think for myself. I don't need anyone to hold my hand and tell me what I should or shouldn't do."

"Of course you—"

"I want to be your wife, Matthew. But not if it means I'll cease to be a person whose opinions matter."

"That's the sort of idiotic blather you've been getting from Katie."

"It's not blather! And it's not from Katie." She pointed at her chest. "This is *me* talking, Matthew. Me. Sophia. The woman you're supposed to care about and listen to. The woman whose thoughts and feelings should matter to you more than anything else."

"Why are you acting so crazy? Have I said I didn't care?"

The anger drained out of her. "I'm not acting crazy. I am trying to tell you how I feel. I'm trying to tell you what's important to me. But you don't hear me, do you?" She shook her head. "Either that or you don't care. Which is it?"

"Sophia, you're tired. Getting ready for the wedding has left you emotionally drained. Why don't you go home and have a nap? You'll see things more clearly when you wake up."

Her heart was breaking, shattering along with her dreams. "I see things quite clearly right now." She removed her engagement ring and set it on the counter. "I'm very sorry, Matthew, but I cannot marry you."

Before he could voice another protest, she turned and fled the Book Shoppe.

NINE

Just as the Susan B arrived at the Rafferty house, Katie saw Sophia walking toward her from the direction of town. Katie slid across the seat and disembarked, waiting beside the automobile. Then she saw Ben's sister dab at her eyes with a handkerchief.

"Sophia?" Katie hurried forward. "What's wrong?"

Sophia shook her head.

"What happened?" Katie insisted.

Sophia offered a weak smile, accompanied by a shrug of her shoulders. "I've broken my engagement."

"Oh no." Katie covered her mouth. Her stomach felt like lead. "It's because of my column, isn't it?"

"No."

"I never thought—"

"It's not because of your column. It's because we weren't suited."

But Katie found the protest hard to believe. She remembered too well how lovesick Sophia had been at the age of sixteen. Back then Katie had been eager for college and new adventures, but Sophia had wanted only Matthew. Katie remembered the letters from home that had said what a perfect couple these two were. She couldn't believe that everyone—including Sophia and Matthew themselves—had been wrong.

Sophia touched Katie's forearm. "This has nothing to do with you." She smiled again, and this time the expression didn't appear as forced. "It really is for the best. I realized earlier this week that Matthew needs a different sort of wife than I can be."

"But you've loved him so very much."

"Yes, I did." The words were spoken softly—and with great finality.

"Oh, Sophia."

Ben's sister glanced toward the house. "I must go in and tell Mother."

"Of course. I'll come back another time."

Looking at Katie, Sophia said, "I know this is going to hurt for a while, but it is for the best. For both of us. We wouldn't have done well together. I would have made him unhappy in the end, and I would have been unhappy, too." Again she smiled gently. Again she touched Katie's arm. "Don't worry about me, and don't blame yourself. I was the one who made the decision. It was my choice."

Katie watched Sophia walk across the yard, climb the steps, and enter the front door of the Rafferty home. She hoped with all her heart that Sophia was right, but even if this was for the best, even if Katie shouldered no responsibility for it, she knew others would blame her. She believed, without a shred of doubt, in what she'd written, just as she believed in the truth of what she'd said during her speech to the ladies of the church circle. But if this breakup was her fault . . .

By rote she went through the motions of starting the Susan B, then climbed into the automobile and drove to the school, planning to talk to Blanche Coleson before returning to the ranch. She parked on West Street and stared at the white building as memories washed over her.

Years ago Katie had envied Sophia, who'd been so sure of what she wanted while Katie had still been searching. Sophia had known she wanted to marry Matthew, to settle down in Homestead and have a family. Katie, on the other hand, had felt a pull on her heart to go beyond this valley, to see more, to learn more, to do more—not knowing what *more* could be, knowing only that she had to find out.

It was while at Vassar that she'd first heard Inez Milholland speak on the suffrage issue. That night she had felt an absolute rightness, a sense of coming into her own, of belonging, of not being out of step. The pieces of her puzzled existence seemed to fall into place. The experience had deepened her faith as she began to understand the Creator's view of her—as a woman, as His daughter, as a fellow heir with Christ. It had made her ever more eager to serve Him by making life better for the women and children of this nation.

The old schoolhouse came back into focus, along with her conviction that she had a mission to accomplish in Idaho.

Would she have said anything different, done anything different, if she'd known Matthew and Sophia might break their
engagement over it? The answer was clearly no. And thus she
could only continue as she'd begun.

The doors of the school opened, and children—from six
to sixteen—ran out, filling the air with shouts and laughter.
They scattered in different directions—some of them on foot,
some of them on horseback. The Susan B drew many a gaze,
and three of the older boys mustered the courage to follow
her brother toward the automobile.

Rick jerked his head toward those behind him. "You don't
mind if my friends have a look, do you, Katie? I told 'em you
wouldn't."

"No. I don't mind." She got out and walked to the front of
the motorcar.

She knew all three of the boys. Shane Rafferty and Rick
had been friends since childhood. Kirby Evans, who lived on
a farm out in the valley, had been only eight years old when
Katie had left Homestead, but she recognized him because he
was the spitting image of his father, Ralph. The last boy, Clarence Yardley, was the druggist's son.

Katie greeted them each by name as they surrounded the
automobile.

"How fast does it go?" Shane lifted the hood to stare at the
engine.

"I've heard the touring car can go as fast as forty miles an
hour," Katie said. "But I've never had the courage to test it for
myself."

"What's keepin' it runnin'?" Kirby inquired. "Pa said

you're bound t'run out o' fuel sooner or later and then you'll have t'let it sit and rust. He says a horse'll never run out o' power as long as there's grass t'eat."

Katie laughed. "I'm afraid your pa will be disappointed. I've had gasoline sent up from Boise City on the train. There's not going to be any lack of fuel for the Susan B."

Clarence leaned over the door to check the interior. "Is it hard t'learn to drive?"

"Not really."

Rick turned wide eyes on his sister. "You reckon you could teach us?"

The others all looked at her, too.

"Sorry, boys." She watched disappointment wash over them, and she couldn't help but respond to it. "Tell you what. You come to the Lazy L sometime, and I'll show you how everything works. I won't let you actually drive, but I can teach you about starting her and what each of the pedals do and so forth."

"We'll be there, Miss Jones," Kirby promised. "How 'bout tomorrow?"

"Yeah. How 'bout tomorrow?" the others all chimed in.

"All right," she relented. "When you're done with your chores and if your folks say it's all right, then I'll do it."

"Swell!" they chorused.

Katie looked at her brother. "I've got a few more errands to do in town. Do you want to wait for a ride home?"

"Naw. I've got my horse over at the Raffertys' place."

The boys bade her good-bye and dispersed in pairs, Kirby and Clarence headed into town, Shane and Rick walking along the road in the opposite direction. Katie watched them go, then turned toward the schoolhouse as the door opened again and Blanche stepped onto the landing.

The schoolmarm grinned when she saw Katie. "Miss Jones, how fortuitous. I was thinking about paying you a call." She quickly locked the door, then descended the steps and closed the distance between them.

Even though speaking with Blanche was the reason Katie had come to the school, she still had the urge to draw back from the woman. Perhaps it was the fervor she saw in Blanche's eyes, a fervor that seemed more than a passion for the cause of suffrage. It almost seemed . . . what? A definition escaped Katie but didn't ease her nerves.

"Your column this morning was truly inspired, Miss Jones. I feared this day would never end so I could send my students home. I did so want to tell you in person my feelings about your column. It was wonderful. Inspired."

"Thank you." Katie's smile was fleeting. "I'm afraid my ideas have caused a bit of trouble in town."

"Of course they have. They should. You have sounded the call of liberty to the women of this valley. You should be proud of yourself."

"I only wrote what I believe to be true."

Blanche nodded. "Of course. And we must do more. We carry the torch of truth, you and I. We must help the misguided see. I can be of real help to you. What should we do next?"

"I haven't decided."

"I'm sure we can come up with something if we put our heads together."

Katie realized suddenly that she didn't want to strategize with this woman. So she murmured a halfhearted word of agreement as she pulled open the door to her motorcar.

Blanche reached to stop her, grabbing hold of Katie's free hand. "You're not going already, are you?"

"I'm afraid I *must*, Miss Coleson." Katie firmly withdrew her hand from Blanche's grasp.

"You must call me Blanche." She took one step backward. "I will look forward to hearing from you soon. And in the meantime, I'll be thinking of ways we might do even more for the cause."

Katie nodded, then started her automobile and drove away from the school.

⊱ ❖ ⊰

Ben left the newspaper early for a change. He didn't want to see or talk to one more person. He'd lost count of how many men had stomped into the office during the day, all of them with the same purpose—to put an end to Katie's column.

What's the matter with them?

Ben followed the sidewalk down Main Street, his hat brim pulled low. He purposely avoided looking about for fear he would make eye contact with someone and then have to stop and listen to another diatribe against Katie and her outlandish ideas.

But they aren't outlandish.

In between interruptions Ben had read the column again, and he'd discovered the same sense of pride in what Katie had written. He'd been able to hear her voice in the turn of every phrase. Her earnest belief in the cause of woman's suffrage was clear, and because of it she'd forced Ben to take an honest look at himself and his own beliefs.

Why can't others see it?

He had passed both the Book Shoppe and the office of Vincent Michaels, attorney-at-law, when he heard his name called.

Not another one. Ben groaned.

He turned to see who had hailed him. It was Matthew. While waiting for his future brother-in-law to catch up, Ben removed his hat and raked his fingers through his hair.

When Matthew stopped in front of Ben, he was breathing as hard as if he'd walked a mile instead of the length of a few store-fronts. "Ben, you've got to talk some sense into your sister."

"Sophia? What's she done?"

"What's she done? She's called off the wedding!"

"No!"

"Yes." Matthew waved his hand in the air. "She's got a bee in her bonnet about that stupid suffragette business."

Ah, there it was. Katie, after all.

"Ben, she doesn't realize how this is going to look. I've never seen Sophia behave this way. This isn't like her." He shook his head. "Not like her at all."

"I don't know. If she isn't ready to get married—"

"She doesn't know what she's doing. You've got to talk to her." Matthew jabbed his finger at Ben's chest. "You printed that blather in your paper. Now you've got to make things right."

Come to think of it, Ben never had warmed up to Matthew Jacobs. He was small-minded and judgmental, intolerant of those who didn't see things his own way. Ben thought his sister had made the right decision, and he planned to tell her so, first chance he got.

Ben took a step backward, then set his hat on his head. "I'll talk to Sophia."

"Good. And what about that column? Is this the last of it we'll see?"

Ben was liking Matthew less by the minute. "Miss Jones will continue to write for the *Homestead Herald* as long as she wishes. Her ideas are thought provoking, which is exactly what this town needs. To make people think when they read the paper." He saw Matthew's face redden with anger. "Good day to you."

It was with a sense of relief, a few moments later, that Ben stepped through the wide double doorway of the Rafferty Hotel. He looked forward to a peaceful evening in the suite of rooms he kept on the top floor. As short-tempered as he felt, he was afraid the next person to say something about Katie was going to get a taste of his knuckles.

Then he saw Katie herself rise from the satin-tufted sofa in the hotel lobby, and he immediately forgot his desire not to talk to another living soul. Instead he felt a sudden pleasure. "What are you doing here, Katie?"

"I wanted to see you."

"Why didn't you come to the paper?"

"I was trying to escape Miss Coleson. The hotel seemed

a good place." Katie wrinkled her nose. "She's rather . . .
odd, isn't she?"

"I think that would describe her."

"Besides, I needed a moment of quiet to think." A frown
knitted her brows, and she pursed her mouth as she dragged
in a breath.

"Trouble?"

"I saw Sophia a little while ago."

"Oh. *That.*"

"You know? About her and Matthew?"

"I know."

"This is more difficult than I thought."

"What is?"

She swept at a wisp of hair that fluttered along the side
of her face and tears glimmered in her eyes. "Everything."

"Come on." He took hold of her arm and guided her
toward the hotel dining room. "You look like you could use
some cheering up."

She said nothing as she allowed him to steer her toward
a corner table.

Ben pulled out a chair. "Sit down, Katie. Please."

She did.

"Now tell me. What exactly is upsetting you?"

Katie looked up, and he was struck afresh by all the
things that made her beautiful and special, both inside and
out.

"It's very different here from the way it was in Washington," she said softly. "It doesn't change how I feel about
things, but I don't want to hurt the people I care about. I

never meant for my words to cause problems between Sophia and Matthew."

He covered one of her hands with one of his. "You're not at fault."

"But I—"

"It's *not* your fault. Sophia did the right thing."

Katie gave him a weak smile. "You're sweet to me, Benjie. You always have been."

He didn't want to be sweet. He wanted to be selfish. He wanted to make her love him as he loved her. But Katie saw a childhood friend when she looked at him, not the man he'd become. She was up to her neck in changing the world. He wanted a wife and children and a quiet home life.

"It isn't only that," she said. "Miss Coleson is eager to help me organize, and Sophia says she wants to help, too. But I can't seem to think of what to do next." Her voice lowered. "I feel so confused. It's not like me."

He wanted to erase her confusion. He wanted to make her smile. Really smile, the way only Katie could. He would do anything to make it happen. "I have an idea." He gave her hand a squeeze.

It was crazy. He shouldn't do this. He should keep quiet. He didn't want or need any more complications. Whatever Katie did, he would find himself smack-dab in the middle of it, and it would be neither peaceful nor tranquil. He would regret getting himself involved with her schemes and causes. He knew it as surely as he knew his own name.

But he didn't heed the small voice of reason in his head.

"Why not invite the candidates to come to Homestead? We'll have a rally of some sort."

Her entire countenance brightened. "A rally?"

He got his wish. She smiled. And before he knew it, he was making another suggestion. "Maybe you should have an Idaho version of the Suffrage Special. You could take the Susan B around Idaho and hold meetings to encourage women to vote."

"Oh, Ben, what a scrumptious idea!"

Scrumptious. A good word to describe Katie.

"I knew I could count on you." She rose from her chair, leaned across the table, and kissed his cheek.

Ben had to remind himself once again that they were only friends, and that was all Katie wanted them to be.

TEN

On Saturday, Homestead fairly buzzed with the news of the broken engagement, and people debated—in homes, in businesses, and on the street—what part "Katie's Corner" had played in the breakup.

From his pulpit on Sunday, Reverend Simon Jacobs reminded the congregation of the Homestead Community Church that marriage was a serious and sacred act into which no one should enter in haste or with doubts. He added that while he would have loved to call Sophia his daughter-in-law, he would not criticize the couple for making a difficult decision. He reminded all those listening to him to heed God's instructions to judge not, lest they be judged.

Although the chasm between the two sides of the suffrage-amendment issue continued to widen as the week progressed—George Blake still slept on the sofa, and Phillip

Carson shot hateful glances at Blanche Coleson whenever he saw her—Katie was too enthusiastically involved in her work to give it much notice. She sent letters to both state and national candidates in Idaho, inviting them to participate in an election rally. She requested literature from NAWSA's offices in Washington. She studied the writings of Susan B. Anthony, Frances E. Willard, and others, promising herself she would be the best-informed speaker at the assembly. She met with her suffrage committee—Sophia, Blanche, and their newest member, Leslie Blake—and mapped the route of the Idaho Special, to be undertaken during August and September. And she wrote her next column for the *Homestead Herald*, blissfully preparing to add more fuel to the already hot fires of disagreement.

Every day she drove her automobile into Homestead, where she met with Ben in his office. He encouraged her, bolstered her, and advised her, and those visits were her favorite part of the day. Ben was the best friend anyone ever had. She was convinced of it.

It was on Friday morning, the day Katie's third column appeared in the *Herald*, that Charlotte paid a visit to the Lazy L Ranch.

"You've caused quite a stir in town." Charlotte settled onto the sofa in the front parlor, looking serene and beautiful. "Benjamin is enjoying it immensely."

Katie nodded, remembering all the ideas Ben had come up with during their meetings in his office.

"I understand Benjamin is assisting you with the rally."

"Yes, he is. I had no idea Ben knew so many people in the government. He's been a great help."

Charlotte leaned forward, her expression earnest. "Miss Jones, I know how fond you are of Benjamin." She smiled briefly. "I am, too."

She loves him.

"Miss Jones." Charlotte shook her head. "May I call you Katie?"

"Of course."

"Katie, I wonder if you're aware that some of the business-men in town are refusing to advertise in the *Herald* as long as the newspaper publishes your column."

Katie caught her breath. "But that isn't fair."

"No, it isn't."

"Are you positive? I've met with Ben every day this week, and he's never mentioned it."

"He wouldn't. He says the paper is in good financial condition and can handle a reduction in revenue. He says he won't have editorial decisions made by—" she allowed another little smile—"bigots and ignoramuses."

Katie found no reason to smile. "Why didn't he tell me what was happening?"

"Because he doesn't want to hurt or worry you." Charlotte's tone was gentle. "Because he cares for you a great deal."

A yearning for something undefined twisted Katie's heart. "I don't want Benjie to be hurt, either."

"Of course you don't. That's why I felt free to come and speak to you." A look of indecision crossed Charlotte's face before she continued. "Because we both love Benjamin, I hope we can become friends, you and I. Between the two of us, perhaps we can be sure he doesn't act unwisely. The *Herald* means more to him than he might admit, and he's much too proud to borrow money from his father to save it, if it should come to that."

Because we both love Benjamin. A lump formed in Katie's throat as Charlotte's words echoed in her mind. *Because we both love Ben.* She looked down at her hands, folded tightly in her lap.

"Miss Jones? Katie?"

Katie glanced up.

"You *will* help me, won't you? Sometimes Benjamin . . . sometimes his deep affection for you affects his better judgment. He has an important position in Homestead. People look up to him. They depend upon him. He's trusted by so many. He mustn't jeopardize that position." Her blue eyes appeared misty. "Not even for friendship." Another pause. Another brief, halfhearted smile. "Not even for you, Katie."

We both love Ben.

In that one terrible moment, she realized the significance of those words. They both loved Ben. *Katie* loved Ben. Not just as his friend. Not the way Charlotte meant.

Or was it *exactly* the way Charlotte meant?

Katie looked into the other woman's eyes and saw the truth. Charlotte had understood Katie's feelings even before she understood them herself.

There was another truth to be seen in those pretty blue eyes. Charlotte was afraid. Afraid of what Katie would do with her newfound understanding. Afraid she would lose Ben to

Katie. Charlotte had come here to plead for Katie not to take Ben away from her.

Katie rose and walked to the parlor window, where she stared at the sweep of land that curved west and north, framed by tall, pine-covered mountains. But she didn't see what lay before her. Instead she imagined Ben—and she wondered why she hadn't realized before the depth of what she felt for him.

And if she had, would it have made any difference? How could it, when they wanted opposite things?

"I suppose, if it would help Ben, that I don't need to write another column," Katie said at last. "Perhaps I've already accomplished what I set out to accomplish with it."

"Thank you."

"Ben will have to report on the rally." Katie glanced over her shoulder. "It will mean nothing if it doesn't appear in the papers, and it will be a newsworthy event."

"Of course he'll report on it. Benjamin is an excellent journalist."

"I'll be terribly busy over the remainder of the summer," Katie said with a pasted-on smile. "My work is of paramount importance to me. It always has been. I won't be able to see much of Ben." She felt as if she'd been kicked in the chest by a horse.

Charlotte rose from the sofa. "He'll miss you."

But he'll have you.

"I must go now."

"I'll see you to the door." Katie led the way out of the parlor to the front entry.

Charlotte paused in the open doorway. "I wish you much success in all your endeavors."

"That's very kind of you." Her reply was wooden. She was eager for Charlotte to be gone. She wanted to be alone so she could sort out her thoughts and feelings.

"Good day, Katie. Thank you for . . . for understanding."

"Good day."

She watched as Charlotte walked to the waiting surrey and climbed in. Automatically she lifted her hand to wave farewell when Charlotte glanced back her way.

Please make him happy. Please.

Ben looked at the clock and wondered again where Katie was. It was well past the hour she usually dropped in at the newspaper. He heard the bleak wail of a train whistle. The weekly Union Pacific, up from Boise City, was on time today. But where was Katie?

He would have thought she'd be certain to come in today, what with her latest column in the newspaper. He would have thought she'd want to learn people's reaction to it, to the announcement of the election rally. He could ring her on the telephone, of course, but he didn't want to simply *talk* to her. He wanted to *see* her.

Seeing Katie had become a vital part of his day. Like breathing.

He raked his fingers through his hair as he faced a hard truth. He wasn't going to fall in love with Charlotte, no matter

how long he waited and no matter how much others thought
he should. He couldn't. He already loved Katie too much.
Time and determination weren't going to change that.

He had to break things off with Charlotte. There would be
more talk in town, more unpleasant gossip, same as there'd
been about Sophia and Matthew. Some would blame Katie,
as they had before. Another Rafferty romance ruined by her
modern thinking, they would say.

But Katie couldn't help it if her enthusiasm was conta-
gious to those around her. And she couldn't help being the
woman he'd fallen in love with.

Which returned his thoughts to Charlotte.

This was Friday, the night of their standing supper
engagement. He would have to tell her tonight. It wouldn't
be fair of him not to.

He remembered the night when she'd kissed him here in
his office. He'd known then he didn't love her, that he loved
Katie, but he'd let her kiss him anyway. He'd hoped there
would be more between them than there was. But he couldn't
fabricate feelings, and more time wouldn't change that either.

"I should go tell her right now." He reached for his hat.

But before he could move toward the door, it opened and
a couple of strangers came through the opening. The man and
woman were both handsomely dressed, although a bit wrinkled from travel—the young woman in a green shirtwaist of
fine lawn, the fellow in a white linen suit and straw hat.

The woman—attractive enough, in an ordinary sort of
way—took another step forward and held out her hand.
"How do you do, Mr. Rafferty?"

"I'm sorry. Do I know—"

"I'm Katie's friend, Penelope Rudyard. I would have known you anywhere from Katie's description." She tossed a smile over her shoulder. "That's my brother, Geoffrey. We've come all the way from Chicago as a surprise for Katie. We've come to help her until after the elections. We thought to hire someone to take us to her home, but then I remembered you would be the logical person to help us find her. So here we are. Can you help us?"

"Penny," her brother interrupted, "it looks as if Mr. Rafferty was about to go out. Perhaps we're intruding."

"No, it's all right," Ben said, glad for a reason to postpone the less pleasant duty of breaking off with Charlotte, even more glad for an excuse to see Katie. "I'd be delighted to take you out to the Lazy L." He motioned toward a pair of wooden chairs. "Make yourselves comfortable while I go to the livery for my buggy. I'll be back for you shortly."

⊷ ⊨◊⊨ ⊷

While Blanche and Leslie stared at the sketches on the dining-room table, Sophia studied Katie. There was something wrong with their fearless leader today. Katie was distracted. There was a decided lack of energy in her voice and in her movements. Sophia hoped she wasn't ill. This fledgling group of suffragettes needed Katie's leadership. Without it, they would flounder.

Katie fiddled with the gold locket she wore around her

neck as she stared into space. Her shoulders lifted and fell with a deep sigh.

"There are several large shade trees behind the hotel," Blanche said in her precise, no-nonsense tone of voice. "It would be the perfect place to hold the rally."

Leslie nodded. "We can hire someone to build a platform." She pointed to the sketch. "We can place benches here. What do you think, Katie?"

"Yes, that will be fine," she answered, her expression distant and unfocused.

Sophia leaned close to Katie and placed a hand on her friend's shoulder. "Are you feeling all right?"

"What?" Katie blinked. "Oh, yes. I'm fine."

Sophia frowned. "You *would* tell me if something was troubling you, wouldn't you?" she asked softly.

"Hmmm."

"Katie?" Sophia's fingers tightened. "You're not upset because of your mother, are you?"

"Mother?"

"Because she's not here? Has she changed her mind about working with us?"

Katie shook her head as she resumed twisting her necklace, flipping the locket over her finger again and again. "No, Mother will be here next time. Today she's trying to convince Grandpa Will to see a doctor in Boise City next week about his back. That's what Dr. Tom wants him to do."

"Are you worried about your grandfather, then?"

"A little, I suppose. But Grandma Addie thinks he'll be all right if he follows the doctor's orders." She released a dry chuckle. "She says he needs to remember he's seventy, not twenty."

"Well, *something* is bothering you, Katie Jones, and I wish you'd tell me what it is."

"Would you two quit whispering and pay attention." Blanche rapped on the table with her knuckles. "We have a great deal to accomplish in very little time."

Katie straightened. "Yes, we do, don't we?" She offered a cheerless smile to Sophia. "I mustn't forget our work. It's the reason I came back to Homestead."

Sophia was more convinced than ever that something was amiss.

Over the next half hour Katie did her best to concentrate on the plans the committee was making. She knew Sophia was watching her, wondering what was wrong. It would be awful if Ben's sister guessed the truth. Nearly as bad as it would be for Ben himself to discover it.

How had she allowed this to happen? His friendship meant the world to her. Now she feared losing it forever. Despite Charlotte's saying she hoped the two of them would become friends, Katie knew it was never to be. How could it, when she would be jealous of Charlotte for what she had?

But Katie didn't want marriage. She was different from Ben in that way. Marriage was a wonderful institution for some, but not for her. Her work had to come first. God had given her this mission, and it was bigger than she was. It demanded her full attention.

"Katie?"

She looked up.

Sophia was frowning at her again. "There's someone at the door. Would you like me to answer it?"

"No." She rose from her chair. "I'll get it."

As she walked toward the front entrance, she scolded herself. She had to put Ben out of her mind. She had to remain focused on what was important. She pulled open the door and felt her heart skitter.

"Benjie."

He grinned like the Cheshire cat in Lewis Carroll's *Alice's Adventures in Wonderland*. "Look who I've brought to see you." He motioned with his arm as he stepped to one side.

Nothing could have astonished Katie more than having Penelope Rudyard step into view.

"Penny!" she cried. "Oh, what a perfectly scrumptious surprise!"

Laughing, the two women hugged each other. Then Katie saw Penelope's brother waiting quietly behind her.

"Geoffrey? You came, too?"

"My dear Katie," he said as he took his sister's place, wrapping Katie in a warm embrace, then kissing her cheek. "I wasn't about to let Penny have all the fun of surprising you."

"I'm so glad you didn't," Katie said. "Come in. Come in, both of you. I want you to meet the ladies who are helping me. And we want to hear everything that happened at the convention in Chicago." She dared to glance at Ben. Against her better judgment, she asked, "Can you stay, too?"

He looked for a moment as if he would decline, then said, "For a while."

✦ ⚎◆⚏ ✦

Hours later, after Ben and the other committee members had left the ranch, Lark Jones insisted that Penelope and Geoffrey stay at the Lazy L. "It isn't anything fancy, but it's got enough bedrooms. Besides, Katie's not about to let you leave until you've told her everything she wants to hear. Mark my words. You'll be up half the night talking."

That was exactly what Katie, Penelope, and Geoffrey did. Katie asked her friends question after question about the convention in Chicago. She could close her eyes and imagine the thousands of women—and a sprinkling of men—who had gathered there to demand the right to vote for all.

"Oh, Penny, I wish I'd gone with you."

"But look at what you've accomplished here in such a short time," her friend replied. "You're much further along than I expected. You've formed a committee, and you're planning a rally, and you've been writing a column for the newspaper."

Katie felt a little skip in her heart. "I may not write another column."

"Why ever not?" Geoffrey inquired. "I've read your latest. It's a truly excellent piece. Had we known what a fine writer you are, we would have put you to work on the association's literature."

Even though warmed by his praise, she shook her head. "All I did was use the words of other women who have fought for suffrage for decades."

"Don't be so modest." Penelope patted Katie's hand with her fingertips. "You have a real gift. Your writing is easy to understand and it has passion. Even those who violently disagree cannot help but keep reading."

"Thank you."

"Surely your Mr. Rafferty doesn't want you to stop, does he?"

Another little skip, this one painful. *My Mr. Rafferty . . .*

Only he wasn't hers.

He belonged to Charlotte.

Geoffrey stifled a yawn. "I'm afraid the days are catching up with me." He rose from the overstuffed chair. "If you ladies will excuse me, I'm going to retire for the night." He stepped to where Katie was seated, leaned down and kissed her cheek, then kissed his sister in the same fashion. "Good night, you two."

"Good night, Geoffrey," they returned in unison.

Once he'd disappeared through the parlor doorway, Katie stood. "You must be tired as well. Come on. I'll see you to your room."

Arm in arm they climbed the stairs to the second floor. They didn't speak, comfortable in their silence.

Penelope and Katie had become fast friends at Vassar, quickly learning they had the same dedication to the suffrage cause. They'd shared a room their last two years at college, and it was there the idea was conceived for the two of them to go to work for the association.

Penelope and Geoffrey were from a prominent family in Massachusetts. Their widowed mother, Eugenia Rudyard, was a leader in the suffrage cause in her own state. It was she who had paid the rent on the apartment in Washington, D.C., where the two young women currently lived. Although Katie had tried to insist she should make her own way, Mrs. Rudyard had waved away her words with an aristocratic flip of her wrist.

"Don't be silly, Katie dear. We need young, enthusiastic workers such as yourself. I am able to do this and much more. You and Penny make a wonderful team. The two of you must use your wages for other than necessities. I'll see to those."

With the memory still drifting in her thoughts, Katie asked, "How's your mother? It's been ages since I last saw her."

"Oh, you know Mother. She's positively brewing over with ideas after the convention. I daresay President Wilson had best watch his step."

Laughing softly, Katie stopped before the entrance to the guest bedroom.

Penelope stepped into the open doorway, then turned to look at Katie. "Is something wrong? You don't seem yourself."

She forced herself to smile. "I don't know what you mean. Nothing's wrong."

Her friend leaned forward and kissed her cheek. "You would tell me if there was, wouldn't you?"

The question was almost identical to the one Sophia had asked that afternoon, but Katie was no more inclined to answer honestly now than she'd been before. "Of course I would. Now get some rest. We'll have plenty of time to talk tomorrow."

Penelope hesitated, looking as if she would say something more. Then she nodded and closed the door.

Thoughts of Ben tried to intrude again, beckoned by Penelope's question, but Katie pushed them away as she made her way to her own room. Things would be different now that Penelope and Geoffrey were here. Katie would be able to put aside her feelings for Ben. Her friends would help keep her focused on what was important.

Everything would be all right now.

⋆ ≖◈≖ ⋆

Ben grew tired of tossing and turning. It seemed sleep was bound and determined to elude him. With a sound of exasperation, he threw aside the rumpled bedsheet and got up. He strode to the window of his bedchamber, looking out on the sleepy street below. Even the billiard saloon was darkened at this wee hour of the morning.

Those fortunate folks with untroubled consciences were fast asleep in their beds. Only Ben was awake.

And he knew why.

Upon his return to town, he'd called Charlotte at the parsonage and cancelled their supper engagement. He'd given no reason, no excuse. He'd simply told her they would talk soon.

Coward!

He should have broken off with her right then. He could have gotten it over with. It would have been better than letting it drag on.

And there was the matter of his raging jealousy. Oh, yes, he recognized the demon that was tormenting him. He'd recognized it the moment it raised its ugly head at the Lazy L Ranch. The moment Katie had hugged Geoffrey Rudyard, and Geoffrey had kissed her cheek and called her "his dear Katie." The moment he'd learned Geoffrey had lived next door to Penelope and Katie for the past three years.

Ben leaned his forehead against the cool window glass and closed his eyes, calling himself all kinds of a fool.

Geoffrey, an attorney, was rich, handsome, cosmopolitan. More important, he was as deeply involved in the suffrage movement as his mother, sister, and Katie. If any man could change Katie's mind about matrimony, it would be someone like Geoffrey—if not Geoffrey Rudyard himself.

Ben gazed once again at the quiet, moonlight-bathed street. He'd chosen to rent these rooms from his father's hotel partially because of the view of the town. He was fond of Homestead and the people who lived here. Big cities weren't for him. This was what he wanted.

But would Katie ever want it too?

He closed his eyes, whispering, "God, is that too much of me to ask? If You've called her to this work, am I wrong to ask that she could love me, that she might marry me, that we could have a home and family?"

ELEVEN

Headed for the parsonage on Saturday morning, Ben stopped when he saw Charlotte's father, his head bent forward, his eyes downcast, his hands clasped behind his back. From the looks of him, Obadiah was deep in troubled thought. Ben watched as the reverend climbed the steps to the back of the small white church with its tall steeple. The older man slipped a key into the lock and opened the door without ever glancing around him. A moment later he disappeared into the dark interior.

Ben drew a deep breath, then with the fateful strides of the condemned on the way to the gallows, he continued to the front door of the parsonage. He didn't allow himself another hesitation; he immediately rapped on the door.

It opened in a matter of moments. Regret for the hurt he might be about to cause tightened his chest as he looked at Charlotte.

"Benjamin." She smoothed the front of her dressing gown. "I wasn't expecting you so early in the day. I must look a sight."

"We need to talk."

Her shoulders drooped and her hand stilled. "Yes, I think we do." She stepped back from the opening. "Come in."

He followed Charlotte inside, closing the front door behind him. She led the way into the small sitting room. Quickly, as if her legs wouldn't support her, she sank onto a wooden rocker. When she looked up at him a moment later, Ben hated himself.

He chose a spindle-backed chair opposite her and sat down. He clenched his hands together, resting his forearms on his thighs as he leaned forward. "Charlotte—"

"I can guess why you've come, Benjamin." Tears swam in eyes of blue. "You won't be calling on me in the future."

"I never meant to hurt you, Charlotte."

"I know that."

"It's just that—"

"You love Miss Jones," she finished for him in a whisper. She tried to smile but was unsuccessful.

Ben raked his fingers through his hair, wishing he did love Charlotte. She represented everything he'd wanted in a wife. She was caring and kind. She would be a loving mother to their children. She would be supportive of his work. She would never want for more than Ben was able to provide because it was not in her nature to do so.

Only God knew what sort of wife Katie Jones would make—if she ever became a wife at all.

"Benjamin?" Charlotte attempted another smile, this one slightly more successful than the last. "There were no promises between us."

"I never intended to mislead you."

"You didn't. You're an honest man. It's one of the things I've admired about you."

"I'm sorry."

Holding herself erect, her chin tilted bravely, Charlotte rose from the rocker. "We shall always be friends, Benjamin, and you shall always be welcome in our home." The dismissal was gentle, but a dismissal nonetheless.

Ben followed her lead, rising to his feet. She'd called him honest, but there were more apologies to be spoken before he would feel honest. He reached out before she could turn away, gently grasping her wrist and holding her in place.

"It's a difficult thing, to be unable to express myself. I'm a man of words, and now, it seems, there aren't any. I wish . . ." He wished his life were going the way he'd planned. He wished he didn't feel like a cad. "I wish things had turned out differently."

"So do I." She eased her wrist from his hand. "But I imagine you and Miss Jones will be very happy. I hope so. I'll pray it will be so." Charlotte turned and retraced her steps to the front door, opening it for him without checking to see if he followed. It wasn't until he paused before her in the doorway that she raised her gaze one more time. "I truly do wish you every happiness," she whispered as he took her proffered hand.

"Charlotte—"

She shook her head. "Please, Benjamin. Just go."

He knew she was right. There were no words that would make the situation better. He'd said what he'd come to say. It was time for him to go.

With a brief nod and a slight squeeze of her fingers, he released her hand, then turned and departed the parsonage.

◆━━◆━━◆

With Katie behind the wheel and Penelope seated beside her, Geoffrey gave the Susan B's engine crank a hard turn, releasing it just in time to avoid the sudden kick for which the Model T's crank was infamous. "Why didn't you buy a Buick or a Cadillac or a Stutz?" he grumbled as he rounded the side of the car and hopped into the rear seat. "A friend of mine broke his arm on a machine like this one."

"Don't criticize the Susan B." Katie patted the wheel as if the automobile were a favored child. "She's perfect."

Penelope looked over her shoulder at her brother and said in a stage whisper, "Besides, this was all Katie could afford at the time."

Although secretly enjoying herself, Katie shot a dour look at her friend. "The Susan B is worth the four hundred and forty dollars I paid for her and then some."

The Rudyard siblings laughed.

Katie accelerated, and the motorcar jumped forward, jolting her passengers.

Once he'd caught himself, Geoffrey reached forward and placed his hand on Katie's shoulder. "My dear girl, in case you haven't noticed, this flivver frequently overheats. It's difficult, when not impossible, to start on cold mornings. It needs a running start to mount hills, and unless you're backing up said hills in reverse, the fuel line goes dry and the car stops altogether." He laughed again. "Penny, help me. What am I forgetting?"

"You're forgetting the one advantage," his sister answered. "There's no need for a speedometer."

"Ah, yes. One can always tell how fast it's going without buying a speedometer. When it's running five miles an hour, the fender rattles; twelve miles an hour, your teeth rattle; and at fifteen miles an hour, the transmission drops out."

Again, brother and sister laughed.

Everything they'd said was close to the truth, of course, but wild horses couldn't have dragged that admission out of Katie. "I'll have you know the transmission has never dropped out of the Susan B, and I drive her quite regularly at a speed greater than fifteen miles an hour. Need I remind you this touring car carried all of us across the country as we followed the Special? And she did it without any serious mishaps."

"Oh, Katie, we're merely teasing," Penelope said. "You needn't get your feelings hurt. We'll apologize, won't we, Geoffrey?"

"Absolutely. We beg your forgiveness, my dear Katie." He thumped the car seat. "Frightfully sorry, Susan B. Do forgive us."

Katie grinned, letting them know she wasn't upset.

"You'll pay for forcing that apology, of course," Geoffrey warned, then said, "So tell us how long it will take to reach your grandparents' farm."

"It's a ranch, not a farm. Grandpa Will was the first person to arrive in Long Bow Valley. He built the Rocking R Ranch from nothing, raising the finest horses within five hundred miles in any direction. The U.S. Cavalary still purchases livestock from him, although not as many as they did before the turn of the century."

Penelope gazed about her. "I've never seen so much wide-open space as I've seen these past few months. The mountains. The rivers. It's all quite spectacular."

Katie agreed with Penelope. The West was spectacular, and few places more so than this valley. A sense of pride washed over her as she saw it afresh through the eyes of her friends.

"You belong here," Penelope added softly.

She thought of Ben. "Do I?"

"Yes, I think you do."

Katie wondered how long she would stay, belonging or not. She didn't think she could bear to see Ben and Charlotte together, married, having a family. Besides, she'd never intended to remain in Idaho after the November elections. She'd always meant to return to Washington and continue her work there. It was good to come home for a short while, but she couldn't stay. Not while there was still so much to accomplish.

She hoped Ben and Charlotte wouldn't marry until after she left Homestead. She couldn't bear to have to watch them as man and wife.

"Tell us more about your committee," Penelope said, intruding on Katie's thoughts.

She was glad for the distraction. As the Susan B continued along the dusty country road, she told her friends about her first two weeks in Homestead and how each woman had come to be a part of the local suffrage committee. She avoided mentioning Ben, leaving out the many times she'd sat in his office, talking and laughing, or the afternoon they'd gone swimming in the pond, or the night she'd seen him kissing Charlotte.

"Do you suppose Sophia Rafferty is still in love with her former fiancé?" Geoffrey inquired when Katie fell silent. "Is it possible they might reconcile?"

"She loved him," Katie said. "I'm sure it will take her a while to get over it."

"I suppose," Geoffrey said.

Something in his voice caused her to glance quickly over her shoulder, then back at the road.

"I would hate to see your committee lose one of its members," he added. "There's too much work for all of you as it is."

Yes, there was too much work. Plenty enough to keep Katie's mind occupied, to keep her from thinking unwanted thoughts about Ben.

At least she could hope and pray that would be the case.

━━ ≡◆≡ ━━

Ben heard the soft ripple of whispers as he entered the Homestead Community Church on Sunday morning, walking behind his parents, his sister's hand in the crook of his arm. He knew folks were wondering why he wasn't over at King of

Glory Church with Charlotte. He knew Sophia and his parents were wondering, too, although they'd refrained from asking.

As his family slipped into their usual pew, Ben glanced across the aisle and up one row. Katie was there, seated between Lark Jones on her right and Penelope Rudyard on her left. Her black hair was swept high on her head, topped by a straw bonnet with a gay yellow ribbon. Her neck was long and delicate, the skin soft gold, the color of honey. He wondered what it would be like to kiss the spot below her earlobe—imagining she might taste as sweet as honey, too—and decided right then and there that she looked far too fetching for her own good.

Katie leaned left and said something to Penelope, causing them both to smile. As she straightened, Katie's gaze caught with his. Her smile vanished in an instant, and her eyes widened. Luminous, beguiling eyes of brown. Had they always been as beautiful as they were now? Was it possible he could see more in them than simple surprise? Or was that merely wishful thinking on his part?

She faced forward again, breaking the tenuous connection between them.

The morning's worship service began with a hymn, accompanied by Priscilla Jacobs on the organ. The congregation's voices melded together, but Ben heard each and every perfect note Katie sang.

With the hymn's "amen" echoing in the sanctuary, Geoffrey leaned around his sister to say something to Katie. She gave him that dazzling smile. Ben clenched his jaw, wishing he were somewhere other than church. The thoughts whipping through his head were anything but suitable for a house of prayer.

Ben heard little of Reverend Jacobs's sermon that morning. He was too busy debating with himself what his course of action should be to win Katie's love. Her love as a woman, not a friend.

I've got to get her away from all these people.

It wasn't going to be easy, wooing and winning Katie. Not when she was so determined not to be wooed or won. Not when she looked at him and saw only a childhood friend and not a man.

But Ben was going to change her mind. No matter what it took. No matter how long it took.

<hr/>

Katie wasn't listening to the pastor. She couldn't hear above the loud hammering of her heart. It was silly that Ben's nearness should cause such an internal commotion. She should have been able to control her rampaging feelings, but she couldn't seem to do so.

When the service was over and Priscilla Jacobs began playing a soft hymn on the church organ, Katie composed herself, then rose from the pew and turned toward the aisle. He was there, standing almost within arm's reach.

"Good morning, Katie."

"Good morning." She searched for something more to say. Anything. "I was surprised to see you here." She felt a flush warm her cheeks. "I understand you usually attend services with Charlotte at her father's church."

A short step brought him closer. He offered his arm. "May I walk you to your automobile?"

Katie glanced at Penelope, then at Geoffrey, and finally back at Ben. In the end she realized she couldn't avoid placing her fingers in the crook of his elbow. She longed to touch him too much to ignore the impulse.

She should have urged him to offer his other arm to Penelope, but she didn't. She wanted him to herself, if only for a few moments.

"I missed seeing you yesterday," Ben said as they walked toward the back of the church.

I missed you, too. "I took Penny and Geoffrey to see my grandparents."

He looked down at her and smiled. "I imagine your grandmother charmed them as she does everyone."

Her heart did a thousand flip-flops in the space of a few seconds. *Why did I have to fall in love with you? Why?*

"Katie, I know you have many demands upon your time, but I'd like to steal you away tomorrow. Do you think you can leave your guests to their own devices for a day?"

Steal me away?

"I'd like us to drive up to the logging camps. We should tell those folks about the election rally that's coming to Homestead. I've heard there are a couple of women loggers in one of the camps. They might make a good subject for one of your columns."

Disappointment washed over Katie. Her column. Of course that was what he wanted to talk to her about. What else? She hadn't yet told him she didn't plan to continue to write the column.

"We ought to be able to make the trip all in one day if we take your motorcar," he said. "That is, if you wouldn't mind taking the Susan B up that rough trail."

A day with Ben. Just to themselves. Just the two of them. She shouldn't. She'd promised Charlotte, although not in exact words, that she would stay away from him. She'd planned to quit writing the column, not wanting him to lose more revenue.

"How about it, Katie? Are you game?"

Her decision was made. She couldn't resist his invitation. Perhaps Tuesday she would be forced to face reality, but tomorrow was for her and Ben.

"Well?" Ben urged.

"Yes, I'm game. It sounds like a perfect story for my column. Let's do it."

"Good. I'll ride out to the Lazy L first thing in the morning."

"I'll be ready."

I'll always be ready to see you, Ben. That's the problem.

TWELVE

Katie was up at the crack of dawn after a long, troublesome night. Whether she was sleeping or not, Ben had remained in her thoughts. A much different Ben from the boy who had been her companion throughout childhood. A tall, strong, and handsome Ben with a devastating grin and masculine appeal.

She knew she ought not to think about him that way. He would soon marry Charlotte, and Katie was married to her life's work. Single womanhood was what she had felt called to. It was what she felt God wanted and what Katie herself had wanted for many years.

In the Gospel of Matthew, Jesus said that the harvest was great but the workers were few. And without workers, would conditions ever change for women in this country? Would women ever have the opportunities afforded to men—good jobs, equal education, fair property rights, the freedom to vote for elected officials?

Staring at her reflection in the mirror while she brushed the tangles from her hair, Katie recalled the words of Miss Anthony: *"There is not one woman left who may be relied on; all have 'first to please their husband,' after which there is but little time or energy left to spend in any other direction. I am not complaining or despairing, but facts are stern realities."*

Yes, facts were "stern realities." If Katie was to give herself, heart and soul, to the betterment of all women, if she was to be relied upon, she could not become fettered by selfish desires. She could not indulge her secret fantasies about Benjamin Rafferty.

But just once, her traitorous heart asked, *wouldn't it be wonderful to experience love? Wouldn't it be wonderful to experience it with Ben?*

With a groan, she dropped the hairbrush and covered her face with her hands. She had to stop this. How could she meet Ben this morning with such thoughts roiling in her head? How could she look at him and believe they were friends and nothing more?

She remembered the day she and Ben had gone swimming at the pond. She remembered the way he'd held her in his arms as she'd cried. She'd felt the shift in their friendship that day, only she hadn't known it was she who had shifted, she who had changed.

When she made the choice never to marry, she'd thought it would be an easy decision to keep. She would be as dedicated to the cause as Susan B. Anthony, her greatest inspiration. She would simply *not* fall in love, and therefore there would be no temptation to wed.

"What a fool I was. What an unmitigated fool."

O God, I want to do Your will. Lead me not into temptation. Deliver me from my own selfish desires. Please, God, deliver me.

She uncovered her eyes, drew a deep breath, and whispered, "Amen." Then she walked across the room to her wardrobe. She selected a brown skirt and cream-colored blouse, unconsciously seeking to look as prim, proper, and spinsterish as possible. She tossed the robe over the back of a chair, then reached for her clothes.

What am I going to do now?

She couldn't leave Homestead. Not now. Not with things progressing so well. The political rally was only a couple of weeks away. Several candidates had consented to attend; many others were expected to do so. Besides, she had made a promise to the leaders of NAWSA that she would do her part in Idaho. This election year was critical if they were going to see the passage of the suffrage amendment.

So that was settled. She couldn't leave Homestead. Not until after the elections in November.

Katie donned a camisole and knickers of crepe de chine, the edges decorated with ribbons and lace. Then she sat on the side of her bed and drew on a pair of beige stockings, her thoughts continuing to churn.

Since she was to remain in Homestead for the time being, she would have to deal with her attraction to Ben on an intellectual level. She could no longer act like a schoolgirl when she was with him. She could no longer throw herself into his arms with joyful abandon and kiss his cheek, nor could she let him hold and comfort her when she was feeling down.

Another treasonous thought snuck past her defenses: *Could I make him forget Charlotte?* Immediately contrite, she closed her eyes. *O Father, forgive me. Banish such thoughts from my head. Help me to be strong. Help me resist my temptations. Help me to be true to the calling You gave me.*

She opened her eyes and reached for her blouse, her thoughts still churning.

What kind of friend was she, to even consider hurting Ben that way? He wanted a home, marriage, family. He wanted all the things Charlotte was willing to give him, all the things Katie could not give him.

She must make sure Ben never learned what she felt in her heart. She must never allow Ben to be hurt because of her own selfishness.

✦ ⊰◈⊱ ✦

Blanche awoke at her usual time. It didn't matter that school was in recess for the remainder of summer. Especially not this year. Other summers she'd found herself with little to occupy her time. She had filled the hours with needlework and mundane chores. But this year was different. This year she was accomplishing something of value.

She drew a robe over her nightgown and cinched the belt around her waist, then walked from her bedroom into the living area of her apartment. She crossed to the kitchen and reached for the coffee grinder while her mind ticked off the things she must do today.

First on her schedule was writing several letters to the

wives of some public officials in the capital city. Katie thought it a poor idea, to rile up the wives against their husbands, but Blanche didn't care what Katie thought. Not anymore.

She had been delighted at first to find a kindred spirit in Homestead. Only Katie didn't believe precisely as Blanche did. While the young woman was passionate about gaining the right to vote for all women, she continued her friendship with Ben Rafferty, telling him the committee's plans, involving him in the rally. And there was that Mr. Rudyard visiting from the East, pretending to be a great supporter of the cause.

Blanche snorted in disbelief. No man wanted women to enjoy the same freedoms they had. Why would they, when the subjugation of females was so beneficial to their creature comforts?

But did Katie understand that? It seemed not.

To make matters worse, everyone treated Katie as if she were a saint. Blanche was growing increasingly tired of the attention they paid to Katie Jones's opinions. Sophia didn't do a thing without first checking with Katie, and Leslie Blake was no better. She hung on every word that fell from Katie's mouth.

If they had any sense, they would have appointed Blanche the first president of the Homestead Woman Suffrage Committee. Anyone could see that Katie was incapable of proper leadership. She was too young, too inexperienced. She needed a good dose of Blanche's common sense.

Blanche poured water from the pitcher into the coffeepot, thinking how unfair life had been to her. She possessed a great deal of intelligence but little else. She'd grown up in poverty and want in a home deprived of love. Fear of her father had been the dominant emotion of her mother and siblings. Not Blanche. She'd felt hate. Hate was what helped her survive.

Throughout her life she had been overlooked by others. Even women preferred friends who had beauty or wealth or both. She hadn't had the opportunity to travel, to attend a fine college, to see much beyond the small towns where she was forced to teach the children of ignorant men like her father.

Oh, what she might have done had she had Katie's opportunities!

Feeling more irritable by the moment, Blanche set the pot on the stove, then stoked the fire before returning to her bedroom to complete her morning ablutions. Then she was going to write those letters. She was going to prove to Miss Jones and the others that she knew what was best.

Ben offered to drive the Susan B before they started out from the Lazy L, but Katie was adamant about being the one behind the wheel. Ben didn't mind. It gave him the freedom to watch her while she concentrated on the mountain road. He took full advantage of the opportunity.

She looked utterly fetching in her brown outfit. On any other woman it would have looked plain and dowdy, but on Katie, it seemed perfect. *She* was perfect, from the dark wisps of hair curling near her temples to the tip of her buttonlike nose, from the top of her straw bonnet to her sturdy brown boots.

It was a pleasure just to look at her.

The question now was, how did he go about telling her what he felt without scaring her away? He wasn't sure what the answer was, but he wouldn't get anywhere by allowing this silence to continue.

"It's a beautiful day for a drive, isn't it?" he said.

The Susan B backfired, drowning out Katie's monosyllabic reply.

He slid a little to his left. "You're sure you don't want me to drive?"

"I'm sure."

It would be easy to slip his arm around her shoulders, but they were likely to end up in a ravine if he did. Katie seemed to be wound tight as a spring today.

Katie, I love you.

He wished he could say it just like that, but he couldn't.

Katie, I'm no longer calling on Charlotte.

That would be a good start. Let her know he had no obligations to anyone else.

But Katie spoke before he could. "Ben, if I asked something personal, would you answer me honestly?"

It seemed an odd question. Maybe she already knew about Charlotte. "I always try to be honest. What is it you want to know?"

"Is it true the newspaper has lost advertisers because of my column?"

That's what she meant by personal? "Yes, it's true."

"What does that mean to the paper? Is it going to hurt you?"

"Hurt me?"

She frowned. "You know. Will it cause a financial hardship? Is the paper in danger because of me?"

If it was possible, he loved her more because of her concern. "No, Katie, the *Herald* isn't in any danger because of you."

"But—"

"And even if it were, I wouldn't do anything differently." He leaned toward her. "You need to understand something. I'm a journalist. I believe in freedom of speech, in people's right to know, every bit as much as you believe in suffrage for all women. I'm not going to have a group of advertisers tell me what's news and what isn't. Nor will I let them tell me who can write for my paper just because they disagree with the point of view expressed in a column."

"But if our friendship is influencing you—"

"I'd want you to write that column even if we'd never met before."

He saw a shadow of doubt cross her face and knew now was his chance to say what was on his mind.

"Katie, I'd like to tell you something. About Miss Orson and me. You see, we—"

He was interrupted by a loud pop, followed by a jerk of the automobile toward the drop-off at the side of the road. He grabbed hold of the door as Katie braked to an abrupt halt. A cloud of dust flew around them, making them cough and sneeze.

Even after the air cleared, Katie continued to grip the steering wheel, her knuckles white. "Dear me." She glanced at him. "I think I was going a bit too fast. We nearly went over the edge."

"But we didn't." He opened the door. "I'll have a look." He got out of the motorcar. A quick check located the problem. The left front tire was flat.

"The tire?" Katie asked, still seated behind the wheel.

"Yes." He began rolling up his shirtsleeve.

"This isn't a very auspicious beginning. Perhaps we should go back to Homestead."

"Don't be ridiculous." He wasn't about to let her get away from him today. Not until he'd said what he needed to say. "It won't take but a few minutes to change it."

And then maybe he'd find the right moment to begin wooing Katie.

But things didn't work out quite as Ben had hoped. After the incident with the flat tire, the Susan B overheated twice and the fuel line ran dry on three different inclines. When it wasn't the automobile causing problems, it was Katie who stopped Ben from speaking his mind. Whenever he tried to bring up his feelings, she quickly changed the subject. The only topics she seemed inclined to discuss were her suffrage committee, what she hoped they could accomplish in the fall elections, her eagerness to return to Washington, and how important her life's work was to her.

By the time they were on their return journey, Ben felt more than a little discouraged. Perhaps he was hoping for something that could never be. Perhaps it would be easier to rope the moon than to win Katie's love.

Katie was never more glad of anything than she was to see the lights of Homestead twinkling in the distance as the Susan B rolled out of the mountains as dusk turned to darkness.

The interview with the two women loggers had gone well, and she knew it would make an interesting story for her column. But the day itself had been a tremendous strain. Try as she might, she hadn't been able to relax, not for a moment. She'd been too afraid Ben might see the longing in her eyes, and then everything would be ruined between them.

It had been a mistake to come with him today. More than once she'd feared she would dissolve into tears, especially when he'd started to tell her about Charlotte. If he'd put his arms around her and tried to comfort her, she would have done something foolish. She knew she would have.

Just as a full moon began to ascend, the Susan B coughed, sputtered, and died. The electric lights dimmed, then went dark.

"What now?" Ben asked.

"I don't know," she answered, feeling again the threat of tears.

"I'll see if I can get her started." He opened the car door and got out.

As he walked to the front of the automobile, moonlight silvered his usually golden hair. The light fell upon his face, revealing the strong angles and lines Katie knew so well.

Was it possible to love him even more tonight than she had this morning?

"Ready?" he asked.

With shaking fingers she set the levers. "Ready."

He gave the crank a hard turn. Nothing. He tried again. Still nothing. A third try brought the same results.

Ben rounded the car to the driver's side. "I don't think she's going to start. Looks like we'll have to leave her here."

Katie nodded, barely thinking about the automobile as she stared at Ben in the moonlight.

"I'll bring Edgar Childers out here in the morning, and we'll tow her back to town." He leaned forward slightly. "At least it's a nice night for a walk."

She found it hard to breathe. He was so very close. She couldn't seem to look away from his mouth.

"Katie?"

She drew back, realizing where her thoughts had been leading. "I'm ready." She slid across the seat and got out. "Let's go."

She set off at a brisk walk, leaving Ben to catch up with her.

"Katie." His fingers closed around her upper arm. Gently he pulled her to a halt, then turned her to face him. "What's wrong?"

"Nothing." *Everything.*

He lifted her chin with his index finger. "Come on. We've always been open with each other. You can tell me."

"There's nothing to tell." *I can't tell you this.*

The earth went suddenly still, the night sounds fading away. A cool evening breeze caressed Katie's cheek, contrasting the warmth of Ben's finger on her skin.

She wasn't sure how it happened.

He leaned down.

She stretched up.

He cradled her face.

She clasped her hands behind his neck.

His mouth grazed hers.

She released a tiny sigh through parted lips.

It lasted forever.

It happened in an instant.

It was more wonderful than she'd dared imagine.

It was more devastating than she'd feared.

Katie stepped back from Ben. His fingers slid across her cheeks until they lost contact. The night turned suddenly cold.

"We shouldn't have done that," she whispered in a shaky voice.

"Why not?"

There was an ache in her chest that made each breath come hard. "You know why not."

"Didn't you want me to kiss you?" His voice softened. "Didn't you like my kiss?"

He wasn't being fair. He had to know good and well what the answer was. He couldn't have helped feeling her response.

"Katie, about Charlotte. You must think—"

"Stop!" She clenched her hands together. "Benjie, we've been friends too long. Don't spoil everything."

"Does it have to spoil things? Can't we be more to each other than friends?"

No! her mind shouted.

Yes! her heart countered.

Katie covered her face with her hands. "I don't know. I don't know anything anymore."

A long silence fell between them while Katie wrestled with what her mind told her had to be done and what her heart told her she wanted to do. There was Charlotte. There was her work. There were promises and obligations and commitments.

"Katie, if you'd let me explain—"

She turned her back to Ben, unable to look at him and think straight. "I don't want to talk about it tonight. I can't. Please." Her voice broke. "Please don't ask me to."

His fingers touched her shoulder, but she pulled away.

"All right, Katie." He sighed. "We won't talk about it now." He stepped up beside her. "Come on. We'd better go. I don't want your folks to get worried about where you are."

Side by side they headed toward Homestead, not speaking, not touching. Two people walking in the moonlight, wondering what the next day would bring.

THIRTEEN

For the remainder of the week Katie took refuge in her work and with her friends. She didn't go into town, not even to retrieve the Susan B; she had Geoffrey bring back the repaired automobile.

Not once did Ben make an attempt to see her. She wasn't sure if not seeing him made things better or worse. She only knew she despised herself for what she had allowed to happen, for what she had discovered about herself. And for what she'd discovered about Ben. How could he kiss her the way he had when he was planning to marry Charlotte? How could he have betrayed his future bride *and* his friendship with Katie?

Even so, she longed to see him, longed to be with him, longed for more of his kisses.

That Friday the Homestead Woman's Suffrage Committee met to go over the final plans for the rally. An undercurrent of expectation charged the air in the dining room as the members of the committee—including Lark Jones and the Rudyards—gathered around the table.

There was good news to share at the start of the meeting. The majority of incumbents running for reelection had accepted the invitation to attend the rally, and one hundred percent of their opponents had agreed to be there as well. It looked as if this would be a hotly contested election year.

"Katie, you should be proud of what you've accomplished," Geoffrey said, and everyone around the table concurred.

She smiled, although there was no real feeling behind it. It was hard to be praised by her friends when she was feeling less than praiseworthy.

Sophia leaned forward. "I have something of interest to share. A reporter from the *Idaho Daily Statesman* is coming to Homestead to cover the rally. My brother told me about it this morning when he stopped by the house."

Katie's heart skittered at the mention of Ben.

"He says Katie's second column was picked up and reprinted in several newspapers in Idaho. It's created quite a stir, as it did here."

Did Ben ask about me?

"He says we can expect lots of folks to come to Homestead next week to hear the candidates. He says people want to know where the candidates stand on the war in Europe as well as on the vote for women. Ben also said we won't be able to stay out of the war much longer."

Blanche stiffened. "There would be no wars if such things

were decided by women." She slanted an accusatory glare toward Geoffrey.

"Unfortunately," he replied, giving his shoulders a shrug, "we don't see any women sitting in Congress, where such things are decided."

"Katie will be the minimum age in September," Penelope interjected. "Maybe she should run for office."

Silence fell around the table. All heads turned in Katie's direction. It took her a moment to register what had been said, since her thoughts had been lingering on Ben. But once she realized why they were looking at her, she said, "That's a preposterous idea!"

"Is it?" Geoffrey asked.

"Of course it is. Utterly preposterous."

"You know more about politics and the way government works than most candidates, Katie," Penelope countered. "You've been living in Washington for three years. What you don't know, my mother could tell you."

Blanche's expression was brittle. "Since it's obvious Miss Jones has no intention of running for political office, I suggest we turn our attention back to the real matter at hand."

Katie quickly agreed. After all, the last thing she ever intended to do was run for political office.

The idea was absurd.

For the second Friday in a row, the weekly train from Boise brought a surprise visitor to Homestead. And just as the

Rudyards had done the previous week, this visitor made his way to the office of the *Homestead Herald*. When Ben returned from the mercantile, he found Uriah Cobbs sitting at his desk, smoking his pipe.

As the door opened, Uriah—a short, wiry man of fifty with a receding hairline and wire-rimmed spectacles—looked up from reading a copy of that morning's edition of the *Herald*. "Nice work, Rafferty," he said, pipe still clenched between his teeth. "This little burg is lucky to have you."

"Thanks." Ben pushed the door closed behind him. "I'm surprised to see you. I wasn't expecting you till next week."

Uriah stood. "Thought I'd better get a jump on the competition. When do I get to meet this Miss Jones?"

Ben considered Uriah one of the best newspaper reporters in the business. He also considered him a pompous parasite. Uriah would be accurate in his reporting, but Katie would be subjected to plenty of cutting questions and snide remarks in the meantime. Ben wished he could get the first without the latter.

"Well?" Uriah prompted.

"Let's get you a room at the hotel first. Then I'll give her a jingle on the telephone to see when she can drive into town to meet with you."

The reporter grabbed his satchel. "Whatever you say, Rafferty. You can tell me about the little lady on our way."

Ben didn't know what he wanted to tell Uriah about Katie. He wasn't even sure what he would say to her when he called. He'd spent the last four days trying to figure out what his next step should be. After the kiss they'd shared, he was fairly sure she was well on her way to caring for him as more than a friend, but he also knew she was determined not to give in to those emotions.

Getting Uriah to cover the rally was Ben's way of showing his support. He hoped she would be appropriately grateful, grateful enough to give him a chance. He believed that once he won her love, all would be well. Of course, marriage to Katie wouldn't be easy. But they would be happy, and life would never be dull. Of that he was certain.

As the two men left the newspaper office, Ben gave a brief sketch of Katie's childhood, leaving out her more outrageous escapades. Of his feelings for Katie he said nothing, other than that they and their families had been friends for many years.

—— ❊ ——

After the meeting of the Homestead Woman's Suffrage Committee adjourned, Katie went to the door with those who were leaving. Blanche and Leslie said quick good-byes, then walked toward the Blake carriage, but Sophia hung back for a moment.

"Katie, do you think you might speak to Ben? Mother and I are worried about him."

"Worried? Why?"

"Ever since he and Charlotte broke off, he's been spending even more hours at the newspaper. He doesn't look as though he's slept all week."

A knot formed in Katie's stomach. "Ben and Charlotte aren't seeing each other?"

"I thought you knew."

"No, I didn't."

"It was a surprise to everyone, especially coming on the heels of my broken engagement. I needn't tell you, the town gossips are having a field day. The scandalous Raffertys— that's what they're calling us."

This is my fault. Katie turned her gaze in the direction of Homestead. *This is all my fault.*

The jangle of the telephone sounded from inside the house. Blanche called for Sophia to get into the carriage so they could be on their way. A fly buzzed against the parlor windowpane, as if trying to gain entry to the house. *Buzz. Click. Buzz. Click. Buzz.*

But all Katie was conscious of was her own echoing thought: *This is my fault.*

Sophia's fingers closed around Katie's wrist. "I'll see you in church Sunday. If you have a chance, please talk to Ben. Maybe there's something you can do. He won't discuss the matter with us." With a final pleading look, Sophia headed for the carriage.

Ben and Charlotte weren't seeing each other. He'd broken off with her, no doubt out of guilt for the other night. Or perhaps Charlotte had guessed about Ben's faithlessness. Perhaps she'd sent him away.

Oh, Ben. What have we done?

"Katie," her mother called from inside. "You're wanted on the telephone. It's Ben."

The knot in her stomach turned to lead. What would she say to him?

"Katie?"

"Coming, Mother." Squaring her shoulders, she opened the screen door and walked down the hall toward the telephone. Reluctantly she picked up the receiver and put it to her ear, then rose on tiptoe to speak into the mouthpiece. "Hello?"

"Katie, could you come into town this afternoon?"

"I just finished a committee meeting. I don't think I could get away—"

"Well then, maybe I could come out to the Lazy L."

"Ben, this isn't a good time. Perhaps—"

"It's important, Katie. There's a reporter here from Boise—Uriah Cobbs. He wants to interview you."

"Mr. Cobbs is here? In Homestead?"

"He's come to cover the rally." There was a pause on the other end of the line. Then Ben added, "This is a great opportunity. I think you should meet with him."

How could she face Ben? But what choice did she have? The cause. There was the cause to think of first.

"Of course, Ben. I . . . I'll meet you and Mr. Cobbs in your office at . . . say, three o'clock."

"Good." Another pause. "Katie?" There was a slight change in the timbre of his voice. "We need to talk. About the other night."

"Yes." Her chest ached. Her throat ached. "I know."

"I'll tell Uriah you'll be in my office at three."

"Three o'clock. I'll be there." She hung up the receiver without saying good-bye.

What was she to do? She placed her forehead against the wall. How could she make things right between them again?

"Katie?"

She straightened. Her father stood in the doorway to the kitchen.

"Papa."

Tears welled up in her eyes, and before she could give a thought to what she was doing, she was in his arms, her face pressed against his chest as she sobbed out her confusion and sorrow.

"What's the matter, kitten?" Yancy stroked her head with a work-worn hand.

The lump in her throat prevented her from answering.

"Here now," her father murmured. "There, there. It'll be all right. You don't need t'cry. It'll be all right."

"No, it won't," she whispered against his shirt.

" 'Course it will." He took hold of her arms and set her back a step from him. "Now, tell me what's causin' those tears."

She sniffed. "It's Ben. I . . . I think I've done something to hurt him. I didn't mean to, but—"

"Whatever it was, Ben'll forgive you, and things'll be right between you two again."

Her father didn't understand. Couldn't understand. And how could she explain it to him when she didn't understand herself? Why had God put this burning desire in her heart to fight for justice for all women, then allowed her to fall in love with Ben? Was this a test of her obedience?

O God, help me make sense of it all.

Ben could tell that Uriah Cobbs was surprised at Katie's youthfulness when he met her. No doubt he'd expected a dried-up old spinster with a sour countenance and her hair combed into a tight bun. Instead Ben had introduced him to a beautiful young woman with intelligent brown eyes and a lovely smile.

"We hadn't known anyone would arrive this soon, Mr. Cobbs," Katie said as she settled onto a leather-upholstered chair. "We're honored you came."

"You've taken on quite a task for a little lady. Are you sure you're up to the work it will take to defeat both an incumbent governor and an incumbent president?"

Ben perceived Katie bristling behind her composed facade.

"Nothing of true importance comes easily. Don't you agree, Mr. Cobbs?"

Uriah wrote something on his notepad. "I suppose not. Tell me, why bring your campaign to Idaho, where women already enjoy the vote?"

"Because if we're to make certain all women share that right, it will be because women of the enfranchised states rise up in support of their sisters who are told, by lack of a right to vote, that they are unimportant, that their needs have no value, that they are less than their male counterparts."

"But why hold Governor Alexander responsible?"

"The governor is a Democrat, and his party has refused to support the cause of woman's suffrage. You've heard of the policy of holding the party in power responsible, Mr. Cobbs?"

She paused long enough for the reporter to nod. "It is the Democratic *Party* that must be defeated in the November elections, not just Governor Alexander and President Wilson. Be assured that should Mr. Charles Hughes be elected president and should the Republicans not then support the amendment, we shall work just as vigorously to defeat his party in the next election."

"I see." Uriah scribbled a few more notes with his pencil. "Why don't you tell me a little about yourself?"

Katie inclined her head and began to speak. As Ben listened along with Uriah, he felt a welling up of pride in his chest. There was so much about Katie that he loved. It went far beyond her pretty face and enchanting figure. He loved her spirit, her nerve, her unwavering faithfulness to the things she believed in. He supposed it was some sort of miracle that the little tomboy had grown into this self-assured young woman. But it was no miracle that he loved her. How could he have helped it?

And love her, he did.

Ben hoped Uriah's interview wouldn't take much longer, because he wanted to talk to Katie privately. He wanted to let her know, if the kiss they'd shared the other night hadn't already told her so, that he cared for her as a man for a woman, not just as her friend.

Uriah rose from his chair. "I would be obliged if you'd show me around Homestead, Miss Jones. I need a better understanding of this place. I'd like to meet the people who live here." He offered his elbow to Katie as he glanced at Ben. "You're welcome to join us."

"Thanks," Ben muttered. It didn't make him feel any more charitable to know he'd have wanted the same thing if he were in Uriah's shoes. What he wanted was to have Katie to himself, to steal another of her sweet kisses, and then declare his love for her.

"I'll be happy to show you Homestead, Mr. Cobbs." Katie took hold of his proffered arm.

Ben had to keep from grinding his teeth in frustration as he reached for his hat, hanging on the coatrack. He set it on his head, then crossed to the door which he held open for Katie and Uriah.

They stopped first at the sheriff's office, where Uriah met both Sheriff Frank Murray and Vincent Michaels, the town's lawyer. Across the street at Barber Mercantile, the reporter was introduced to Leslie and George Blake, as well as Ophelia Turner, the postmistress; Annalee Leonhardt, Leslie's sister; and Fanny McLeod, wife of the town's doctor.

After introductions were completed, Uriah asked a few questions, innocuous questions that seemed no more than polite chitchat. But Ben could see the wheels turning in the reporter's head.

Zoe's Restaurant was their next stop, and it was there the course of things changed for them all.

FOURTEEN

When Katie entered the restaurant, she was surprised to find Geoffrey and Sophia sharing a table, deep in conversation.

After Katie introduced Uriah to Geoffrey, the reporter said, "You're from Massachusetts, Mr. Rudyard. Any relation to Mrs. Jonathan Rudyard?"

"My mother."

"Well, well." Uriah made a notation. "I had no idea Miss Jones's committee included anyone such as yourself."

Geoffrey cocked an eyebrow but said nothing.

"Do you plan to remain in Idaho long, Mr. Rudyard?"

"My plans are open at this time." Geoffrey glanced at Sophia, then back at Uriah. "I'll remain as long as Miss Jones needs or wants my assistance."

"If you're such a strong supporter of this woman's suffrage business—" Uriah's eyes narrowed—"why aren't you doing something back in Washington? For instance, why aren't you running for political office? Perhaps you haven't the gumption to stand behind your mother's convictions?"

Sophia gasped, and Katie opened her mouth to give Mr. Uriah Cobbs a piece of her mind.

But Geoffrey responded with a bored smile, saying, "I'm not the least bit afraid to stand behind either my mother's or my own convictions, sir. However, I should much rather see Miss Jones run for Congress. I'm merely an attorney, and the government is filled to overflowing with attorneys. Miss Jones, on the other hand, has an understanding of the issues and concerns of women that I could never have." He winked at Katie. "Being a woman herself, you understand." His expression sobered as he looked once more at the reporter. "In truth, Mr. Cobbs, Katie Jones is highly qualified to serve in office. We were just discussing it this morning, weren't we, Katie? That you should run for Congress."

"Miss Jones?" Uriah turned to Katie. "Surely Mr. Rudyard jests. You aren't considering such a ridiculous stunt?"

This morning Katie had considered the idea ridiculous, too. But looking at Uriah's mocking expression caused her temper to overheat as quickly as the Susan B on a summer day. "Do you think a woman incapable of filling such an office, Mr. Cobbs?"

"As a matter of fact, Miss Jones, I do." Chuckling, he gave his head a slow shake and looked at the notes he'd written. "But since it isn't likely any women will ever sit in the United States Congress, I won't have to worry about it, will I?"

Katie balled her hands into fists, and before she could stop herself, she said, "I hope I shall prove you wrong come November."

"You don't mean—"

"That's exactly what I mean, Mr. Cobbs." Oh, it was impulsive—even insane—but she continued speaking with growing resolve. "I plan to declare my candidacy for office. I'm going to run for the U.S. House of Representatives. And I'm going to *win,* too."

Geoffrey leapt to his feet. "Bravo, Katie!"

"That's wonderful!" Sophia joined in.

Katie glanced toward Ben to see what his reaction might be, but his expression was impossible to read. Perhaps he thought she'd lost her mind. If so, he could be right, but there was no taking back her declaration now, not with Uriah Cobbs writing furiously on his notepad.

"And do you plan to make this announcement public at the rally?" the reporter queried.

It was Ben who answered the question for her. "Yes, she does." His smile was mercurial, there and then gone, but it shored up her courage nonetheless.

Uriah turned a dubious look upon Ben. "Don't tell me *you* support this idiotic stunt?"

"Not only do I support it, Uriah, but I intend to manage Miss Jones's campaign. If she'll have me."

"Benjie," she said softly, her heart *rat-a-tat*ting in her chest.

Uriah spun on his heel and headed for the door. "Excuse me, folks. I've got to call this in to my editor. He's never going to believe it. Not in a million years. A woman running for the U.S. House. Unbelievable!" He was out the door in a flash.

Katie's knees suddenly went weak. She grabbed for the nearest chair and sank onto it. "What have I done?" She hadn't prayed about it. She hadn't sought godly counsel. She hadn't done any of the things she knew she ought to have done before making such a decision. All she'd done was react to the ridicule of an adversary. *O God, what have I done? And what should I do now?*

Geoffrey intruded on her thoughts, saying, "Katie, this is a stroke of brilliance. A woman running for Congress when most women can't even cast a vote at the ballot box. It will get the attention of people across the nation." He leaned down and kissed her cheek. "Wait until Mother hears."

Katie's stomach roiled as if she were at sea in the middle of a violent storm. She looked at Ben again. "What do you think?"

He drew her from her chair. "Come on. We're going to talk in private." He didn't bother to look at Geoffrey or Sophia. He didn't make any excuses. He simply escorted Katie out of the restaurant and down the street.

She dreaded what was coming. Ben was going to read her the riot act, and she would deserve everything he said. She'd done some crazy things in her life, but this was certainly the craziest one yet.

She expected him to take her to the newspaper office, but he turned on Barber Street and headed out of town, not stopping until they'd reached a tiny copse of trees along the banks of Pony Creek. Then, one hand on each of her arms, he turned her to face him.

She had a hard time thinking about the scolding she

deserved or Uriah Cobbs or running for office when she was standing so close to Ben, looking up at his mouth and remembering the way his lips had felt pressed against hers. She seemed to recall there was something else that should be troubling her, too, something she'd known they needed to discuss, but she couldn't recall it either.

Ben's fingers tightened. "Before we discuss your campaign, Katie, we need to come to an understanding."

Charlotte. It was Charlotte she needed to talk to him about.

"The other night—," he began.

"Ben, I—," she said at the same time.

Then, as had happened a few days before, she was somehow in his arms, kissing him. The world slowed on its axis. The creek's gurgle turned into a melody of love, joined by the songbirds in the trees.

When the kiss ended, Ben nuzzled Katie's hair as one hand stroked her back. Then he whispered, "Katie," and the sound of her name was as sweet as any confection she'd ever tasted.

But she mustn't indulge in that sweetness, she told herself. She had to try to make things right, not make them worse.

She drew back from him. "Sophia told me that you and Charlotte . . . that the two of you . . ." She turned away, her gaze locked on the fast-running stream. "I don't know why this is happening, Ben. I never meant to come between you and Charlotte. You're my dearest friend. I never meant for you to be hurt, to ruin your plans. I never meant—"

"If I'd loved Charlotte, you couldn't have come between

us." He drew up close to her back, leaned down to whisper in her ear. "It's you I love, Katie."

Her eyes widened. She held her breath. She couldn't have heard him right. She couldn't have.

She turned slowly. "What did you say?"

"I said I love you."

She shook her head. It couldn't be true. Everyone had told her they expected Ben to marry Charlotte. Everyone had said—

"I love you, Katherine Lark Jones."

He kissed her again—thoroughly, wonderfully, deeply kissed her until the feel of his mouth upon hers was the only reality left in her topsy-turvy world.

"I love you, Katie," Ben whispered as their lips parted, "and I want to marry you."

＊ ⊫◈⊨ ＊

Ben heard her gasp as she stepped back from him. He'd known he shouldn't move this fast, but he hadn't seemed able to stop the words. Now she was staring at him as if he'd sprouted a second head.

"Come over here," he urged, guiding her toward a boulder beside the creek. "Sit down. You're shaking like a leaf."

A nervous laugh escaped her as she sank onto the rock.

It was too late for him to take back his proposal, so he pressed forward. "Will you marry me, Katie?"

"Ben, I don't know what to say. I'm totally confused." She rubbed her forehead. "I just told Mr. Cobbs I was running for office, and you said you were going to manage my campaign, and now you're asking me to marry you." She drew a deep breath as she lowered her hand. "How could I possibly marry you if I'm going off to Washington as a congresswoman?"

He could have told her he thought it unlikely she would win the election for a national office. He didn't think enough people would support a woman for the United States Congress. He didn't doubt Katie was deserving, however. He above all people knew she could do anything well that she set her mind to.

"And even if I'm not elected, there's my work," she continued, more to herself than to him. "I never intended to stay here in Homestead. I don't know where God will call me next."

"You're doing the work you came here to do, aren't you? You're doing it here, not in Washington."

Confusion swirled in the brown depths of her eyes. "But that's temporary."

Ben wanted to take her back in his arms. He wanted to persuade her with kisses and caresses. He wanted to make her feel what he was feeling—love, desire, tenderness, passion. But something held him back. Something told him not to push any further.

"Did you mean what you said, Ben? Will you help me run for office?"

"If it's what you want to do." He would do whatever it took to make Katie happy.

Katie closed her eyes, and Ben suspected she was praying. He said a quick prayer of his own: *Show her we belong together, God. I'll make her happy. I promise.*

Katie opened her eyes, squared her shoulders, and tilted her chin. "Yes, I think it is what I want to do. I know it's a quick decision, but I wonder if God didn't make the way for this moment. I can do this job, Ben." Her eyes narrowed slightly. "Don't you think I can?"

"Yes, Katie, I know you could do it."

She rose to her feet. "And you'll help me win the election?"

As had been true throughout his life, it was impossible for him to deny Katie whatever she asked. "I'll do what I can." He took hold of her arms once again. "And what about us?" He was positive he saw love in her gaze.

With a note of sadness, she answered, "I can't marry you, Ben."

He nodded, as if accepting her decision. But silently he rejected it. *You will marry me, Katie. I don't know what it will take to convince you, but you will marry me. I can have enough faith for the both of us.*

⊶ ✦ ⊷

Later that night Katie drove home, her thoughts churning, her emotions in a continuing state of confusion. So much had happened that day, she could scarcely assimilate it all.

By the time she and Ben had returned to the restaurant, word of her candidacy had spread throughout Homestead. Those who had not come to Zoe's to congratulate Katie on her decision stood in the doorways of the shops and businesses and stared at her with looks of horror or derision or a combination of the two. She knew it was just an inkling of what the next few months would be like.

She refused to consider what others thought of her. She had enough to ponder—her candidacy for the U.S. House, Ben's proclamation of love, his proposal of marriage.

Ben's proposal of marriage.

Nothing could have shocked her more than the moment he'd said he wanted to marry her. Not even her announcement in the restaurant had surprised her as much as that.

Ben loved her.

He wanted to marry her.

Katie braked to a halt, then closed her eyes and rested her forehead against the steering wheel.

"Let us lay aside every weight, and the sin which doth so easily beset us, and let us run with patience the race that is set before us."

That was the verse she'd heard in her heart as she'd prayed beside Pony Creek this afternoon, after Ben had asked her if running for office was what she wanted to do. It was the answer, she was certain, that God had given her. Woman's suffrage was the race God had set before her. She had to run it.

Frances Willard had once said that every woman who vacates a place in the teachers' ranks and enters an unusual line of work does two excellent things: She makes room for someone waiting for a place to teach, and she helps to open a new vocation for herself and other women. Well, Katie wouldn't be vacating a teaching position, but she most certainly would be entering an unusual line of work.

Will you marry me, Katie?

She loved Ben. She couldn't deny it. She loved him with everything within her. But marriage? No. She couldn't turn her back on everything she'd believed, everything she'd been saying for years. Marriage could only be a complication, a hindrance to the race she was meant to run.

Wouldn't it?

Marriage to Ben would distract her. Look how he distracted her already. She'd made promises to others that she had to fulfill. She'd made a promise to God that she had to fulfill. There was no room in her life for anything more. No, marriage to Ben wasn't a possibility.

Was it?

Katie drew a ragged breath.

It would be better if she left things as they were. Ben would help her in the election, as he had helped her in the past. He was her dearest and most beloved friend. It was better that they be friends alone. Better for everyone.

FIFTEEN

The Homestead Weekly Herald
Homestead, Idaho
Friday Morning
June 23, 1916

Local Woman Announces Intention to Run for U.S. House of Representatives on the Republican Ticket

Katherine L. Jones, daughter of Yancy and Lark Jones, has declared her intention to seek the office of United States congresswoman from Idaho. Her announcement has caused considerable interest from politicians, constituents, and the press, especially as it comes in conjunction with the election rally being held in our town this Saturday, June 24, behind the Rafferty Hotel on Main Street.

Local merchants report a significant increase in business as visitors arrive in Homestead in advance of the rally. . . .

The week following Katie's decision to run for Congress was a complete blur of activity. Ben participated in daily meetings with the Homestead Woman's Suffrage Committee. He and Geoffrey mapped out a strategy for Katie's primary campaign, beginning with a trip to Boise to officially file for office in the second week following the rally.

By the next Friday, when Katie's name first appeared in the *Herald* as a candidate for office, every available room in Homestead—at the hotel, at the boardinghouse, and every private room anyone was willing to rent out—had been filled by reporters, candidates for office, and interested citizens from other cities and towns. The two restaurants in Homestead were doing a booming business, as were the other small shops. Folks gathered on street corners, in the billiards saloon, the barbershop, the drugstore, and in homes to discuss Katie Jones and her candidacy.

Everyone had an opinion, and most people spoke those opinions freely. New divisions arose between husbands and wives, between neighbors, between old friends. Women who hadn't objected to the suffrage issue expressed shock at one of their own running for national political office. Others saw a new hope because of one young woman's courage. Men who'd thought Katie's suffrage talk unnecessary but harmless suddenly saw what her candidacy could mean for their futures and quickly ridiculed her. Others, though smaller in number, expressed support for her actions and offered to help however they could.

Katie didn't have a good night's sleep all week. She slaved over a new speech for the rally because everything had changed after her declaration for office. She appreciated, more than she could say, the encouragement she received from Ben and Geoffrey, Sophia and Penelope, her mother and Leslie Blake. Blanche Coleson was the only member of the committee who didn't seem enthusiastic, but Katie never asked her why. She didn't want any more doubts to wrestle with. Her own were quite sufficient.

On the Saturday of the rally, Katie drove the Susan B into Homestead, the Rudyards and both of her brothers riding along with her. Her parents followed in the surrey, and the ranch hands came in on horseback.

A platform had been erected behind the Rafferty Hotel.

People milled around it, waiting for the rally to start. Wagons, buggies, and automobiles filled the open field south of the Homestead Community Church.

As Katie parked the Susan B, she shot a nervous glance toward Penelope, but her throat was too dry to speak.

Her friend patted her hand. "You're going to be wonderful, Katie. Just wait and see. I promise it's true."

"Penny's right," Geoffrey joined in from the backseat. "You were born for this moment."

Sam leaned forward. "Yeah, and if Andy Henderson says anything more about you, I'll black his other eye."

Katie groaned. "Don't tell me you've been in another fight because of me?"

Sam shrugged, not bothering to deny it.

"What have I done?" Katie mumbled to herself as she turned her gaze toward the platform.

That was when she saw Ben striding toward the Susan B. He wore a smile, and she knew it was meant just for her. A smile of encouragement and love. Her heart quickened. Ben stopped beside the car, placed his hands on the stationary door, and leaned in, bringing his face close to hers. Too close for Katie's comfort.

"You've cost some folks a bit of spare change." His smile broadened. "They were laying odds you wouldn't show up."

Her back stiffened and her temper sparked. "I hope you won a bundle, Benjie."

"I did."

"Good." She glanced at her passengers. "I believe it's time we got this rally started."

Everyone piled out of the automobile. Katie's brothers dashed off to join friends their own ages, leaving the others to cross the street toward the platform at a more sedate rate.

Ben took Katie's hand and slipped it into the crook of his arm, then covered her fingers with his opposite hand. "No matter what happens today or after, Katie, you can be proud of what you've accomplished." His voice lowered a notch. *"I'm proud of you."*

━━◆━━

Two hours later, when it was Katie's turn to speak, Ben's words continued to warm her heart. She stepped to the podium, feeling a strange calm settle over her. At the same time, a hush gripped the audience in the field below. All eyes were locked on Katie.

"My friends." She looked from face to face, recognizing the myriad emotions she found there—anger, anticipation, ridicule, hope. "Our republic has believed in no taxation without representation since its birth one hundred and forty years ago. In 1896, six years after gaining statehood, Idaho became the fourth state to extend full voting privileges to women, recognizing that native-born women should be at least as politically equal with native-born Chinese and Indian men. Most important, the people of Idaho affirmed that the ballot is a badge of equality for all classes."

She didn't need the notes for her speech. Every word was memorized, in her head and in her heart.

"In the two decades since this enfranchisement, Idaho women have been elected as the legislative chaplain, as the state superintendent of public instruction, to the Idaho legislature, as county treasurers, and as deputy sheriffs, to name a few offices. The Idaho legislature has also—at the urging of women legislators and lobbyists—adopted acts prohibiting child labor, giving married women the same right to control and dispose of their property as married men, requiring saloons to close on Sundays, establishing a state library commission, providing a domestic science department at the university, and establishing an industrial reform school. These are positive changes for the people of our state."

Were they listening, or were her words falling on deaf ears? Did the people understand the importance of what she was saying?

"Now it is time to make a difference for our country. It is time for all women in America to share the same rights as we have in Idaho."

Katie grabbed the podium, and fervor filled her voice. "Many of you are asking why I'm running for office. Wouldn't it be enough for me to work to elect men who support an amendment for woman's suffrage? No, that's not enough. It's time for a woman's voice to be heard in Congress. I want to feel that I have done something of consequence in my life. I should like to champion the causes that will better the lives of all women in this country, and to do so, I must be able to address the lawmakers of this land as an equal, as one of them."

"You belong at home!" a woman at the back of the crowd shouted.

Katie looked in the direction of the voice. Try as she might, she couldn't understand why all women didn't believe in the importance of suffrage, why they didn't believe a woman could be as effective as a man in government. Hadn't Deborah in the Bible been a judge in Israel?

"It is not my intention to make a long speech today. You have heard many speeches. You have listened patiently to many candidates, some with vast experience in government. Certainly much more experience than I myself have."

"You've talked too long already!" a man jeered.

"Get a husband!" another yelled.

"I will close with words from a woman I have so greatly admired, Susan B. Anthony. When asked what message she had for the new century, Miss Anthony answered, 'We women must be up and doing. I can hardly sit still when I think of the great work waiting to be done. Above all, women must be in earnest, we must be thorough, and fit ourselves for every emergency; we must be trained, and carefully prepare ourselves for the place we wish to hold in the world. The twentieth century will see as great a change in the position and progress of women in the world as has been accomplished in the previous century, but it will have ceased to cause comment, and will be accepted as a matter of course. There will be nothing in the realm of ethics in which woman will not have her own recognized place, and all political questions, and all the laws which govern us will have a feminine side, for woman and her influence, in making and shaping of affairs, will have to be reckoned with.' "

Again Katie paused and let her gaze sweep over the crowd. When she continued, it was with a strong, sure voice. "I want to be a part of what Miss Anthony foresaw for this nation and for its women. I want to be a part of the work God is doing in America. And this is my promise to each one of you. Should I be elected to the House, I will represent the people of Idaho with integrity and a vision for a better future for all."

Her gaze met with Ben's. He'd spoken earlier of his pride in her. Now she could see it in his eyes. "Thank you," she ended, speaking to all but meaning it for Ben.

Then she picked up her notes and left the platform.

+ ＝◆＝ +

Sophia had been spellbound by every word Katie spoke. Never had she heard anything more wonderful or inspiring.

"Look at them, Sophia!" Geoffrey exclaimed as he hugged her shoulders. "Katie's won them over." Then he lifted Penelope off the ground and kissed her cheek. "She did it, Penny. She really did it. By Jove, Katie's a marvel."

"We must send a telegram to Mother." Penelope straightened her hat, which had been knocked askew by her brother's enthusiasm. "She'll be waiting to hear. So will everyone."

"I'll go at once." Geoffrey took off toward South Street with long, purposeful strides.

Sophia watched as he walked away and found herself

wondering about the handsome lawyer. She'd liked both of the Rudyards from the moment they'd met, but it was only now she wondered why Geoffrey had made woman's suffrage his cause, too.

As if she'd read Sophia's thoughts, Penelope said, "Our mother took us with her everywhere when we were young. Geoffrey and I saw the terrible squalor so many women and children are forced to live in because of unfair property laws. We saw what happens when a man decides to cast his wife aside. Geoffrey swore, while he was still a boy, that he would help change things when he grew up. It's why he studied law. It's why he's helped work for the suffrage amendment."

"I don't think I ever thought of anything except what I wanted for myself," Sophia confessed. "I've been terribly selfish."

"I don't think you've been selfish. Look what you've done, once you saw the need."

"I haven't really done anything."

"You're wrong, Sophia. Change doesn't happen because of one person doing one big thing. It happens when many people do their own small parts."

"I wish I could do more."

Penelope took hold of her hand. "Why don't you come to Washington when this is over? Katie will need her friends after she's elected. You could live with us and work for the association."

"Washington?" Sophia's eyes widened. Could she really do something so daring? "I don't know. I never—"

"You wouldn't be sorry. I can promise you that."

"I don't know." She felt her heart racing. "But I'll think about it, Penny."

<hr />

Blanche observed the commotion following the close of the rally from her spot near the rear entrance of the hotel. She watched as people crowded around Katie, reporters asking questions and writing her answers on their notepads. Even some of the other politicians had gathered near her.

Ben Rafferty stayed close by her side, watching her with an adoring gaze. It was obvious that there was more going on there than simply his managing a political career.

Disappointment washed afresh over Blanche. Katie was not at all what she'd expected her to be. Any suffragette worth her salt would do her utmost to avoid men. Men were inferior and worthless. A wise woman kept her distance from them. If Katie was *really* concerned about the welfare of her own sex, she would have ended her association with Mr. Rafferty long ago. Instead she seemed to encourage it.

Blanche turned and slipped through the crowd unnoticed, making her way to her apartment above Yardley's Drugstore.

Jealousy and envy ate at her soul. Katie Jones was young and pretty, and her family had money and prestige. If it weren't so, no one would have paid her any attention. Katie would have been as invisible as an old maid schoolmarm.

Bitterly Blanche thought of the letters she'd written two weeks before. Only one response, and that one from a woman who called Blanche a few unkind names, then told her to mind her own business.

But Katie Jones? She had people gathered around her like a pack of jackals, hanging on every word as if each utterance was a droplet of gold.

It was so unjust.

—— ❈ ——

Ben waited patiently while Katie answered question after question. He understood people's desire to draw close to her. She had a charismatic, vivacious, infectious personality. Today people had also seen her intelligence, her caring, her commitment to her beliefs.

He'd been proud of her before she'd given her speech. He was even more proud now. But he was also concerned. Listening to her, he'd realized it was not an impossibility for her to win the election as he'd at first believed.

And if she won, what would happen to the future he'd envisioned for them? She would, indeed, be going back to Washington. Would she ever want to return to Homestead? Would she ever be willing to settle down in a quiet, small town, have a home, have a family?

His own wants and desires warred with Katie's dreams. He'd promised he would help her in her campaign. He would keep his promise. But he couldn't deny the secret hope within him that she would be defeated.

Because if she won, Ben was afraid everything that mattered most to him would be forever lost.

SIXTEEN

Uriah Cobbs, Katie decided, was a weasel of a man, sneaky, underhanded, and not to be trusted. While the other reporters and political candidates left Homestead in their automobiles and horse-drawn carriages within two days of the rally, Uriah lingered—like a bad cough.

Twice he came to the ranch to interview Katie, asking the same questions time and again, doing his best to trip her up in some manner. If she went into town, he dogged her steps, pad and pencil in hand. When she went to church, he observed her from another pew. He talked to her girlhood friends and to her neighbors. Katie felt as if she couldn't keep a single private thought from the intrepid reporter.

In the meantime, the dining room at the Lazy L became campaign headquarters for the Elect Katie Jones to Congress Committee. Morning, noon, and night, there was no escaping the ringing telephone or the onslaught of telegrams and letters or the plans that had to be made.

And although Ben came out to the ranch daily, there was never a time when they could be together, just the two of them. Katie longed for a few minutes to be herself with him, to be able to laugh and tease, to go swimming with him at the pond or horseback riding up in the mountains.

Most of all, she wanted to step into Ben's arms and feel his heart beating near hers. The memory of his kisses filled her dreams, both waking and sleeping. Her subconscious teased her with the knowledge of his love. Charlotte was no longer a factor. Ben was free to love and be loved.

Even when they were briefly alone together, Ben didn't mention his proposal of marriage again. Not even once. He didn't try to change her mind about running for Congress. Nor did he list all the reasons she should marry him.

It was oddly disturbing that she should want him to do so.

June rolled into July, temperatures climbing. Rain was a thing of distant memories. Whenever anything moved in the valley, a cloud of dry, fine dust rose above it. Tempers grew short, even among friends.

Blanche no longer attended the committee meetings. She'd given no reason for her absence. She'd simply stated she no longer wished to participate. Because no one on the committee had felt particularly close to the schoolmarm, they didn't try to change her mind, especially since other volunteers had begun to show up at the ranch, offering their help.

Yancy steered clear of the political plotting and planning going on beneath his roof, but Lark participated fully—often with tears in her eyes and sentimental comments about her daughter as a child. Katie knew it was hard on both of her parents, the idea that she wasn't going to stay in Homestead, that she was going back to Washington, and she was grateful for the love and support they showered upon her while she was here.

There was, however, no cause to rejoice about the chasm in Homestead between her supporters and those who thought she should be locked in her father's woodshed until she came to her senses. Phillip Carson refused to shop at Barber Mercantile or to cut George Blake's hair now that George had decided Katie had every right to run for office. Norman Henderson and his sons were attending First Church because of Reverend Jacob's refusal to speak against Katie from his pulpit; in her own small protest, Rachel Henderson continued to burn the meals she prepared for husband and sons. A group of boys threw eggs at the windows of the *Homestead Herald* office one night, but they ran off before the sheriff could catch them. Everyone suspected that Frank Murray knew who the perpetrators were but didn't want to punish them.

On the Fourth of July the town held its annual celebration, with a community picnic planned for the afternoon and a display of fireworks scheduled for nightfall. By an unspoken agreement the opposing sides of the election and suffrage issues called a temporary truce so the townsfolk could celebrate the nation's independence without rancor.

As had happened the day of the rally, Katie drove her touring car into Homestead with the Rudyards and her brothers for passengers. But this time Ben wasn't waiting to greet

Katie when she parked the automobile near the Homestead School. Today he was standing in the shade of a box elder tree . . .

With Charlotte.

"Why didn't you tell me your father was ill?" Ben asked Charlotte as he took hold of her hand. "I had no idea."

"Neither did I. Father never said a word. If Dr. McLeod hadn't come to me and insisted Father take a rest . . ." She let her voice drift into a strained silence.

"Everyone will be sorry to see you and your father leave Homestead."

She made a brave attempt at smiling. "Perhaps it's for the best."

"I'm sorry, Charlotte."

"You needn't be, Benjamin. All things work for good for those who love the Lord." She drew a deep breath. "I don't know when Father will be able to pastor another church, and with so much time on his hands, he'll need me to see that he follows the doctor's orders."

"But why California?"

"Father wants to see the Pacific Ocean. This is his opportunity." Her voice lowered. "He may not have many more opportunities if his heart—" She broke off abruptly, fighting tears.

"I'm sorry," he whispered again.

She pulled her hand free and turned her back toward him.

He saw her wipe furtively at her tears with her fingertips. Then she faced him again. "What about you, Benjamin? Are you happy?"

"Katie's running for office changed some of my plans."

This time Charlotte's smile was more earnest. "I was impressed by what she had to say at the rally."

"So was I."

"But?"

"But she doesn't want to discuss marriage because of her campaign."

It was Charlotte's turn to take hold of Ben's hand. "And even so, you're doing your best to help her win. You're a special man, Benjamin. But then, I always knew that about you."

He shrugged, uncomfortable with the compliment, especially knowing, down deep in his heart, that he wanted Katie to lose.

"I understand you're driving down to the capital on Thursday."

"Yes. Katie's going to officially file for office. She'll meet with members of the press and talk to the suffrage leaders, too."

"Then this will be my last opportunity to tell you good-bye. Father and I leave on Friday's train."

"So soon?"

She nodded.

"The community will miss you. Your father's congregation. Everyone."

"Thank you, Benjamin. We'll miss Homestead." She

squeezed his hand one last time, then released it. "I'd better get back to Father. He shouldn't even be out in this heat, but I couldn't convince him to stay home, not today of all days." She walked away, headed toward the picnic tables set up near the banks of Pony Creek.

Ben watched her go, wondering again why he hadn't fallen in love with her. Odd, the twists and turns that happened in life. She'd asked him if he was happy, but he hadn't really answered her. Perhaps because *happy* wasn't the right word. He didn't know if Katie would ever agree to marry him, but he knew she was the only woman for him. He knew he'd done the right thing in ending his relationship with Charlotte and pursuing the woman who held his heart.

Loving Katie was worth the risk.

⊷ ⟨◊⟩ ⊶

Katie's chest hurt, as if something inside had shattered in two. She pasted a smile on her face and went through the motions of greeting people, of making polite conversation. But all the while she kept envisioning Ben and Charlotte, standing so close together beneath that tree, holding hands.

It was for the best, she tried to tell herself. She hadn't been willing to marry him. She wanted Ben to be happy, and she was quite certain Charlotte would be able to make him happy. Yes, this was for the best.

From the corner of her eye Katie saw Uriah Cobbs start toward her. Unable to bear the idea of answering one more of his intolerable questions or listening to another of his condescending comments, she quickly slipped into the crowd, then made her way toward the tall cottonwoods and underbrush growing along the banks of the creek. She followed a well-worn path, a path beaten into the earth by generations of children who'd come to play by the cool stream on hot summer days. As she walked, the trees seemed to close in behind her, shutting out the noise of the townsfolk as they shared food and enjoyed one another's company. She kept walking. And walking and walking and walking.

She was nearly to the lumber mill before she stopped her hasty retreat. With a great sigh she sank to the ground, her back against a tree trunk, her knees pulled to her chest and her arms wrapped around her legs. She pressed her face into the folds of her skirt.

Truth washed over her. She wasn't escaping Uriah and his interminable questions. She was trying to avoid seeing Ben and Charlotte. She realized she'd been waiting for them to come walking into the picnic, holding hands and smiling at each other. The couple everyone had known should marry, together again.

Why couldn't she be glad for them? Was she so selfish, so small-minded, she would begrudge Ben his dream when she was so determined to achieve her own?

She didn't much care for the small voice inside her that said yes in answer to her silent question.

"Mind some company?"

She raised her head as Ben stepped into view from between two trees. *Where's Charlotte?* she wanted to ask but couldn't. Her throat was too tight to speak, so she simply shook her head in agreement.

Ben chose another tree trunk to stand against, crossing one leg in front of the other and resting the toe of his shoe on the ground. He folded his arms over his chest. He'd removed his suit coat sometime earlier. His white shirt seemed rather startling amid the earthy tones of trees, grass, and soil that surrounded them. The brightness hurt Katie's eyes, so she turned away.

"Feels good to find some quiet, doesn't it?" he asked.

She nodded.

"Looks like those who oppose you are calling a truce for today. No speechifying. It'll be nice for a change."

"Yes," she whispered, not caring at the moment if everyone in Idaho opposed her.

"I've asked Childers to go over the Susan B tomorrow to make sure she's ready for the drive down to Boise."

Three days with Ben. A full day's drive to the city. A day in the capital, registering her candidacy, talking to officials, meeting with other supporters of woman's suffrage. And then another long day's drive back to Homestead. Three days with Ben—and he'd be thinking about Charlotte.

"Katie." He stepped across the short distance separating them and sank to the ground beside her. "Why don't you tell me what's wrong? Is it Cobbs? Has he said something he shouldn't?"

Oh, Ben. Why do I have to feel this way?

He sighed. "All right. I won't press." He settled against the trunk beside her, so close she could feel the heat of his skin beneath his shirtsleeve. "Did you hear about Charlotte and her father?"

Katie's heart nearly stopped beating altogether.

"The reverend has been having trouble with his heart. He and Charlotte are leaving Homestead, moving to California. Dr. Tom thinks it will do him good."

She turned to look at Ben. "They're leaving Homestead?"

"On the next train."

"Charlotte's leaving Homestead?" She stared hard at him, trying to read what lay behind his eyes. "Will you miss her?"

* * *

When Ben realized what Katie was asking and why she was asking it, he had to work hard to suppress a grin. She was jealous. She must have seen him talking to Charlotte. She'd seen him and she'd jumped to the wrong conclusion. And she was jealous. Which meant she cared far more than she was willing to admit. Which meant she might love him the way he loved her.

With a firm grasp he took hold of her shoulders, pulling her toward him, turning her until she lay across his lap, his left arm supporting her back while his right hand caressed her cheek.

She stared up at him with wide eyes, eyes filled with a love she refused to admit.

"Katie, didn't you believe me when I told you I love you? Charlotte is special, and I hope she finds a man who deserves her and who will make her happy. But that man's not me.

Because I'm in love with you, and it's only you I want to be with."

He'd tried for so long—eighteen days, to be precise—not to pressure Katie. He hadn't told her again that he loved her. Hadn't asked her again to marry him. Hadn't kissed her. But there was a limit to his self-control, and he'd reached it.

"Marry me." It was a demand rather than a request.

"I can't, Benjie. You know I can't and you know why."

He brought his face close to hers. "You're too stubborn for your own good."

"I know." Her smile was uncertain. "I've been told so quite often."

"Marry me."

"No." She freed herself from his embrace, rose to her feet, walked to the water's edge.

Ben let his head fall back against the tree trunk. A deep sigh escaped him. "You win. But only for now. I'm not going to give up until you agree to become my wife."

She spun to face him, a spark of defiance replacing the look of love and longing that had been in her eyes only moments before. "Have the things you want changed, Ben? Don't you still want to live in Homestead and run your news-paper? Are you willing to live in Washington with a wife who leaves a rented house every day to serve in Congress? Do you understand the sort of ridicule you'd have to endure?" She gestured expansively, exhibiting her frustration. "I'm not ready to be a wife. To you or anyone else. I cannot stop fight-ing and working until suffrage is a reality for all women. I can't and I won't."

He got up but didn't move toward her. "You know what I think, Katie?" His tone was serious, his voice deep. "I think you love me. I think you want to say yes. Only you're afraid. You don't trust that I'll support you in whatever you want to do. Marriage is about compromise. At least the good marriages are."

She crossed her arms over her chest, as if to stave off his words.

"Yes," he continued, "I still want all those things you mentioned. I want to live in Homestead and have a home and a family. But I think we can find a way to have what we both want. I don't know how, but I think we can do it because we love each other. When God makes two into one, I'm sure He also guides them into the life they're meant to live as a couple."

"I'd only make you unhappy, Ben. I wouldn't make you a good wife." She tried, unconvincingly, to smile. "I'm too stubborn. You said so yourself."

He couldn't stay away from her any longer. He couldn't bear the distance between them. He stepped forward and saw her lean slightly back, as if suddenly fearing his touch.

When he stopped a few feet from her, he asked, "What makes a *good* wife? If I love you and you love me, doesn't that make it good?"

"Don't, Ben."

"You do love me, don't you?"

"Stop it." She covered her ears.

"Ah, Katie," he urged gently, "at least tell me you love me."

Tears welled in her eyes a split second before she turned and ran away, disappearing beyond the trees.

He wanted to chase after her, hold her, kiss her, force her to say the words he needed to hear. He wanted to, but he didn't.

"You can run all you want, Katie. You still can't run away from your feelings or from my love. Not today. Not ever." With determination in his voice, he added, "I *will* catch you, Katie."

SEVENTEEN

On the night before Katie was scheduled to leave for Boise, her father found her in the barn's loft, sitting with her legs dangling out the open hay doors. Wordlessly he sat beside her, and together they watched the sun sink behind the craggy mountain peaks. The clouds turned pink as shadows spilled across the valley floor. With dusk came a cooling breeze, a relief from the heat of the day.

"Nothin' quite so pretty as an Idaho sunset," he commented at last.

She didn't look at him. "No, there isn't. I missed them when I was away."

"I remember the first time I saw this valley, clear as if it were yesterday. Clearer, probably. Never planned to stay longer than a year or two. I'd never stayed any place much longer than that." He took hold of her hand, still staring at the fading colors of the sky. "I lit out on my own when I was younger'n Rick. Never knew what a home was. Never knew what a family was like. Took your ma t'teach me those things."

Katie laid her head on his shoulder.

"I reckon most fathers only want what's best for their children. Raise 'em up healthy and happy. Make sure they got an education and a portion o' common sense."

"I'm sorry I've disappointed you so often, Papa."

"Disappointed me? No, kitten, *disappointed*'s not the right word. You're a puzzle t'me, that's true. I don't understand the way you think at times, and I don't reckon I ever will. But I've never been disappointed in who you are."

She straightened and looked at him.

Her father squeezed her hand. "Your ma says you see things better than most folks, that you got a vision 'bout what things should be like. I think maybe she's right."

"Do you? Really?"

"Yep. You should know I'm mighty proud of you, Katie. I still don't know why you do some of the things you do, but I'm proud of you, all the same."

"Thank you, Papa."

"Kitten, you've bitten off a mighty big chew, runnin' for Congress an' all."

"I know."

"You sure this is what you want? You've had a small taste of what some folks, like the Hendersons or Mrs. Percy, will say about you. But it's gonna be worse when you get out away from Homestead. You got lots o' friends here. You got your brothers to fight for you, and Ben and the Rudyards and others to help you with your plannin' and all. But when you get out there, it's gonna be different. It's gonna be harder."

"I know," she whispered. "But I've got to try."

"Well, if you're dead set on it, at least I know Ben'll do his best to protect you, any way he can."

She blinked quickly, then turned her head to stare out at the darkening valley once again.

Her father took a deep breath, then let it out slowly. "Sometimes life makes us choose betwixt two things. Sometimes we want 'em both but can only have one. Times like those, choices can be mighty hard to make." He released her hand and got to his feet. "Times like those, kitten, you'll have t'follow your heart or your head, and only you can figure out which is right."

The air was filled with the sounds of night. Crickets chirped a familiar tune. A coyote howled from a faraway hill. A horse nickered in the corral beside the barn; another responded. A gentle breeze rustled the tree limbs, carrying the scent of pine with it.

Yancy stroked his hand over Katie's hair. "You'd best get yourself a good night's sleep. You'll have a long day tomorrow." He turned and strode toward the ladder.

"Papa?"

He glanced back at her.

"What if you don't know what you want most?"

He gave her a tender smile. "Just keep listenin' to your heart, kitten. You'll figure it out. Just keep listenin'."

"Just keep listenin' to your heart."

As Katie drove the Susan B into Homestead the following morning, her father's words repeated over and over again in her mind, as they had throughout the night.

"Just keep listenin'."

It had been much easier when she was in Washington. There, she'd been surrounded by women who had dedicated themselves, body and soul, to the cause of suffrage. She had also witnessed how difficult it was for those women who had husbands and children. No matter how committed they were to the cause, they were torn in different directions. Katie hadn't wanted the same sort of confusion for herself.

The Bible said that no one could serve two masters, for either you'll hate the one, and love the other; or else hold to the one, and despise the other.

"Ye cannot serve God and mammon," her reason whispered.

Why had she allowed herself to fall in love with Ben? How could she have been so reckless? He was like mammon to her, like temptations of wealth, like golden honey, sweet upon her tongue.

"A double minded man is unstable in all his ways."

Katie brought the automobile to an abrupt halt, then squeezed her eyes shut. She mustn't be double minded. She mustn't try to serve two masters. She must remember the course she'd embarked upon, the course to which she'd been called.

Purposefully she recalled an article about Miss Anthony written by Ida Husted Harper: "Had Miss Anthony married, she would have been a devoted wife, an efficient mother, but the world would have missed its strongest reformer and womankind their greatest benefactor. It will be of far more value to posterity that she gave to all the qualities which in marriage would have been absorbed by the few."

I don't want to be absorbed by you, Ben. And I would be because I love you too much.

There was the crux of the problem. She loved him too much. No matter what else she was doing, no matter what else was happening around her, Katie's thoughts turned to Ben. She was already being absorbed by him. If they married, it could only become worse.

She'd made a grave mistake, agreeing to have Ben drive with her to Boise. He'd convinced her and everyone else that he was the logical person to accompany her. He was managing her campaign. Katie should have a man with her during the drive—which would take place during the daylight hours and so would not subject her to undue criticism. They would be able to make plans for her campaign leading up to the primaries. His reasons were all valid.

But she should have insisted someone else go with them. She never should have allowed herself to be alone with Ben for so many hours. How would she be able to keep from weakening in her resolve?

"God, help me," she prayed softly as she once again started the automobile down the road to Homestead.

Fifteen minutes later she'd nearly convinced herself she would be able to deal with Ben for the long hours ahead, that this would be a time to restore their friendship to its former lightness. Then the Susan B rolled into town. She saw Ben standing on the sidewalk in front of the *Homestead Herald*, and she knew she'd deluded herself.

These were going to be the worst hours of her life.

* ◄►◄►◄► *

Water bubbled and splashed over the rocky river bottom, sending up a fine spray to cool the occupants of the Susan B as the automobile followed the rough road south toward the capital city. Neither Ben nor Katie had said a word in hours, not since they'd stopped to eat their lunch. Silence seemed to be what Katie wanted most, and Ben had obliged her.

Now, as the motorcar jounced and rocked over more ruts, nearly jerking the steering wheel from his grasp, Ben spared a quick glance toward Katie. She was seated as far to the right as she could get without hanging out the door. Her chin was tilted up, her mouth set in a firm line, her back stiff as a rod. She stared straight ahead with the resolve of a general perusing the battlefield.

Man alive, she was stubborn!

And oh, how he loved her.

Breaking the intolerable silence, he said, "We ought to be there in another hour or so."

She jumped, as if startled by gunfire.

Why wouldn't she admit she loved him? Why couldn't she be sensible?

He tightened his grip on the wheel, determined to draw her into conversation, even if only a mundane one. "Good thing, too. It's been a while since we ate lunch, and I'm getting hungry. The hotel's supposed to have a fine restaurant."

"It has been a long, hot day."

"Too bad we can't take the time for a dip in the river to cool us off." Not too long ago he would have suggested they stop and do just that. And not too long ago she would have agreed. But he knew it would be useless to try now.

Without warning, the Susan B sputtered and died. They rolled to a stop, the only sound that of the rushing water.

"What's wrong?" Katie asked.

"I don't know. I'll have a look."

For the next hour Ben checked everything he could think of. He knew a fair amount about automobiles, but he wasn't a mechanic, and he finally had to admit he was stumped.

"I don't know what else to try," he said as he turned toward Katie.

She had a smudge of grease on the tip of her nose and another larger grease stain down the front of her bodice. Her hair had tumbled free of its pins and was falling about her shoulders like an ebony waterfall. She looked hot, tired, and far too lovely. He glanced skyward. The sun had moved past the canyon rim, and shadows had grown long.

"Maybe she'll start again after it cools off," Katie said.

"Maybe." But he doubted it.

"Then we'll have to walk. We can't stay here and hope someone comes along. Besides, I've got to register tomorrow. Otherwise I'll have to wait until Monday, and neither you nor I wish to remain in Boise until then."

Ben sighed inwardly. There was no point in arguing with her, and he knew it. "All right. We'll walk."

* * *

The heat of the day disappeared with the blanket of night, and the darkness was all-encompassing. Ben, burdened with the suitcase Katie couldn't leave behind, had suggested more than once that they wait for the moon to make its appearance so they could see the road before them. Katie had refused to listen, which was why she now found herself sitting on the ground, her right ankle swelling, the pain causing her eyes to tear.

"I don't think it's broken." Ben turned her stockinged foot slightly to the left. "But you're through walking for the night."

"But I have to be—"

"Katie, be reasonable. I can't carry you *and* your suitcase all the way to Boise in the dark. You'll be lucky to get that shoe back on by morning."

He was right, of course. Again.

He stood, then bent down. "Put your arms around my neck. I'll carry you over to the trees. The ground will be softer there from all the old needles."

The moment Ben straightened, holding Katie against his chest, was the same moment the moon made its appearance. The silvery-white light fell across his face, a face she loved to look at, just for the sake of looking. She loved the sharp cut of his jaw and the way his nose was shaped. She loved the deep set of his eyes, so blue by day but black tonight. She loved the tousled look of his golden hair and the almost straight line of his eyebrows.

"Just keep listenin' to your heart," her father had said. The only problem was, her heart was telling her the wrong thing.

She had obligations.

She'd made commitments.

And she couldn't be what Ben wanted her to be.

She pressed her face against his shoulder as he carried her from the side of the road and up the slight incline to the nearest cluster of trees. There, he set her down, her back near the trunk of a tall pine.

"You're shivering," he said. "As pretty as it is, that dress wasn't meant to keep you warm. Here. Take my jacket."

She took it.

"I'll go get your suitcase and your shoe."

Katie pressed the jacket against her face, feeling the lingering warmth of his body, breathing in the scent of him. *Oh, Ben. Oh, Ben.* Never in her life had she felt such a strange keening in her heart. *Oh, Ben.*

This night promised to be both long and sleepless.

EIGHTEEN

Katie came slowly awake, aware first of the sounds of
nature, then of the crick in her neck from sleeping in an
upright position with a tree at her back. She was debating
whether or not to straighten and open her eyes when she
heard a woman's voice call, "Ben Rafferty, is that you? Are
you all right?"

Almost instantly, Ben was on his feet. "Marge?"

Marge?

Ben moved through the underbrush down to the road.
"Are we glad to see you. How'd you find us?"

Who's Marge?

Katie managed to stand, despite the pain in her ankle.

Ben leaned against an automobile, talking to the driver,
his back blocking Katie's view of the woman at the wheel.
Finally, he looked over his shoulder, and Katie could see he
was frowning. After another brief verbal exchange with the
woman, he headed back to where Katie was.

"We've got trouble," he said, his voice grim.

"Trouble?" *Who is that woman, Ben?*

"Uriah Cobbs's got wind that we didn't arrive last night, even though we left in plenty of time to reach Boise. He's tried to discredit you in his column."

"Discredit me? Whatever with? Is it a scandal to have trouble with an automobile?"

"It doesn't matter what the truth is, Miss Jones. People believe what they see in print." The woman stepped into view. With an apologetic smile, she held her right hand toward Katie. "I'm Marge Kline, a friend of Ben's. I work as a clerk at the *Idaho Daily Statesman.*"

Katie shook Marge's hand, all the while wondering what she'd meant by "a friend of Ben's."

"Mr. Cobbs doesn't like the idea of a woman running for Congress. An unmarried woman alone on the road at night with a man . . . well, you can imagine . . . " Marge handed the morning edition of the paper to Katie; then she looked at Ben. "Kenneth sent me to look for you two. He thought if I could find you . . ." Her voice drifted into silence.

Katie scanned the article. It was filled with innuendos of a none-too-flattering kind. She didn't know what to think, what to feel. How could she possibly be blamed for car failure? "Can you print a retraction?"

Marge hesitated before saying, "Yes . . . but that won't stop people from thinking—"

"Katie?" Ben took hold of her shoulder and turned her to face him. "Marry me."

"What?"

"Marry me. If we're married, no one can say a thing against you. This will all go away."

"Ben, I—"

"You want to run for office, right?" He didn't wait for an answer. "Then let me help you. We'll have Marge drive us into town where we can get married. Even Uriah won't be able to say much then."

"But—"

"I'd say that's your only option, Miss Jones," Marge interrupted. "If you want to avoid a public scandal, that is."

"But we didn't do anything wrong." The moment Katie's protest was out of her mouth, two sayings—she thought they were from the Bible—popped into her head: "Avoid even the appearance of evil" and "It is better to marry than to burn." She found the second more disturbing than the first. Was this what God wanted her to do after all? Could she do the work He had called her to do *and* be Ben's wife?

Ben drew closer to her and lowered his voice. "Katie, you know I love you. You know I've wanted to marry you even before this. You refused because you wanted to run for office. Well, now if you *don't* marry me, you may lose that chance."

She didn't want to lose her chance at serving in office. It seemed it was what she was supposed to do. If this was the only way she could salvage the situation, then—

"Say yes, Katie."

"Oh, Ben—"

"Say yes."

"I—"

"Katie?"

She released a little sigh, then softly said, "All right, Ben."

"Splendid!" Marge Kline exclaimed. "Then let's make haste before one of Mr. Cobbs's bloodhounds locates you."

"Sophia, stop that pacing and sit down this instant," Rose Rafferty demanded.

"Something must be wrong," Sophia said as she obeyed her mother, sinking onto a chair beside the kitchen table. "Katie said she would call just as soon as she'd filed. Something must have gone wrong."

"If something was wrong, we'd have heard." Rose resumed shelling peas, popping open the pods and, with her index finger, scooping the peas into the bowl on her lap.

Sophia knew she should be helping her mother with their supper preparation, but she couldn't stop fidgeting. Finally she jumped up from the chair. "I think I'll walk over to the newspaper office. Maybe Ben has called there."

Her mother merely shook her head and went on with her work.

Outside, the midday sun was blistering the streets and buildings of Homestead. The few horses that were tethered to hitching posts stood with heads hanging low, tails flicking slowly at flies. Dogs slept in the shade of awnings and beneath the boardwalks. The bench outside the hardware store was empty, and Sophia suspected the usual gathering of men was inside the billiards saloon, washing away the heat with glasses of beer.

Sophia had just passed the bank and was preparing to cross Barber Street when she saw Geoffrey Rudyard and his sister come out of the newspaper building. When Geoffrey saw her, he waved.

"Have you heard anything?" Sophia asked as she drew closer to the brother and sister.

Penelope answered, "Not a thing. This isn't like Katie."

"Or Ben either." Sophia's glance darted to Geoffrey.

"I think the two of them can handle whatever problems might arise," he reassured the women in a calm voice.

"But what if they've had an accident?" Sophia persisted, her anxiety increasing with each word. "What if they're lying somewhere, injured?"

Geoffrey placed an arm lightly around her shoulders and smiled at her. "I think it's far more likely your brother has grabbed the chance to woo his girl." He put his other arm around his sister. "It's what any red-blooded fellow would do, given the same opportunity."

Penelope poked him in the ribs. "I wish you had tried to woo Katie, my dear brother, but you never had the good sense to do it. Now you're too late."

Sophia wasn't sure she understood what they were saying. Ben and Katie? "But they're just friends."

"I find that highly unlikely, Sophia, my girl," Geoffrey responded with a laugh. His arm slipped easily from Sophia's shoulders; then just as easily he placed her hand in the crook of his elbow. As he offered his other arm to Penelope, he said, "Allow me to escort you two lovely ladies to Zoe's Restaurant.

Perhaps Miss Potter has some cold lemonade to quench our thirst while we wait to hear from Katie and Ben."

Sophia let herself be guided across the street, her thoughts churning. *Katie and Ben? But how could that be?* She'd thought her brother was still mourning his broken romance with Charlotte.

And Katie? Katie had made it clear she wasn't ever going to marry. She wouldn't be foolish enough to fall in love with her best friend nor foolish enough to marry him. Would she?

＋—⫤◆⫤—＋

"And now, by the authority vested in me by the state of Idaho," Reverend Osgoode intoned, "I pronounce you man and wife." He paused a moment, staring at the bride and groom. When neither of them moved, he added, "Benjamin, you may kiss your bride."

Ben turned toward Katie. Tenderly he took hold of her shoulders and drew her toward him. "I hope someday you'll know how much I love you, Katie," he said softly, for her ears only. "I'll do my best to prove it to you." Then he leaned down and kissed the center of her forehead.

For the first time since they'd walked into the church, Katie met his gaze. He saw a flicker of something in her dark eyes that caused hope to rise in his chest. Somehow he would make it up to her, this hastily arranged marriage of theirs.

He turned toward Pastor Osgoode. "Thanks, Robert." They shook hands. "We appreciate this."

"No trouble at all. Mrs. Rafferty, I wish you well in the elections. I mean that with all sincerity."

"Thank you, sir."

Ben took her arm and walked her toward the door. "We'll slip over to the secretary of state's office. If our luck holds, we won't run into the members of the press until after you've filed."

"Our *luck?*" She cocked an eyebrow, her expression dubious. "Any more luck like we've had already and we're likely to end up in jail."

His heart lightened at her teasing sarcasm. "I suppose it could still happen, Katie. Don't give up yet. Nothing like a jail cell to start a marriage off right."

She rolled her eyes. "Very funny."

Mentally Ben renewed his vow. Somehow he would make it up to her for the way their marriage had begun. He would prove he only wanted to make her happy. Even if it took him a lifetime, he would prove it.

And a lifetime was exactly what he wanted with Katie Jones Rafferty.

＊―＊ ⚜ ＊―＊

A delegation from the Boise City Chapter of the Woman's Christian Temperance Union, with sashes worn over their shoulders identifying their affiliation, awaited Katie and Ben when they emerged from the secretary of state's office an hour or so later. Behind them was an eager-looking group of reporters, Uriah Cobbs among them.

Ben's grip on her arm tightened slightly. "Looks like

someone inside made a few telephone calls while you were filing your papers," he whispered near her ear. "Are you ready for this?"

Katie felt a moment of doubt and fear. Then, drawing a quick breath for courage, she stiffened her spine and forced a friendly smile onto her lips as she moved toward the women.

After a few words of welcome from Mrs. Walter J. Smith, president of the local WCTU, Katie was introduced to the other members of the delegation. She spoke briefly about her support for issues regarding women's property and guardianship rights and earned applause when she quoted World WCTU founder Frances Willard without benefit of notes.

Looking once again at the formidable Mrs. Smith, Katie said, "I sincerely hope I'll enjoy the support of your members, Mrs. Smith." She offered her hand to the woman.

"I believe you shall, Mrs. Rafferty, judging from what I've just heard." Mrs. Smith's handshake was firm. "I look forward to hearing more from you in the weeks to come."

"Thank you."

Mrs. Smith glanced at the rest of her group. "Come along, ladies. We have our own work to do."

Unable to delay her meeting with the members of the press any longer, Katie turned toward them. She gave each of the men a smile, although the expression was more difficult to maintain when she met Uriah Cobbs's piercing gaze. Again she felt Ben's fingers tighten on her arm, and again she took courage from it.

"Gentlemen, I imagine you have questions for me."

For what seemed ages, she responded to their queries. Most had to do specifically with her candidacy for the United States House of Representatives—why she was running, what she hoped to achieve, her thoughts on the war in Europe. Some delved into her college education and her work with the National American Woman Suffrage Association. One man wondered if her husband shouldn't be the one running for office, given that his father had once been mayor of Homestead.

Uriah Cobbs, however, seemed more interested in her married status. "Why were your plans to marry kept a secret, Mrs. Rafferty?"

"My husband is a respected journalist in Idaho, Mr. Cobbs. His pieces are read in many other newspapers besides his own. I don't want our marriage to influence voters on my behalf. I want to be considered for office on my own merits." She was relieved she'd been able to speak the truth and still answer his question.

"Gentlemen," Ben interjected, "if you don't mind, I'd like to take my wife to dinner. You'll have plenty of opportunities to interview her during the next couple of months." With a hand placed firmly in the small of Katie's back, he propelled her away from the reporters.

As soon as they were out of earshot, Katie released a deep sigh. "Thank you. I really do detest that man."

Ben said, "I'll have the hotel send our supper to our room so we can eat in peace."

She was grateful for his thoughtfulness and knew she should tell him she didn't hold him to blame for anything.

Ben had married her in order to protect her reputation from scandal, even if it had given him what he'd wanted in the bargain.

She glanced at him as they entered through the wide doors of the hotel. She thought about all the years they were apart, all the times she'd missed him. She could talk to Ben about her deepest secrets. He understood her as no one else ever had—not even her parents, not even Penelope. She'd loved Ben as her dearest friend for as long as she could remember. And since returning to Homestead, she'd fallen in love with the man he'd become.

Need it be so awful, this hasty, unplanned marriage of theirs?

They climbed the stairs, and she became newly aware of the feel of his hand on the small of her back, of the warmth of her skin beneath it. She looked down the hall at the door to their hotel room and realized they would be alone in that room tonight.

Alone as man and wife.

A shiver shot up her spine, reminding her how easy it was to forget everything except Ben.

The moment he opened the door for her, she moved away from him, crossing the room to stand before the window. She heard the door close softly, heard the click of the lock as it turned.

Alone as man and wife.

"Katie."

She pressed her forehead against the windowpane. The glass was still warm from the touch of the late-afternoon sun.

In the street below, she saw a man place a Closed sign in his shopwindow. Going home, probably to his wife and children.

"Katie, we need to talk."

"I know."

"Come and sit down," he urged gently.

She turned. He now stood near the sofa and chairs. He'd removed his hat. His hair was slightly mussed, and she knew he'd raked his fingers through it only moments before. He had a habit of doing so whenever he was troubled.

And he was troubled about her.

She drew a deep breath and let it out. "None of this is your fault, Ben. I have only myself to blame. I should have insisted Penelope or my mother come along."

"I think we can share the blame."

"Oh, Benjie." She sank onto the sofa and stared at the thick carpet beneath her feet.

He sat on the chair opposite her. "What is it you want, Katie?"

She glanced up, wishing she knew how to answer him. "I don't know." Tears pooled in her eyes. "I suppose I want things to be as they've always been."

"It won't happen. They won't ever be the same again."

"I know," she whispered.

He took hold of her hands, drew her gently from the sofa and onto her knees before him. Then, with a tender touch, he cradled her face with his palms, tilting her head back slightly. He brushed the tears from her cheeks with his thumbs, then kissed the moist tracks left behind.

With his mouth now hovering near hers, he said, "I make you this promise, Katie. I won't ever try to change you. I love the woman you are." He lowered one hand and placed it just above her heart. "I love the woman you are in here." He kissed her lightly, then added, "All I ask is a chance. Just a chance."

Her skin tingled. Her breathing was shallow.

It isn't that I fear you trying to change me, Ben. It's myself I fear.

But for the moment, she didn't care.

With just a slight movement, she brought her lips in contact with his. A languid warmth spread through her veins as she pressed closer to him. She wanted the kiss to go on forever. She wanted things she couldn't even put names to, and that frightened her.

"I think," Ben whispered when their mouths parted at last, "I'd better order up our supper." He smiled tenderly. "We'll not rush things tonight, Katie." He stood, bringing her with him. He wrapped her in his arms, kissing her again until she was breathless. When the kiss ended, he took a short step back from her. His voice almost gruff, he said, "I'll go see about our food."

She nodded, unable to speak.

"I won't be long."

She shook her head.

He touched her cheek with his fingertips. "I love you."

I love you, too.

Ben hesitated, seeming to wait for her to say with her mouth what he could see in her eyes. But she didn't speak, didn't say the words he wanted to hear.

Finally he turned and left the room.

When she heard the knock on the door sometime later, Katie almost decided against answering it. She wasn't in any frame of mind to talk to anyone. If it was Ben, he could use his key. If it was a reporter, he could jolly well go away.

But the caller knocked a second and then a third time, and finally Katie resigned herself to facing whoever was on the other side of the door. She wasn't expecting who—or rather what—she found.

Three men stood in the hallway, all of them obscured by enormous bouquets of red roses. Roses and roses and more roses. Large vases filled to overflowing with greenery and long-stemmed, bloodred roses.

"Are you Miz Rafferty?" asked a voice from behind the nearest bouquet.

"Yes."

"Then these are for you, ma'am."

"*All* of them?"

"Yes, ma'am. You mind if we bring them in? They're kind of heavy."

"No." She stepped back, opening the door fully. "Of course. Bring them in."

They paraded by her, setting the vases on a large table near the bedroom doorway. Then one of the men brought her an elegant white envelope. "This here's for you, Miz Rafferty."

She stared down at Ben's familiar handwriting as a cloud of rose perfume filled the room. Forgetting about the delivery men, she slipped her finger beneath the flap and opened the envelope, then removed the note card.

In the true marriage relation, the independence of the husband and wife is equal, their dependence mutual, and their obligation reciprocal.
—Lucretia Mott
So shall it be.
Ben

Her vision blurred as she stared at the card. He knew her so well. Perhaps he understood, after all, what made her afraid to give in to the love she felt for him. And perhaps her fears were unfounded. Perhaps—

"If you'll excuse us, ma'am, we'll be on our way."

She looked up, surprised that the men were still there. She blinked away her tears. "Let me get something for your trouble." She glanced around for her purse.

"No need, ma'am. We've been paid." He tipped his hat as he backed through the doorway. "A pleasure, ma'am. And might I say, the mister is a right lucky fellow."

Katie turned her eyes toward the table laden with roses, scarcely aware of the sound of the closing door as the men left. Misty eyed, she crossed the room. With her fingertips she cradled a blossom and lowered her nose to breathe in its heavenly fragrance.

"American Beauties for an American beauty," Ben said from the doorway.

She straightened, turned, and blinked her eyes so she could see him clearly.

"They're your favorites," he added.

"How did you know?"

"You said so in a letter. I think it was after Amelia Christopher's wedding."

"That was years ago. You remembered all this time?"

He walked toward her. "I remember everything about you, Katie. I always have."

As naturally as if she'd done it for a lifetime, she stepped into his embrace, tilted her head, received his kisses.

When at last they broke for air, he whispered, "Our supper is on its way up."

Tell them to take it back to the kitchen, she wanted to say. Perhaps her eyes said it for her. Perhaps Ben heard her with his heart. His eyes darkened as he stared down at her. His handsome face grew taut with controlled passion. Katie felt a thrill spiral through her, accompanying a new realization, a sense of power in her womanhood.

A knock on the door announced the arrival of their meal, as Ben had predicted. With obvious reluctance he released her and went to answer the summons. A moment later two white-coated kitchen servants carried large trays into the room.

"Just put them there," Ben instructed, indicating a pair of parlor tables set on either side of the sofa.

It seemed to Katie the servants moved much too slowly. It seemed forever before they accepted Ben's gratuity and left, and she and Ben were once again alone.

He smiled at her—a secret smile, full of promise—and held out his hand. "Come over here."

She went, placing her hand in his, allowing him to draw her to the brocade sofa.

"You may not know this, but the hotel has a fine chef." Ben lifted a cover off a platter. "Lobster a la Newburg." He selected a bite-size piece of meat, picked it up with his fingers, and carried it to her mouth. "Try it," he encouraged softly.

She had only a moment to savor the succulent flavors of cream, Madeira, and lobster before Ben leaned forward and kissed her. The ensuing sensations first surprised her, then stole her breath away.

Tonight was her wedding night, and they were alone as man and wife.

NINETEEN

Within minutes of each other, telegrams were delivered the next morning by employees of Homestead Telephone and Telegraph to the Lazy L Ranch and the Rafferty home. Both were read by stunned members of the bride's and groom's respective families. The missives were identical:

> *Katie and I married. Newspapers announce on Saturday. Katie has filed her candidacy. Will return to Homestead on Sunday evening, following repair of automobile. More information upon our return. Benjamin*

Phone lines began to hum as the news spread across Long Bow Valley. Some folks were surprised by the sudden turn of events. Others nodded knowingly, as if they had always assumed the two friends would one day marry.

The schoolmarm was disgusted. Such weakness. But she kept her opinion to herself.

━•━ ✠ ━•━

For an idyllic, unexpected thirty-six hours Ben and Katie locked themselves in their hotel suite. Both had a secret wish to hold the morrow at bay, to have this time to savor, knowing instinctively they would need it as a foundation against a still uncertain future.

But they couldn't remain hidden forever. On Sunday they checked out of the hotel, taking with them a bevy of treasured, rose-scented memories.

Outside the hotel, Katie stood on the sidewalk as Ben set the levers, then went to the front of the Susan B. She thought she heard him say, "Thanks," as he patted the hood with one hand. She might have asked him to repeat what he'd said if she hadn't been suddenly interrupted by the appearance of Uriah Cobbs.

"Good morning to you, Mrs. Rafferty. I see you're about to leave our fair city."

She truly disliked this man, but she tried to hide her feelings as she replied, "Yes. Our automobile is running again, and it's time we returned home."

As if to prove it, Ben turned the crank, and the Susan B roared to life.

"I would have thought you'd make a few more public appearances while in Boise City." He peered at her with a gaze that missed nothing.

Her glance went to Ben as he jumped on the running board and reached into the motorcar to reset the throttle lever. He looked so handsome, so wonderful this morning, it was hard to focus on anything else.

"Another time," she answered the reporter absently.

"Are you aware you've captured the interest of the nation with your candidacy for office? The *Statesman*'s received inquiries from nearly every state in the Union. This election promises to make you sort of a celebrity."

Katie didn't want to listen to Uriah. She didn't want to be reminded of the campaign or the election, nor did she want to be a celebrity. She only wanted to think about Ben.

"You seem distracted, Mrs. Rafferty. Maybe you're having second thoughts about running for office? Maybe now that you're a married woman—"

The pleasant images fled as she turned her gaze upon the reporter a second time. "No, Mr. Cobbs, I have *not* had second thoughts. I am in this race to the finish."

Ben stepped onto the sidewalk just as she made her sharp retort. Taking hold of her arm, he said, "You'll have to excuse us, Uriah. We've a long drive ahead of us."

The reporter tipped his hat. "Of course, Benjamin. I understand. I'm sure I'll be seeing you and your lovely wife again soon."

"Yes, I'm sure you will. Good day."

Katie's temper seethed, but Ben's grip on her arm kept her silent as he helped her into the front seat of the motorcar. However, the moment he put the automobile in gear and they pulled away from the curb, she spluttered, "The unmitigated gall of that man! Just because I'm married, he thinks I'll have no more interest in running for political office. It's probably what they all think. Why can't they understand what this is about?"

"I suppose it's natural some folks would assume you'd want to settle down with your husband rather than going off to Washington, D.C."

She looked at Ben, and her anger faded. "That's what you'd like, isn't it?"

He was silent for a long time before he answered, "Yes." He cast a quick glance in her direction, then turned his gaze to the road. "I can't lie to you, Katie. I wish you wanted the same things I do. But I believe we'll find a way to work it all through. I have to believe it. I love you."

But did he love her enough to let her go on being herself, to let her go on chasing her dreams? When would he start making demands she couldn't fulfill?

Perhaps that was one more reason she had yet to tell him she loved him. So many times during those blissful hours in the hotel room, she'd been tempted to say the words. She'd seen in his eyes his need to hear them, but she hadn't been able to do it. Not then. Not now. The campaign. The fight for suffrage. Those had to come first. That was her calling. She had to remain steadfast and true.

⊷ ▰◆▰ ⊶

"No, Michael!" Rose called to her husband from across the Rafferty Hotel dining room. "Not there. Center the banner above the column." She pointed. "Over there."

"And higher, too," Lark chimed in.

"I'll give him a hand," Geoffrey offered, then wove his way through the tables toward the hapless man on the ladder. "Is there something I can do to help, sir?"

Michael let out a frustrated laugh. "I doubt we'll get it right, no matter what we try." He sat on the top step of the ladder and looked down at Geoffrey. "Yancy had the right idea. Hightail it into the hills for the afternoon. Between his wife and mine . . ." He let his voice trail off, ending with a shake of his head.

"They are intent on doing it all up brown." Geoffrey grinned.

Michael raised an eyebrow, obviously finding nothing amusing about the turmoil all around him. "Young man," he said dryly, "you're enjoying yourself entirely too much."

Geoffrey tried to contain his laughter but failed. The older man was right. He was enjoying himself. He thought it grand that Ben and Katie were married. He thought Ben Rafferty was just what Katie needed. He'd always adored his friend's forthrightness, her ability to focus on an issue and pursue justice with the tenacity of a bulldog. He enjoyed her sense of humor and the pleasure she took from the simple things in life. But secretly he'd also believed she needed to fall in love and discover that there was more to life than her causes. As important as they were, they were not *everything*.

"As a matter of fact," Michael said, intruding on Geoffrey's thoughts, "there's another ladder out behind the hotel. Why don't you get it, and we'll have a go at this banner together.

With any luck, we can hang it to the women's satisfaction before the newlyweds arrive."

"Right away, sir."

"Go through the kitchen. It'll be quicker."

Geoffrey walked to the swinging doors that joined the hotel kitchen to the dining room and pushed one of them open before him. As he passed into the kitchen, he was stopped by the sight of Sophia standing beside a table, an apron tied around her waist, a scarf covering her pretty gold hair. Her mouth was puckered in concentration as she decorated a large single-layer cake.

"Hmm. Looks good."

With a gasp, she jumped backward. Her hand flew to her scarf, and she tugged it off, then held it behind her.

"Sorry. Didn't mean to startle you."

"I didn't hear you come in." She smoothed her hair away from her face.

He stepped forward, smiling when he saw the smudge of icing on her cheek. Sophia Rafferty was a beguiling young woman. It wasn't simply because she was pretty, although that was certainly true. Nor was it because she believed in woman's suffrage and was working to see it become a reality, although that was important to him, too. No, it was something much simpler, yet more complex, than either of those reasons.

"I must look a sight," she said as he drew closer.

"Indeed you do." He stretched out his arm and brushed at the icing on her cheek with his fingertips. "And it's a very lovely sight you make."

She blushed.

Maybe that was it. Too few women of Geoffrey's acquaintance remembered how to blush. They were far too sophisticated—or at least they pretended to be. He doubted Sophia would know how to carry on such a pretense.

"Are you and Penny settled into your rooms here at the hotel?" she asked as she took a step back from him. "Are they to your satisfaction?"

"The rooms are fine."

"You're probably glad to be in town."

"We enjoyed our stay at the Jones ranch, but it was time we stopped imposing on their hospitality. Ben and Katie's wedding gave us a good excuse to leave without offending our hosts."

Sophia glanced down at the worktable. "I hope they like their cake."

"I'm sure they shall."

"And I hope the Susan B doesn't break down again."

"I'm certain they hope so, too."

Odd that he hadn't recognized his attraction to Sophia before today. "Tell me, have you decided to come to Washington with us when we leave? Penny is counting on you."

"I'm thinking about it. It's a bit frightening. I'd never planned to live anywhere but right here in Homestead." The color deepened in her cheeks. "All I'd planned to be was a wife and mother."

He wondered if Matthew Jacobs had ever had the nerve to kiss her as she ought to be kissed. From what he'd seen and heard of the gentleman in question, he doubted it. Sanctimonious fool.

"I'd like to thank you, Geoffrey."

"Thank me? Whatever for?"

She gave a tiny shrug. "It's hard to explain. I think I've been jealous of Katie, the way Ben always listened to her and thought what she had to say was of value." She tipped her head slightly to one side and offered a smile. "Not many men do that, you know. Listen to women, I mean. But you do. You listen to all of us on the committee. I just wanted you to know I appreciate it."

I hope you come to Washington, Miss Rafferty. I'd rather like listening to you on a regular basis.

There wasn't a soul in sight when the Susan B arrived in Homestead. The thought crossed Ben's mind that the town looked quieter than usual—which seemed almost an impossibility, even to him.

He drove the motorcar to the front of the hotel, then turned off the engine. "Well, Katie," he said into the sudden silence, "we're home."

She glanced over at him, surprise in her eyes. She hadn't thought about this being her home, he realized, about home being anywhere except the Lazy L. She must not have given any thought to Homestead, to what their lives would be like after their return.

Katie looked at the front of the hotel, saying softly, "I

suppose we should have gone out to the ranch first. I'll need to get my things, and I'll have to talk to my parents."

He guessed the reality of their marriage had hit her afresh and wondered if she was wishing for a reason to avoid going up to his suite.

A glimmer of a smile curved her mouth, dispelling his doubts. "I suppose tomorrow will be soon enough."

He hopped over the side of the car, then went around to open the door for Katie. She took his hand, letting him help her out. Then he held her elbow, and they walked into the hotel together.

"That's odd," he said as they entered the lobby. "There's no one behind the desk."

Just before his concerns could deepen, the doors to the dining room flew open, and there was a great shout of voices: "Surprise!" Suddenly he and Katie were surrounded by people—half the town, it seemed like—hugging and kissing and all talking at once.

Ben's father slapped him on the back, then shook his hand. "I'm glad for you, Son," Michael said. "I suspect the women are upset you didn't get married here, but we're all mighty glad for you both."

"Thanks, Dad."

Rose was the next to hug him, tears running down her cheeks. "I wish you all the happiness your father and I have had, Benjamin."

I hope your wishes come true, Mother. He returned her hug.

Sophia was next and then Ben's brother Shane.

After that came Geoffrey Rudyard. "About time someone

had the good sense to snap Katie up. She's a real find, Ben. But I expect you already know that."

He glanced toward his wife, who was at that moment being kissed by her grandmother. "Yes, I know."

From the dining-room doorway, Michael raised his voice above the din. "Everyone come back in here where there's more room. Give the newlyweds a chance to see what we've done."

Ben reached quickly for Katie's arm before she could be swept away from him. If this party was for Mr. and Mrs. Benjamin Rafferty, he wanted them to go in to it together.

"Oh, look!" Katie exclaimed, causing him to turn his gaze away from her and toward the dining room.

Ribbons and streamers hung from the ceiling. Bouquets of bright midsummer flowers—yellow and red and purple—festooned every table. A large white banner hung above the back wall. "Congratulations, Mr. and Mrs. Rafferty!" it proclaimed in bold blue letters.

"Come and cut the cake," Katie's mother instructed, motioning for them to follow her. Lark Jones led them through the crowd, and as they went, they continued to acknowledge all the good wishes and kind words that were being showered upon them.

The party lasted for over two hours, but eventually people had to return to their own homes. They left in groups of twos and threes until only the Raffertys and the Joneses remained.

For the first time that evening, Katie was able to be with her father without a crowd around them. He took her hand

and led her to a corner of the room, where he wrapped her in a tight embrace. "Are you happy, kitten?"

She found herself fighting tears.

He drew back and looked into her eyes. "It'll be good for you t'have Ben beside you while you're out there fightin' whatever it is you feel you gotta fight." He kissed her forehead. "I won't have cause to worry about you so much."

"You never needed to worry so much anyway, Papa," she managed to say despite the lump in her throat. "I've always been okay on my own."

"Do you love him?"

Strange, how she could keep from saying the words to Ben but not to her father. She nodded as she whispered, "I love him."

Yancy looked as if he would say more, but Lark joined them at that moment, and whatever he might have said was lost.

Her mother gave Katie another tight hug. "We'd best be on our way. You and Ben must be worn out from your trip."

Katie nodded.

"Your father and I brought some of your things from the ranch. We put them up in Ben's rooms." She squeezed one of Katie's hands. "Be happy, dearest."

"I will, Mother."

As her parents stepped away from her, Ben moved in to fill the void, placing his arm around her shoulders, holding her close. Together they bade their parents good night, then watched as the Joneses drove away in their carriage and the Raffertys walked down the street toward their home on the edge of town. Finally, with nothing else to delay them, they climbed the stairs to Ben's suite of rooms on the top floor.

Their suite, Katie reminded herself as she entered what served as the parlor.

"I've never done much with it," Ben said with a note of apology as she walked slowly around the room, touching the furniture. "You can change anything you like, do whatever you want to make it feel more like a home."

Home. My new home.

She opened the door to the bedroom. Her best nightgown had been laid across the spread of the large, four-poster bed with its heavy oak headboard and footboard.

Our bed.

She felt a moment of strangeness, knowing this wasn't a temporary stay in a hotel, realizing this really was her home now, that the bed really was her bed. She wouldn't be returning to the Lazy L. She wouldn't be sleeping in her familiar bedroom. Everything was changed now and would never be as it once was.

Then Ben stepped up behind her, putting his hands on her shoulders. He brushed aside the hair at the nape and nuzzled the tender flesh he found there, and she forgot her worries for the night, knowing tomorrow would have enough worries of its own.

TWENTY

The Homestead Weekly Herald
Homestead, Idaho
Friday Morning
July 21, 1916

Republican Race for Congress Heats Up; Local Candidate Scheduled to Make Several Idaho Appearances

As of last week, there are now five candidates in the Republican race for the two at-large seats in the U.S. House of Representatives. Congressmen Addison T. Smith and Robert M. McCracken are both running for reelection. The challengers are Burton L. French of Moscow, E. E. Elliott of Sandpoint, and Katherine Jones Rafferty of Homestead.

Mrs. Rafferty, who was recently married to Benjamin Rafferty, owner and publisher of the Homestead Herald, has scheduled a comprehensive tour of Idaho, with speaking engagements confirmed for Sandpoint, Moscow, Boise, Twin Falls, and Idaho Falls. Mrs. Rafferty is the first woman candidate for a national office from the state of Idaho. . . .

It would have been so easy for Katie to give in to the love she felt for Ben. Little by little he chipped away at the protective wall she'd put up between them. There were times she forgot completely the fight for the suffrage amendment and even her own campaign, times when all she thought about was Ben and the love he showered upon her, times she ached to tell him she loved him, too.

She couldn't even blame Ben for her forgetfulness. From the time of their return, he was true to his word. He did everything in his power to help her win the election. He worked tirelessly, masterminding an energetic and innovative campaign. When a delegation of men called upon him at the newspaper demanding he take his new bride in hand and stop this outrageous and unseemly stunt of hers, he invited them to mind their own business and stay out of his. If he was worried about the effect of her campaign on the newspaper's revenues, he didn't tell Katie. In a dozen different ways every day, he showed her how important she was to him.

Thus it was easy to forget everything except Ben. Too easy.

They'd been married two weeks when Katie had the nightmare. She dreamed of Ben holding her in his arms. Then slowly—ever so slowly—she faded away. She simply ceased to exist, evaporating into thin air.

She awakened, heart pounding, her body damp with perspiration. She lifted her hand, staring at it to make sure it was there, that she could see it and prove she existed. Then she sat up and looked at Ben, asleep beside her. It was happening already. He was absorbing her—minute by minute, day by day—just as she'd feared he would.

She sank slowly back onto the bed, rolling onto her side, her back toward Ben. *I won't forget everything I'm meant to do and be,* she promised herself as she closed her eyes. *I can't forget who God made me to be as easily as that.*

The next morning Katie was on her way to the general store when she met up with Blanche Coleson.

The schoolmarm's glare was as stiff and unyielding as her spine. "Good day, Mrs. Rafferty." She made the name sound offensive, meant as an insult rather than a form of address.

Katie forced herself to be pleasant. "Hello, Blanche. I haven't seen much of you lately. I hope you're doing well."

"Well enough."

"I'm sorry you've been unable to continue helping on the committee." It was a lie, and she suspected Blanche knew it.

The woman's demeanor became even more censorious than before. "Mrs. Rafferty, I had high hopes when you first returned to this town. I assumed you would be of a serious nature, intent on helping other women free themselves of the unfair rule of men. I assumed you would help women see they needn't subject themselves to the impulses of men. But when you continued your *friendship*—" the word dripped with sarcasm and suggestion—"with Ben Rafferty, I suspected you are, instead, a woman who is ruled by her basest nature." She crossed her arms and jutted her chin into the air. "You may have fooled others, Mrs. Rafferty, but you have not fooled me."

Katie was rarely left speechless, but this was one of those times.

"I'll have you know I've been writing letters to the fine leaders of the association," Blanche went on. "Now they know about you, too. They won't continue to put their faith in you. They'll soon withdraw their support. You'll see."

A tiny warning bell rang in Katie's head. She'd never warmed to Blanche, but she hadn't thought the woman unhinged. Now she wondered.

The schoolmarm pointed toward the newspaper office. "That man has poisoned your thoughts, and he uses his position in this town to make others believe you're something you're not. Well, it won't work. It won't work, I tell you."

"I think I've heard enough," Katie said quietly but firmly.

"You've sold yourself to the enemy. *Jezebel!*"

"Good day, Miss Coleson." Katie turned and immediately crossed the street.

As she hurried along the sidewalk toward the hotel, she told herself she shouldn't be surprised by the venomous words Blanche had spewed. She'd known the schoolmarm resented men, that her support of woman's suffrage had more to do with that resentment than with truly wanting women to be free to choose their own paths, paths that would naturally take many of them into marriage.

Her footsteps slowed, Blanche forgotten.

Choices. Wasn't that one of the things she loved most about Ben? His love didn't stifle her, didn't control her. He'd left her free to make her own choices.

Katie recalled the words of Miss Mott that Ben had sent to her on their wedding day. *Equal. Mutual. Reciprocal.* Ben had been living those words. Had she?

No, she answered her own question. *I haven't been. What's the answer, Lord? How do I serve You and be a good wife to Ben at the same time? What's the answer for us? I'm so confused. I feel like I've lost my way. I used to be so sure of Your call but now . . . now I feel lost.*

⊷ ⊷⬦⊶ ⊶

When Ben opened the door to their suite in midafternoon, he found Katie seated on the sofa, her feet tucked up beside her as she read a book. He strode quickly over to her, leaned down, and gave her a kiss.

"I have a surprise for you."

She gave him a mock frown. "Ben, you really must stop spoiling me." Then she grinned like a schoolgirl. "What is it?"

"Get your hat. We're going for a drive."

"Now?"

"Now."

"But we're expecting Penny and—"

"I've told Geoffrey we'll be late. He'll let the others know." He drew her to her feet, took the book from her hand, and tossed it onto the sofa. "Come on. Get your hat, Katie. I want you to see something."

"All right." She smiled at him. "If it's that important." She went into the bedroom, reappearing moments later, bonnet and scarf in hand. As she put the hat in place and tied the scarf beneath her chin, she asked, "Do you mind telling me where we're going?"

"I told you. It's a surprise." He took hold of her arm. "You wouldn't want to spoil it, would you?"

There was a twinkle in her eyes as she said, "No. But if

it involves the old water hole, I think we should take some blankets."

"What a delightful thought." He kissed the tip of her nose. "However, the water hole will have to wait for another time." With a flourish of his hand he opened the door and motioned her out of the room.

Within minutes they were in the Susan B, driving west out of town, Ben at the wheel of the automobile. He could feel Katie watching him and knew she was wondering what this was all about. He also knew she would never guess. Not in a hundred years.

For Ben, the last couple of weeks had been almost perfection. He loved being married, and he liked being with his bride. Sometimes, when they were meeting with the other members of the election committee, he would listen as Katie talked and he'd feel a welling up of pride in her intelligence, her dedication, her keen perceptions.

"What's going on in that head of yours, Ben Rafferty?"

He glanced at her. "I was thinking how much I love you."

She smiled, but he saw the conflict in her eyes, the wish to repeat those same words to him and the fear that stopped her from doing so.

It didn't matter, he told himself. It would happen. He just needed to give her more time.

Looking ahead, he said, "We're almost there." He slowed the Susan B, then turned north off the main road onto a rarely traveled track. "Hang on. It's bumpy."

As if to prove his point, the right front tire dropped into

a rut, violently jerking the passengers from side to side. Katie grabbed hold of the door with her right hand and her hat with her left as they followed the track toward the tree-lined banks of Pony Creek, the terrain gently but steadily rising before them.

It took another ten minutes of rough travel before Ben braked to a halt. "We're here."

Katie looked around. "We're *where?*"

"Come on. I'll show you."

They got out of the car, and Ben guided her up a grassy slope. At the top he turned her to face the east. From here they had a fine view of sleepy little Homestead. Katie stared at the town obediently for several moments, then glanced at him in question.

"This is where we're going to build our home." The words filled him with pleasure and warm contentment. He envisioned a two-story house with porches on two sides and shutters framing the windows. He pictured a rope swing hanging from a tall tree's thick branches in the front yard, deep green in summer, stark and gray brown in winter. He imagined children playing there while he and Katie watched them from the porch.

"Our home?" she asked softly.

"I met with Leroy Smith over at the bank this morning. He owns this piece of property. He'll let us have it for a reasonable price. With a bit of effort, we could have the house built before October."

"But why build a house when we hope to be in Washington after the election?"

He'd hoped she would be as excited as he was. She wasn't.

"We won't be there forever, Katie. We'll want a house to come back to." It was as close as he could come to saying he hoped they wouldn't be going back East.

"But building a house is an enormous undertaking, Ben. Haven't we enough to worry about this fall? We'll be traveling often in the weeks to come, and you're already putting in too many hours at the newspaper and on my campaign. Besides, no matter how much you've tried to keep it from me, I know you've lost more advertisers because of me. How can we afford to build a house?"

Her reasons all made perfect sense, yet they left him feeling out of sorts. His reply was sharper than intended. "We can afford it."

She didn't pay his words any heed. "What's wrong with the rooms we have at the hotel? They're more than adequate for the two of us."

"They won't always be adequate, Katie. A hotel's no place to raise children."

With a look of regret, she turned away from him. "There'll be time enough to worry about children and where we're going to live after I've won this election."

It was on the tip of his tongue to remind her she might not win the election, but then he thought better of it. These weeks had been happy ones for them. He wasn't ready for that happiness to be spoiled by an argument. He was certain she would see the wisdom of building a home here. She only needed a little time to think about it.

"Tell you what, Katie." He touched her shoulder. "I'll ask Leroy to let us have until after the primary in September. If you win that election, we'll let the land go. The bank can sell to another buyer when they have one. But if you lose, we'll go ahead with the purchase. Agreed?"

He could see her internal struggle in her eyes.

Ah, Katie. Can't you see what I'm offering you? Can't you let go and realize you want it too?

After a lengthy silence, she finally replied, "All right, Ben. That sounds reasonable enough. We'll wait and see what happens in September."

TWENTY-ONE

That August was the hottest month on record. Ben sometimes wondered if the heat might account for his mood, but he knew it had much more to do with Katie than with the weather.

Leaning his forearm against the window casement, he watched dusk settle over Homestead, but his thoughts weren't on the dusty, deserted street that ran in front of the newspaper office. They were on his bride of seven weeks.

To the folks of Homestead, it must seem he and Katie had a picture-perfect marriage. No one would guess his wife had yet to tell him she loved him. And if they knew, he was certain no one would guess how heavily that omission weighed upon his heart.

In the month since Ben had shown Katie the land where he wanted to build their home, he'd poured himself into the work involved in her political campaign, spending long hours in his office or meeting with other members of the committee. When it seemed he and Katie were too seldom alone, he didn't voice his complaint to her. When it seemed they never talked of anything unrelated to the election, he kept his opinion to himself. When he wondered about their future together, he kissed her and pretended all was well. Occasionally he allowed himself to dream about the house on the western slope, to envision it finished and lived in. Sometimes he closed his eyes and imagined that yard full of children, their children.

Often he prayed that his efforts to help Katie win the election would fail—and then he felt guilty for his prayers.

"Well, it'll be over soon, my friend," Geoffrey Rudyard said, interrupting Ben's troubled thoughts. "At least, the first step."

Ben glanced over his shoulder. Geoffrey's long legs were stretched out in front of him, ankles crossed. His arms were folded over his chest, his head rested on the back of the spindle-backed chair, and his eyes were closed. The two of them had spent the last four hours hammering out plans for Katie's final campaign appearance before the primary, and Geoffrey looked as tired as Ben felt.

Stifling a yawn, Geoffrey added, "I don't believe anything can stop Katie from winning in the primary now."

Sadly, Ben had to agree with him. As Katie had traveled the length and breadth of the state, from the panhandle to the southeasternmost corner, she had gained more confidence, spoken ever more eloquently and effectively about her goals and what she hoped to achieve in Congress, about her vision for the women and men of Idaho and the nation. The gentlemen of the press, at first skeptical and often derogatory, had begun to write some positive articles about her. A few newspapers had even come out in support of her candidacy.

Just as Geoffrey had said, it seemed nothing could stop her, not even the secret prayers of her husband.

"Have you ever thought of going into politics yourself, Ben?"

He laughed sharply, then said, "No."

"So, what are you going to do with yourself after Katie's elected?"

That same question had plagued Ben for weeks. "I don't know." Again he looked out at the empty, dusty street.

He'd promised Katie he would help her win this election, and that was exactly what he'd been doing. But that didn't mean he didn't hope she would lose. He'd promised he wouldn't try to change her, and he'd kept his word. Yet secretly he hoped she would discover their marriage was more important than her causes.

He loved Katie more every day. When he awakened in the morning, he gazed upon her and thought how unhappy he'd be without her. When they were apart, he often stopped whatever he was doing to think about her and wondered if perhaps she was thinking about him, too. Every evening when his work was done, he hurried back to their hotel suite, eager to hold her and kiss her and remind her that she was his wife.

If only he could be sure they would one day build that house and spend the rest of their lives there, then all would be perfect.

He quickly reminded himself that he'd known what Katie wanted when he married her. But, he added silently, in the beginning he'd been certain she would lose.

The idea of living in Washington for the next two years—or more—was a grim one. He'd never liked the hustle and bustle of big cities. He didn't care for the social activities required of those in business and government or the accompanying artificiality he so often found. He liked even less the notoriety he would have as husband of the first woman elected to the nation's legislature.

Geoffrey yawned, then said, "Well, I believe it's time we called it a night. Doesn't seem to be anything more we can do here, and Penny and I are expected for supper at your parents' home."

"Growing tired of hotel fare?" Ben turned around. "Or have I detected some interest in my sister?"

"Whatever do you mean, my good man?" Geoffrey grinned as he rose from the chair and jauntily placed his hat on his head.

"I'm not blind."

Geoffrey's expression sobered. "To be honest, Ben, I do have a certain affection for your sister, but I'm afraid she doesn't return it. Is it possible she's still in love with Mr. Jacobs?"

"With Matthew? I doubt it."

"He's a rather self-righteous fellow, isn't he? I've had the dubious pleasure of a lengthy conversation with him. He implied Sophia is suffering some sort of nervous female condition that has altered her judgment. Had the nerve to warn me off her, among other things."

"Oh, did he?"

"I considered showing him what I learned as a pugilist at the university, but Penny saw what I was about and dragged me away before I could strike the first blow."

"Now *that* would have been something for the town gossips to feast on." Ben chuckled. "I can see it now: 'Geoffrey Rudyard accosted local bookstore owner Matthew Jacobs this last week in Homestead. Mr. Rudyard, an attorney from Washington, D.C., is a member of Katherine Rafferty's election committee.' "

"That's precisely why my sister had the good sense to stop me. It wouldn't have done Katie any favor to get into a battle of fisticuffs."

Wishing Penelope hadn't stopped her brother, Ben pulled open the door. The two men left the office and started toward the hotel, walking side by side in silence.

With the coming of evening, electric and gas lamps flickered to life inside homes and the few businesses that stayed open late. Light spilled through windows onto the sidewalk in front of the two men as they walked. For most folks, supper had been eaten, dishes washed and put away. Young children had already been tucked into their beds for the night. Women sat with their baskets of mending, men with their pipes and newspapers.

Quiet, comfortable Homestead.

"Have you thought of getting a job at the *Post* once you're settled in Washington?" Geoffrey asked. "They'd be interested in a man like you."

Ben didn't reply, not certain what his answer should be.

He would need something to keep himself occupied while his wife was about the affairs of state. But none of the obvious choices appealed to him.

Geoffrey's hand alighted on Ben's shoulder. "It won't be easy for Katie, being a woman in Congress." He shook his head. "She'll need you more than ever. She's lucky to have your support in all this."

Although he nodded, Ben knew he wasn't supporting Katie the way she needed him to. Did she, or anyone else, suspect how heartily he wished for her defeat even while he worked toward her victory?

As if in answer to his silent questions, he remembered Reverend Jacobs's sermon the previous Sunday. " 'A house divided against a house falleth,' " the reverend had warned. Ben had squirmed in the pew as he'd listened, feeling as if the minister were speaking directly to him.

A house divided . . .

He raised his eyes toward the hotel, toward the windows of the rooms he shared with Katie. She, Penelope, and Sophia had spent the day in a neighboring county, drumming up votes, but Katie had called him at the newspaper upon their return an hour ago. She would be waiting for him now.

Would he destroy their house, their future, their happiness, because of his secret hopes?

⇥✦⇤

Katie hadn't felt well for the last couple of weeks. The very thought of food in the mornings had left her queasy and unable to eat. She'd been losing weight, and her dresses didn't fit as they should. She'd told herself it was only because of the demands of her campaign, the visits to strangers' homes, and the countless cups of coffee or tea. Besides, she'd been overtired, wanting to sleep longer at night and wishing to take naps in the afternoon. She was certain she would be more herself as soon as all her gadding about was over and done with.

But tonight, within moments after the waiter from the restaurant wheeled in their supper, Katie succumbed to the sickness that had threatened for days, vomiting into the toilet until she was left shaking, too weak to rise.

That was how Ben found her.

"Katie?" He knelt and placed a hand on her back.

She shook her head, unable to speak for the burning in her throat.

He handed her a towel.

She wiped her mouth slowly. Another time she might have been embarrassed for him to see her like this. Tonight she was too sick to care.

"I'll get you a glass of water." He rose and left her but was back in less than a minute. "Here."

She took the glass and rinsed out her mouth, then whispered, "I don't think I care to eat any supper tonight."

Ben drew her up from the floor, cradling her in his arms as he carried her to their bed. She let him help her into a nightgown, neither of them speaking the entire time.

Once she was settled, a pillow at her back, Ben sat on the edge of the bed and took hold of her hand. "What brought this on?"

"Too many sweets maybe. Too much time in the hot sun."

"I should send for Tom."

She tried to smile. "That isn't necessary, Ben. I don't need a doctor. All I need is a bit of sleep, and I'll be fine. It was so hot and dusty on the road today. I'm just tired. Honest."

"Are you sure?" He brushed stray wisps of hair from her face.

"I'm sure."

He hesitated a moment, a frown furrowing his forehead as he looked down at her. Then he leaned over and turned off the lamp. "I'll leave the door open. Call me if you need anything."

"I will."

He kissed her cheek before getting up from the bed and going into the connected parlor, leaving the door ajar.

Katie released a sigh as her eyes closed. This was nothing more than indigestion. A good night's rest would do her wonders.

⊁ ⊰◊⊱ ⊁

The next morning Ben paced the parlor of their hotel suite, impatient to learn what was going on in the bedroom, where Tom McLeod was examining his patient.

Katie had vomited again this morning. Violently, it had seemed to Ben. There had been circles beneath her eyes, and her face had looked drawn and pale. He couldn't recall ever seeing Katie sick, and seeing it worried him. She'd told him he was overreacting. She was probably right. But he hadn't let her talk him out of calling Tom to have a look at her.

The door to the bedroom opened, and the doctor stepped into the parlor.

"Well?" Ben demanded immediately.

Tom raised his hand, then reached behind him and closed the door.

"What is it? What's wrong?"

The doctor removed his eyeglasses and cleaned them with a towel. "Nothing that won't take care of itself in a matter of months."

"Months?" His heart nearly stopped. "Is it that serious?"

"As the father of four daughters, I can assure you it's quite serious. Bringing a child into this world is an awesome responsibility. But Katie is a healthy, strong young woman, and I don't expect any undue problems with the pregnancy itself."

"Katie's *pregnant?*"

"It seems to catch us all by surprise the first time," Tom answered as he walked over to where Ben stood. He patted him on the back. "Congratulations."

Katie was pregnant. Katie was going to have his baby. He stared at the closed door to the bedroom. She wasn't sick. She was pregnant.

She would drop out of the race now. They would buy the land west of town and build their house. He'd plant trees around it, lots and lots of fast-growing trees, suitable for climbing and building a tree house in and swinging from. He'd buy a puppy next summer, and the two—child and dog—could grow up together.

"It's clear it isn't me you want to talk to," Tom said. "Go on. You can see her. I'll let myself out."

"Thanks," Ben answered, already heading for the bedroom.

He heard the doctor laugh. "Don't thank me."

But Ben ignored him as he turned the doorknob and entered the bedroom, seeking Katie with his eyes.

She was sitting up in bed, several pillows plumped at her back. Her hair flowed loose about her shoulders, the way he liked it best, a dark contrast to the stark whiteness of the bedsheets. She still had circles under her eyes, still looked pale and peaked.

She was pregnant with his baby.

She looked more beautiful than ever before.

"Did Tom tell you?" she asked as he closed the door.

"Yes." He moved toward her, searching for the words to explain the joy that was in his heart. But there didn't seem to be any words appropriate for the occasion. Anything he thought of seemed inadequate.

She looked up, her eyes wide and filled with misery. "This couldn't happen at a worse time."

She isn't happy about the baby. The knowledge caused a hard knot to form in the pit of his stomach.

"I'm sure to win a seat in the primary, Ben. Everyone says so. Even you say so. And if I do, then there are all those weeks of campaigning before the November election. By then, my pregnancy will be showing. Voters will think me unable to fulfill my duties. If they elect me despite that, by the time I'm sworn into office, I'll be as big as a cow. How can I—"

"Then drop out of the race."

The room fell silent. They stared at each other, both of them surprised by his suggestion. Or had it been a demand? Even Ben didn't know for sure.

"I can't," she said at last. "You know I can't. You've always known it."

"I think the correct word is *won't*. You *won't* withdraw from the race." He knew his voice sounded harsh. He *felt* harsh. This was their baby, the child of their union they were talking about, and all she could think of was her campaign.

"All right," she whispered in agreement. "I won't withdraw."

He turned on his heel and abruptly walked out, not trusting himself to speak again.

⊷ ⊨◈⊨ ⊶

Katie stared at her husband's back as he disappeared through the doorway. Profound regret burned in her chest. Regret for what she'd said. Regret for the way she'd reacted. She placed her hands on her flat stomach. Ben's baby was growing inside her, a result of the love they shared.

How could she make him understand what she was feeling when she didn't understand it herself? If being Ben's wife was a threat to all that she needed to accomplish, all she'd been called to do, how much more of a threat would be this child that was a part of each of them? Ben would never know how she longed to rejoice over the creation of this new life. But she couldn't. She'd made promises—to herself and to others.

Withdraw from the race, an internal voice urged. *Tell Ben you love him and withdraw from the race.*

I can't, another whispered.

If she dropped out, she would lose an important piece of herself.

If she didn't, she might lose Ben.

Katie sank down in the bed, rolled onto her side, and buried her face in the pillows. Then she wept over the choice she couldn't make.

⊷ ⋈⧫⋊ ⊶

Ben stood where the living room would have been, looking out where the large picture window would have been. He could see Homestead clearly, even as the shadow of a summer storm fell over the town. Forks of lightning spiked from clouded sky to craggy mountain peaks, accompanied by the distant rumble of thunder.

He'd thought he would spend many an afternoon looking at Homestead from this spot. He'd pictured Katie standing beside him, their arms around each other. Just a pair of contended married folks. He'd thought their children would grow up in the house they would have built on this site.

But Katie didn't want his children, not even the baby she was already carrying in her womb.

He'd been fooling himself all along, it seemed. He'd thought time would take care of everything. He'd told himself

Katie loved him, despite her silence. He'd told himself she would one day understand that she could be herself and love him, too. But he'd been wrong. Desperately, foolishly wrong.

He wished he could hate her. Or at least be indifferent to her. Indifference would have made things much easier. Problem was, he loved her still.

Lightning flashed over the mountains again, leading the way for the deluge to come. The cooling air smelled fresh and wet. The wind rose, bringing with it the first drops of rain. But Ben didn't move. He couldn't. Not yet. Not until the storm was over. Not the storm he could see rushing toward him, but the one he could feel on the inside. The one in his heart. The storm that had come with the shattering of the hopes for his future.

He looked up at the sky as the rain began to come in earnest. In moments he was soaked. Rivulets of water ran into his face and eyes. His clothes clung to his skin. Around him, long field grass bent beneath the onslaught from heaven. Dirt turned to mud. A thousand tiny streams formed at the top of the hill, racing down the slope toward the banks of the creek.

Standing there in the rain on that isolated hillside, Ben faced the truth: He *had* meant to change Katie. He'd planned to prove to her that the things he wanted were more important than what she wanted. She was supposed to have become the wife and mother he'd envisioned all along.

He raked the fingers of both hands through his hair.

He loved Katie, but if she didn't meet him halfway, could he live life her way? He wasn't sure anymore.

He wasn't sure he even wanted to try.

❖

The instant she heard the key turn in the lock, Katie spun from the window where she'd been standing vigil for hours. With her hands clasped in front of her waist and scarcely daring to breathe, she watched the door swing open and Ben enter. He was soaking wet, but it was the resolved expression on his face that caused her heart to nearly stop beating.

She took a hesitant step forward. "Are you all right? I was worried."

"I'm fine."

"Mr. Trent was looking for you. He called hours ago."

The look in his eyes was as black and stormy as the roiling clouds in the sky.

"I thought you'd gone to the paper from here. I didn't know what to tell Mr. Trent. He said it wasn't like you not to be in the office on Thursdays."

He nodded, but his hard, ungiving expression didn't alter. "I'll change and then head over there. Excuse me." He strode across the parlor and disappeared into the bedroom.

Katie sank onto a nearby chair, feeling chilled. His anger wouldn't last, she told herself.

What's going to happen to us, Benjie?

They'd been happy the way things were. They would be so again. Ben wouldn't remain angry with her. He'd never been able to stay mad at her.

When Ben reappeared minutes later, dressed in one of his suits, his damp hair slicked back on his head, Katie looked at him hopefully. He was her best and dearest friend. He loved her. He'd never been able to stay mad. Surely he would forgive her this time, too.

"I don't know how late I'll be," he said as he headed toward the door.

"Benjie?"

He glanced over his shoulder.

"Don't you think we should talk?"

"Not yet."

"But—"

He jerked open the door. "Not yet, Katie. We'll talk about it later." His voice lowered. "When I know what it is I'm going to do."

When I know what it is I'm going to do.

Katie felt icy fingers of fear move along her spine. "What do you mean?"

"Just what I said."

When I know what it is I'm going to do.

He pushed the door closed again. "You won't withdraw from the race, will you?"

"We've been over that. I can't."

"You won't."

"You're right. I won't."

A few quick strides brought him to her. He took her by

the shoulders and drew her to her feet. "Is it worth it, Katie? Is any of this worth it?"

She was too shocked to form a reply. She'd never seen Ben like this, never felt the heat of his anger in this way.

"Can't you see beyond your *cause*? What about me? What about our baby? What about the two of us becoming one in God's eyes?"

"Benjie, I—"

He released her and stepped back. "Maybe that's part of the problem. You still think I'm Benjie. Well, I'm not. I haven't been Benjie for a long time."

"I don't know what you mean."

He stared at her, the silence thickening between them. Then it seemed the anger drained from him, leaving an icy calm in its wake. "No, I don't suppose you do." He turned and walked to the door. As he took hold of the doorknob, he said, "I'll stay with you until after the baby's born, Katie. Then I'm taking my child to that house I'm going to build."

"But what about Washington? If I win the election—"

"I'm not going to Washington. I belong here. And so does our child."

Her chest hurt. "What about me?"

"You've already made your choice." He paused. "*Haven't* you, Katie?" He didn't wait for an answer. He opened the door and left.

"Don't go," she whispered, already too late.

She sat down again, fighting tears, trying to calm herself. It *had* to be all right. She'd always been able to count on Ben. When her father had disapproved of her, Ben had been there to tell her he was proud. When she'd despaired of following her dreams, Ben had urged her on. When almost everyone else had said it was crazy for her to run for Congress, Ben had told her she could do it and had promised to help her. He *had* helped her, every step of the way. Ben had always been there to help her. Always.

No, he wouldn't stay angry with her. They would get past this.

They had to.

TWENTY-TWO

On the eve of her final campaign appearance before the Republican primary, Katie drove the Susan B to her parents' ranch. She felt a compelling need to be with her mother, to hear Lark's calm voice as she spoke of normal things.

"Katie!" her mother exclaimed when she saw her. "What a wonderful surprise. I wasn't expecting you today." Lark wiped her floury hands on her apron before giving Katie a hug.

The warm, rich fragrance of fresh-baked bread filled the kitchen, bringing with it images of other days when Katie and her mother had worked together in this same room.

Katie said, "My speech is written. Our clothes are packed. We're all ready to go. There's nothing more to be done except catch the train tomorrow." She sat on one of the kitchen chairs. "I wanted to drive down in the Susan B, but Ben said we couldn't take the chance of her breaking down again." *"Not in your condition,"* had been his exact words.

Lark filled two glasses with iced lemonade, then brought them to the table, setting one in front of Katie. "At least the hot spell has broken. Your trip to the capital won't be as miserable as it would have been. It'll be nice for you to have Sophia's and the Rudyards' company."

Katie agreed, but she didn't want to think about her trip or her speech or the election or even her friends. She didn't want to think about anything. For just a few minutes she wanted to pretend she was fifteen again, sitting in her mother's kitchen, carefree and happy.

She took a sip of the lemonade, and when she set the glass on the table, she touched a deep scar in the surface of the wood. "I remember when this happened."

"So do I. Sam nearly cut Rick's finger off with that knife. I was so scared. Oh, how I wanted to paddle their backsides!"

"We weren't any of us model children. Seen and not heard and all that."

Lark laughed. "I should say not."

"Remember how angry I was because Sam wasn't the sister I wanted?"

"You hid in that old line shack near the river. We didn't find you until it was almost dark. That day nearly turned my hair gray."

"I know. And remember the time Ben and I ran Mrs. Percy's drawers up the flagpole after she called us a pair of barbarians?"

Her mother shook her head, still chuckling. "You *were* a pair of barbarians."

"There must have been times you hated being a mother.

I mean, you spent all your time taking care of us, and there wasn't any left just for you."

Her mother's laughter ended abruptly. She leaned forward and covered Katie's hand with her own. "You couldn't be more wrong. I never felt that way."

"Not ever?"

"Not ever."

"But you must have realized there was so much else you might have done if you hadn't married and had children. You could have traveled. You could have gone to Europe or—"

"Things like that can't even compare, Katie. The moment I laid eyes on Yancy, I knew he was my future, my whole life. There wouldn't ever be anyone else for me. I still feel that way. We'd walk through fire for each other. We *have* walked through fire a few times, I guess."

Katie realized she was jealous of her mother. She'd never doubted the love her parents shared, but she had under-estimated its power. For the first time, she understood fully the joy and strength her mother and father had discovered in each other, the rewards they found in the little things in life. They were content, no matter their circumstances.

Was this what Ben had hoped they would share? Could she feel the same satisfaction as her mother if she were to give up her dreams?

Lark's smile was sure. "Sharing my life with my husband and my children has been a blessing, even in the hardest of times. There isn't a day of your childhood I would trade for anything else in the world." She paused, then asked, "What greater thing could I have accomplished than you?"

Katie couldn't think of a reply.

Lark squeezed Katie's fingers. "What is it? What's troubling you?"

Katie shrugged as she pulled her hand free, then rose and turned to look out the window above the worktable. Beyond the glass she could see Drifter, the oldest of the Lazy L cow dogs, lying in a strip of shade. Inside the corral several horses milled, snorting occasionally, their tails swatting at flies. It was a scene like dozens of others through the years. Just the sort of familiar day Ben liked best, this quiet sameness.

Oh, Ben.

"Katie?"

"I don't know. I've been thinking about you and Papa and everything. And me, I suppose. Wondering why I am the way I am."

"What way is that?"

"Different."

"It isn't that you're different, Katie. It's that you're special. You've tried to do what's right for you. And look at all you've accomplished in your short life. The people you've met. The places you've seen."

But Katie didn't feel as if she'd done anything of importance. She felt like a fraud. Even her faith seemed fraudulent of late. She picked out the Scriptures that suited her at the moment, that justified her actions and thoughts and feelings. It wasn't as it should be, and yet she felt helpless to change it. Her whole world was crumbling around her, and her confidence, her certainty in her calling, were crumbling with it.

Her mother came to stand beside her, offering silent support by her nearness.

"I was never satisfied to be like other girls in Homestead. I was always going to make my mark on the world."

"You are. You have."

"I was going to make a difference. Change things." Her voice fell. "I was going to follow in the footsteps of Susan B. Anthony and Frances Willard."

Lark put her arm around Katie's back.

Katie leaned her head on her mother's shoulder. "But I'm not anything like them. I'm not as strong as they."

"But you are, Katie. You're very strong. Why would you think you're not?"

"Because I can't do this alone," she whispered.

Her mother tightened her arm. "Needing others doesn't mean you're weak, and you're certainly not alone anyway. You have God looking out for you, and you have many friends. Penny and Geoffrey and Sophia. You have your father and me and your brothers. You have your husband. Ben is always there for you."

But Katie didn't have Ben. She'd lost him days ago. The distance between them was as far and vast as the distance between Washington, D.C., and Homestead, Idaho. They might share those rooms at the Rafferty Hotel, they might work together during the day, but a great distance yawned between them all the same. He never touched her anymore, never tried to hold her hand, never kissed her. He even slept on the sofa in the parlor. The one thing they spoke to each other about was the campaign and then only when others were around. Otherwise they were silent, separate camps, each waiting for the election to be over, each waiting for the months to pass.

Each waiting for the baby to be born.

I'm going to have a baby, Mother. She wished she could say the words aloud, but she couldn't. Not yet. Not when she couldn't say it with the same joy that had been in her mother's voice when she talked about her own children.

Lark stared hard at her. "You know you can tell me anything, Katie. Anything at all."

"Yes. Yes, I know."

"You're just nervous about the elections. You'll feel better after next Tuesday has come and gone. I'm very proud of you. Your father and I both are."

"Thanks." Katie forced a smile. "I guess I *am* nervous. And tired."

Her mother gave her one more squeeze, then went to check on the bread in the oven.

"It smells so good in here," Katie said, eager to think of something besides her own worries. "Nothing smells as good as baking bread."

Lark pulled the hot loaves from the oven. "Well, it won't be long before you'll have a kitchen and can bake bread in your own oven. I hear Ben is almost ready to start building on that piece of land he bought."

So, he'd bought the land. He hadn't waited until the primary was over. But then, last week had changed everything.

"Yancy says Ben's ordered the lumber and hired some men to begin digging the basement next week." Lark turned the pans over one at a time, letting the loaves fall onto a clean cloth on the worktable. "It's a shame you won't get to live in the place long before you go to Washington, but it will be here waiting for you when you get back."

No, she thought, it would be waiting for Ben. For Ben and the baby.

It wouldn't be waiting for her.

◆

"Nothin' more you can do here, boss," Harvey Trent said as he reached for his hat. "You better git yourself a good night's rest. Next few days're gonna be hard ones for you and the missus."

Ben leaned back on his chair, rubbing his eyes with his knuckles. "Yeah, I know."

"I figure next week's edition will be all 'bout your wife's win in the primaries."

"Yeah."

"Don't you go worryin' none about it, neither. I can manage t'put one edition together by myself. You send me what you want it t'say, an' I'll see that it's done right."

Ben nodded. "I wasn't worried, Harv."

"Well—" the typesetter pulled open the door—"good night, then, and good luck to the missus. See you tomorrow at the station."

"Good night."

Long after the door had closed behind Harvey Trent, Ben remained on his chair behind the desk. He was reluctant to return to the hotel. Reluctant for this night to pass.

Tomorrow they would be on the train to Boise—he and Katie, Geoffrey, Penelope, and Sophia. Tomorrow night Katie would address the Boise Chapter of the National Council of Women Voters. There would be a great deal of fanfare. All the reporters would be present. Ben would be expected to stand beside his wife and show his support. On Tuesday the polls would open. On Tuesday Katie would win her place on the Republican ticket. Then would begin the plotting and planning, the making of final strategies for her ultimate win to the U.S. House of Representatives.

Ben didn't think he had the stomach for any of it.

He rose, dimmed the lights, then left the office, locking the door behind him. He walked slowly toward the hotel, enjoying the cool of the evening, feeling the promise of fall in the night air.

It seemed impossible that summer was gone. It had still been spring when Katie had driven her flivver into Homestead, bursting into his office with grand schemes for a woman's column. If he'd told her no that night, how different things might be now. If only he'd refused her. But refusing Katie had always been hard for him.

A lot could change in three months.

A lot *had* changed.

His footsteps slowed, and his gaze lifted to the windows of their hotel suite. The lights were on. Katie was there.

Spring. The baby would be born in the spring of next year. In April, when the crocuses flowered and the bare tree limbs began to bud. Spring, with its promise of new life, new beginnings. The new house would be completed and furnished by then. There would be a nursery and a room for the housekeeper he would hire—a woman to watch over the baby as well as to cook and to clean.

Not exactly what he'd hoped for when he decided to build the house. He'd wanted Katie to be there with him, but she wanted other things.

More than him.

More than their child.

Releasing a sigh, he entered the lobby and headed up the stairs. When he reached the door to their suite, he paused before putting his key in the lock. He drew a slow, deep breath, preparing himself for that first glimpse of her for the day. He tried always to be up and gone before she awakened in the morning. It made things easier. But she was invariably still up when he returned at night. Sometimes he wondered if she did it to torture him.

Smiling grimly at the thought, he opened the door and stepped inside. A quick glance revealed an empty parlor. Perhaps he was lucky tonight. Perhaps she'd retired. But the door to the bedchamber was open, the light still on.

Foolishly he moved toward it.

She was standing before the cheval glass in a white night-gown trimmed with lace and blue satin ribbons.

Katie's gaze met his in the mirror. "I'm all ready to leave tomorrow," she said softly.

"So am I."

She turned to face him. "Mr. Trent will get out the paper?"

"Yes."

"I'll call for your supper."

"Don't bother. I'll do it myself."

She turned her back toward him again. "Then I'll go to bed. Tomorrow will be a full day."

"Yes. Good night, Katie."

He knew he should turn and leave, but he couldn't seem to do it. It was as if he wanted to torment himself a little longer, watching as she lifted the blankets and climbed into the four-poster where their child had been conceived.

The child Katie didn't want.

He turned and walked away.

From her apartment above the drugstore, Blanche had watched Ben Rafferty walk to the hotel. Now, a short while later, she saw the light dim in what she knew was the bedroom of that suite.

How she hated and despised them both!

Blanche knew Katie Jones wasn't fit to represent the women of Idaho. If she were, she never would have married. Blanche had told others that Katie Jones had failed in her duties. She had written letters, dozens of them, but no one paid her any heed.

It was that man's fault. If Ben Rafferty hadn't enticed her, perhaps Katie would have been the woman Blanche had expected her to be. It was his fault all had gone awry.

She turned from the window, bitterness filling her chest.

"It should have been me," she told the cat. "I tried to tell them, but they wouldn't listen." She sat on the chair and pulled the animal onto her lap. "It's his fault she doesn't listen to me. If she was rid of him, I could help her. Then she'd listen to me. Then I could prove to them all I was right."

Blanche's life seemed more terrible, more unbearable, than ever. School would return to session next week. She would be trapped in that hideous schoolroom with another bunch of unruly heathens.

Trapped. She was trapped. All her life she'd been trapped.

"It's his fault."

It was a merry-looking group on the train-station platform the next day. The three young women were dressed in their finest traveling attire, the two men in suits with vests. Family and friends were there to see them off and wish them well. There was a great deal of backslapping, good-natured joking, and laughter.

Katie hoped the train would leave soon. She feared someone would see through her masquerade and recognize the unhappiness beneath her carefully constructed facade. But no one did. Everyone expected her to be cheerful, and therefore that was what they saw. After all, everything she'd wanted, everything she and others had been working toward, was about to come true. How could she not be excited and happy?

"All aboard!" the conductor cried, causing a flurry of activity as one last round of hugs was exchanged.

"We'll be praying for you, darling," Katie's mother promised.

"You've done your best, Katie," her father said. "In the end, that's all that matters."

She nodded, not trusting herself to speak.

"Come on, Katie," Sophia called from the passenger-car steps.

"Take care of her, Ben," Yancy added a bit gruffly.

Ben took hold of her arm. "I will."

Her heart fluttered. It was a simple act, the taking of her arm. The sort of thing husbands did all the time. Yet to Katie it was like a drenching rain after a long drought. She soaked up his touch and wished he might never let go.

But he did. The moment they were on the train and out of sight of their families and seated, he released her. "I'm going to the dining car," he said. "Geoffrey, care to join me?"

Geoffrey looked a little surprised at leaving the ladies so soon but agreed to go along.

"Ben's awfully edgy lately," Sophia commented as the two men made their way to the back of the passenger car and through the doorway.

Penelope waved a fan in front of her face. "It's no wonder. He's been burning the candle at both ends. Working on Katie's campaign, writing all those articles, putting out the *Herald* every week, and now starting that new house." Her hand stilled as she looked at Katie. "I was at the paper when he showed the plans to Geoffrey. It's going to be a beautiful house. When you tire of your political life, you'll have such a wonderful place to come back to."

Katie smiled and nodded, unable to confess that she hadn't seen the house plans. "Yes, when I tire of it."

A cloud of steam billowed from the underside of the train, accompanied by a loud hiss; then the car jerked as the wheels were set in motion. Katie looked out the window at the people still standing on the platform. Her parents and grand-parents. Leslie Blake. Reverend and Mrs. Jacobs. Tom and Fanny McLeod and their daughters. Harvey Trent. So many people to wish her well.

Her parents waved. Her grandmother blew her a kiss. She lifted her hand in return. "Bye," she mouthed and saw them all do the same.

"But, Sophia, that's wonderful!" Penelope exclaimed.

Katie turned from the window to see her two friends hugging. "What's wonderful?"

"Sophia has decided she's coming to Washington with us. Isn't it scrumptious? I was afraid I would have to share our place with a stranger, now that you're married. But Sophia will be there with me."

"Scrumptious," Katie whispered, only half listening.

She remembered the evening she'd returned to Home-stead. She remembered how Ben had looked, staring at those papers on his desk, his brow creased in concentration. She remembered taking him outside to show him the Susan B. "Isn't she scrumptious?" she'd asked, and he'd raised an eyebrow and replied, "Scrumptious."

It seemed a very long time ago. Those two people in her memory seemed so young and carefree. Strangers to her now.

"Maybe that's the problem, Katie. You still think I'm Benjie."

She looked out the window again. Already Homestead had disappeared from view. In another minute or two the train would carry them out of Long Bow Valley and into the mountain canyons, the tracks following the river on its way south toward the capital. She listened to the *clackity-clackity-clackity* of the turning wheels, wheels that were taking her swiftly away from home.

Swiftly, swiftly away.

⊷ ⊨◊⊟ ⊶

In the past two months Katie had become an old hand at campaigning. She knew how to speak to the press. She knew how to smile at leering old men and how to look austere in the presence of prune-faced women. She knew when to kiss babies and had become adept at avoiding the sticky fingers of toddlers. She was as comfortable talking to a large group as to a single voter. She was used to seeing her photograph in newspapers, grainy reproductions that looked little like her.

Thus Katie wasn't nervous when she addressed the assembled hundred or so women—and a few brave men—in downtown Boise's Carnegie Hall that night. She'd written her speech weeks ago and knew the words by heart. No one guessed she wasn't thinking about suffrage or other issues of concern to women. She smiled and pretended an enthusiasm for her topic that she wasn't feeling. Judging by the rousing applause she received at the close of her talk, she had fooled them all, even those who knew her best.

Before other members of the audience could get to her, Penelope was at Katie's side, whispering, "You were wonderful. Congratulations."

"Mrs. Rafferty, you are an inspiration," gushed the president of the local chapter of the National Council of Women Voters as she arrived at the podium. "You're so knowledgeable, so composed."

"Thank you."

"The Republicans couldn't select a better person than you to run for Congress, Mrs. Rafferty," the chapter's secretary proclaimed as she pumped Katie's hand.

"You're very kind."

Her eyes scanned the crowd, but she couldn't find Ben. She'd seen him at the back of the hall when the meeting had begun. He wasn't there now.

Apparently understanding, Penelope leaned forward and told her softly, "He said he had work to do back at the hotel."

From the beginning of her campaign, Ben hadn't missed a single speech or a single meeting with the press. For over two months he'd been beside her every step of the way, encouraging her with a glance or a smile or a gesture. But he wasn't here now.

Katie forced herself to keep smiling, to keep saying words of thanks when she was complimented, to keep shaking hands and nodding and answering questions. But she felt no joy when others told her she was certain to win in next week's primary, certain to be elected to Congress in November. That was what she'd worked toward all summer. She should have been happy. It was what she'd wanted. It was what God wanted.

Wasn't it?

An eternity later Geoffrey escorted the three women to the

hotel. Sophia and Penelope, leading the way, carried on a lively conversation about Sophia's impending move to Washington, D.C.

"I do believe Ben's sister may one day run for Congress herself," Geoffrey said to Katie.

"Sophia?"

"You've been an enormous influence on her."

He'd meant it as a compliment, but Katie wasn't sure she was fit to influence anyone. She'd made a mess of things.

"Have you watched the way she handles the press?" Geoffrey continued. "She's nearly as adept as you are."

Katie cocked her head to one side as she looked at him. "Do I hear a note of affection in your voice?"

He grinned. "You do indeed."

"And Sophia?"

"A bit gun-shy yet, but I think she's coming around."

She squeezed his arm. "I'm glad for you both. Sophia's a lucky girl."

"I'll be the lucky one if she ever returns my feelings."

Sadness washed over Katie, tightening her throat. Not so very long ago she'd heard that same sort of love in Ben's voice. Now he scarcely spoke to her.

Geoffrey's smile faded. "You look tired, Katie."

She shook her head, then shrugged.

"What do you say we forget the campaign completely for a change? We could take the streetcar out to the warm springs tomorrow afternoon. I hear the natatorium pool is spectacular. And maybe we could take in the theater in the evening."

Katie remembered the last time she and Ben had been for a swim. She remembered the sound of his laughter as he'd chased her into the water. Would she ever again hear him laugh like that?

"Get a good night's sleep tonight, Katie," Geoffrey encouraged as they climbed the steps to the hotel entrance.

"I will," she promised. But she knew she wouldn't. Not with Ben so close and yet so far away.

* ⚜ *

Ben had watched Katie and the others approach the hotel from the window of their third-floor room. Even in the darkness, even from this distance, he'd seen the moonlit sheen in her ebony hair. He'd seen the gentle sway in her walk. He'd seen the way her dress fit her trim figure and wondered how long it would be before her pregnancy showed.

He remained at the window long after the foursome disappeared from view, staring down at the wide street below. He didn't turn even when he heard the door open.

"You got a warm reception tonight," he said as Katie entered the bedroom.

"Yes."

"Mr. Elliott is ready to concede before the election begins." Unable to refrain any longer, he glanced over his shoulder. "I met him in the lobby this evening. Says he'll support the entire Republican ticket, no matter who wins."

"Oh?" She removed her hat and laid it on the bureau.

"I also saw Mr. French. You remember. He's the candidate

from Moscow, Idaho. Good man, but I believe you have a chance of defeating him. So does he, I believe."

"Ben?"

"Yes?"

"I—" she seemed to be struggling with words—"I'm sorry it's all turned out the way it has."

It nearly killed him to see her look so sad. He longed to hold and comfort her. But he couldn't. Katie was going to have to decide what she wanted, what meant the most to her. He'd given all he could without her giving some back. If she didn't love him . . .

Staring out the window once again, Ben heard her sigh, heard the creak of the bedsprings.

"I'm sorry," she whispered. "So very sorry."

He knew she was crying by the sound of her voice.

Anger, his only defense against her tears, sprang to life. "What do you want from me, Katie?" He turned, pinioned her with a hard gaze where she sat on the bed. "I'm a man, not some faithful childhood companion you turn to when you need cheering up. I wanted a woman to share my life with. To share *everything* with—the good and the bad. I never expected you to be some docile homemaker with nothing more on your mind than what to fix for supper. I only wanted you to love me. To think of *us* instead of just *you*."

Tears streaked her cheeks, but she didn't look away from him.

He took a step toward her. "I *did* hope you would discover that Homestead was where you wanted to be. I hoped you would welcome your pregnancy with joy instead of thinking it an inconvenience. I even hoped you would lose the election." He raked his fingers through his hair. "But we could have overcome all that. We could've found a way to make it work, Katie, if you'd only tried to meet me halfway."

"I'm sorry," she whispered again.

The fight drained from him. "I don't want your apologies." He reached for his hat. "I'm going out." Then he headed for the door before he weakened and tried to kiss away her sorrows.

TWENTY-THREE

The Idaho Daily Statesman
Boise, Idaho
Wednesday Morning
September 6, 1916

Smith Has Big Lead for Congress; French and Rafferty in Close Race

At 4 o'clock Wednesday morning scattering returns from 233 of the 742 precincts located in 31 of the 37 counties of the state practically assured the nomination of the following Republicans for the November election:

For Congress~Representative Addison T. Smith of Twin Falls and Katherine Jones Rafferty of Homestead.

For governor~D. W. Davis of American Falls.

For lieutenant governor . . .

"By Jove!" Geoffrey exclaimed as he looked up from the newspaper. "You've done it, Katie."

She tried to smile as she was expected to do. "I lead Mr. French by only seven hundred votes. I could still lose."

"Perish the thought!" Penelope interjected.

Perish the thought? Katie wasn't so sure.

She glanced at Ben across the breakfast table in the hotel restaurant, but his expression was as closed to her as ever. Two weeks of pretending had made them both experts at deception.

"Whoa! Listen to this." Geoffrey cleared his throat as he began reading from the paper:

"Women Make War on President Wilson, National Chairman of Woman's Party Says Western Women Voters Are Opposing Democratic Leaders.

Chicago—Miss Anne Martin, national chairman of the Woman's Party, issued a statement here Tuesday in which she said, 'Feeling against President Wilson for his continued opposition to the national suffrage amendment is steadily growing among women voters. In California, members of the Democratic and Progressive leadership have joined the Woman's Party in their fight against the president. The state will be carried by a united Republican and Progressive vote against President Wilson.' "

Geoffrey let out a long, low whistle. "Pity poor Mr. Wilson. All those angry women."

Penelope harrumphed. "Pity him indeed. Perhaps now he'll stop mouthing support and actually do something."

"Katie will see to that once she's sworn into office," Sophia added with confidence.

"I should say she will," Penelope concurred.

Will I? Katie forced another smile and nodded, then rose from her chair. "I think I'd like some air."

"We'll come with you." Geoffrey said, starting to rise.

"No. I'd like to be alone for a while."

Penelope frowned. "Are you sure?"

"I'm sure. You stay and enjoy your breakfast. I won't be long."

She left the restaurant, stepping into the bright morning sunshine. The streets of Boise were bustling. Wagons, buggies, streetcars, and automobiles vied with each other for space. Men in business suits and farmers in coveralls passed each other on the sidewalks. Women in oversize hats chatted near the doorways of dress shops. Boys in short pants and girls in short skirts chased hoops down a side street. A pack of scruffy mongrels fought over scraps of food in an alley outside a restaurant.

So many people. So much activity. So much noise. Boise City seemed a major metropolis to Katie after a summer in Homestead. But Idaho's capital city was a mere speck on the map in comparison with Washington, D.C., and she knew it. She'd loved the big cities back East once. Would she love them again?

She walked all the way to the front steps of the Capitol building without stopping. Once there, she stared at the imposing stone structure.

"I only wanted you to love me. To think of us instead of just you." Ben's words haunted her now, just as they'd haunted her for the past four days. *"We could've found a way to make it work, Katie, if you'd only tried to meet me halfway."*

She wanted to meet him halfway. She wanted to love him. But she'd sworn to serve the suffrage cause. Weren't the needs of others more important than her own wants and wishes?

"Spectacular building, isn't it?"

Startled from her reverie, Katie looked at the man who'd spoken to her.

"My apologies, Mrs. Rafferty." He doffed his hat. "Do you remember me? I'm Burton French."

"Of course. My worthy opponent from Moscow."

He smiled. "Yes."

She offered her hand. "It's a pleasure to see you again, sir."

"I've been following your campaign since I attended the rally in Homestead last June. Looks like the voters have been following you, too."

"Have you always been interested in politics, Mr. French?"

"Not always."

"But you knew this was the right time to become involved? You wanted to win this election a great deal?"

"Yes, but no more than you, I suspect."

Katie studied Burton French. He was a distinguished-looking, middle-aged fellow. He appeared the sort of man who smiled often. She thought she might have liked him, had they the time to get better acquainted.

"Are you married?" she asked after a protracted silence.

"For twenty years."

"Do you have children?"

"Five. Three daughters and two sons. Our eldest daughter is married. The rest are still at home."

For a moment Katie thought of that plot of ground near Pony Creek and the house Ben was building there. The *home* Ben was building there.

"They're going to be disappointed," Mr. French continued. "About not moving to Washington, I mean. The entire family's been involved in my campaign from the beginning. Great little team, I'll tell you. I'm proud of them all."

Katie nodded. "I've had a lot of help, too."

"I spoke with your husband the other night. I imagine he's been a great source of support to you."

"Yes." She remembered the countless hours Ben had devoted to her campaign, all because he loved her. Abruptly she changed the subject. "How do you feel about the national woman's suffrage amendment, Mr. French? Do you favor it?"

"I didn't at first," he answered. "It took my wife doing some hard talking to convince me of its merits. But Mrs.

French has a way of showing me when I'm in the wrong. She reminded me what could happen to our daughters in the future, and that finally made the difference."

"How was that?"

He removed his hat and scratched his head before replying. "The girls are growing up fast. Before I know it, they'll be married and gone from the nest. What if their husbands choose to move them to an unenfranchised state? My girls would lose the right to vote, a right I've taught them is important. I don't want that to happen. If it's left up to each state, that's what *could* happen."

"Then you would fight for the national amendment if you were elected?"

"That's what I'm saying."

"I'm glad to hear it."

"Are you afraid there'll be some sort of upset when the last ballots are counted?" He released a soft chuckle. "You needn't worry. My wife's already told me we can pack our bags and go home. She's certain you've won, and Mrs. French is rarely wrong."

Katie offered her hand once again. "Nonetheless, I wish you good luck, Mr. French."

"And the same to you, ma'am."

She bade him good day, then started back toward the hotel, pondering the chance encounter and wondering why she felt as if something were about to change because of it. What could it possibly change? She was almost guaranteed to have won a place in the primaries.

And she and Ben were still estranged.

The Idaho Daily Statesman
Boise, Idaho
Thursday Morning
September 7, 1916

French and Rafferty Race Undecided as Count Drags

With complete returns in from 375 of the most populous precincts in both the northern and southern parts of the state, the results of the Republican primaries confirm the forecasts made in Wednesday morning's Statesman as to the Republican state ticket. Wednesday night's returns account for about 29,300 votes, which is held to be more than three-fourths of the total ballots.

One place on the ticket is still in doubt. In the contest for the second of the two at-large congressional seats,

> Katherine Jones Rafferty has 12,678 votes to her credit, and Burton L. French has 12,084. This close race, with a difference of only 594 votes between the two candidates, will probably have to wait on an official count for a decision.

＊━≡◈≡━＊

After six days in Boise City, one thing was undeniably clear to Ben: He would never be able to carry off this farce until the baby was born in the spring. It was too hard to pretend whenever others were around and even harder to be alone with Katie. He would never be able to continue feigning happiness and contentment for the rest of the campaign. He wouldn't be able to go to Washington and make believe there was nothing amiss in their marriage.

Marriage? They didn't have a marriage. They were two miserable people sharing a hotel room. That was all.

He wondered when he would stop loving her. When would the hope die completely? When would he look at her and be able to think fondly on the past without wishing for more?

Ben spared a glance at the others around the breakfast table. They were gathered once again in the hotel dining room, the five of them. As usual, Sophia and Penelope were talking about Sophia's move to Washington, and as usual, Geoffrey was observing Sophia with an affectionate gaze. Katie wasn't participating in the conversation. She was turned toward the window, staring into space, obviously as lost in thought as Ben had been moments before.

His chest tightened at the sight of her, so lovely in the golden sunlight spilling through the windows. She was wearing a white toque decorated with several osprey feathers. It wasn't a particularly pretty hat, yet on Katie it took on a beauty of its own. Her dress was also white, the simple tubular skirt elaborately swathed in extra fabric around the legs and draped vertically down the back with a black satin scarf.

Katie looked sophisticated, every inch the height of current fashion, a woman suited to be a candidate for Congress. But Ben couldn't help wishing she were wearing bright pink cycling bloomers instead.

He smiled to himself, remembering how shocked Matthew and Sophia had been the day Katie had shown up in such an outfit. They'd thought her outrageous. So had he, for that matter, and he'd loved her for her very outrageousness. How he missed that lighthearted Katie. She'd become so serious since entering this race for the Congress.

Or maybe—his own smile faded—it was marrying him that had made her so serious, caused her to forget how to laugh. Maybe he was at fault for her unhappiness. Maybe once they were apart, her sparkle would come back.

Dearest Katie. Wonderful, madcap Katie. What's happened to you? What's happened to us?

"Great Scott!" Geoffrey exclaimed as he jumped up from his chair, drawing all eyes to him. "It's Mother!" Their gazes swung toward the entrance of the dining room as Geoffrey hurried forward. "Mother, we weren't expecting you. How did you get here?"

Eugenia Rudyard was a buxom, imposing woman of uncertain years. Her manner of dress was stylish but under-stated—except for the enormous hat crowning her head. "I came by train, of course," she said in a deep, rich voice as she approached the table, using her closed parasol like a cane. "Don't look so surprised, Geoffrey. I've traveled many places without you, you know." She winked at him, then looked at each person seated around the table. Finally she dropped a kiss on Penelope's cheek. "Hello, dear one." Then she kissed Katie in the same manner. "You've been busy, my girl."

Katie nodded. "I know."

Eugenia glanced back at her son expectantly.

On cue he began, "Mother, may I introduce Katie's husband, Ben Rafferty?"

Ben had already risen from his chair, and he took Eugenia Rudyard's proffered hand. "How do you do, Mrs. Rudyard?"

"Quite well, thank you." The older woman seemed to look at him with approval. "It's a pleasure to meet you at last, Mr. Rafferty. I've heard your name from Katie often these many years."

"Likewise, madam."

"And this is Ben's sister, Sophia Rafferty," Geoffrey contin-ued, his tone softening.

Eugenia smiled. "Geoffrey and Penny have mentioned you

in their letters, dear girl, and I expect we shall get on together famously."

"Thank you, Mrs. Rudyard. This is an honor."

"Sit down, Mother," Penelope urged, "and tell us why you've come here instead of attending the convention in Atlantic City."

"I'd much rather be here with Katie than listening to Mr. Wilson spout his support for suffrage while refusing to do anything concrete to bring it about." She settled onto the chair Ben pulled out for her. "And I understand a celebration will soon be in order."

Katie lifted her shoulders. "It's not decided yet. I could still lose." Her glanced flicked toward Ben, then away before he could read the thoughts behind them.

Suddenly he longed to be able to read Katie's mind, as he'd been able to do not so very long ago.

The Idaho Daily Statesman
Boise, Idaho
Friday Morning
September 8, 1916

Primary Aftermaths

An official count of the vote cast in the recent primary election will be made within the next 10 or

12 days at the secretary of state's office. The vote must be canvassed within 15 days after election, but the board may begin its work within 10 days if it wishes.

* ❈ *

As the train rushed north toward Homestead, Katie stared out the window, lost in thought.

She recognized the spot where the Susan B had broken down. At the time, she'd thought she wanted independence. She'd been wrong. She'd thought she could keep the love she felt for Ben to herself. She'd been wrong about that, too.

"Katie, my girl, we need to talk."

She turned toward Eugenia Rudyard, seated across from her in the nearly empty passenger car. Ben had retreated to the dining car before they'd pulled out of Boise. The others in their party had disappeared, too. Katie suspected Eugenia had sent them away.

"You aren't happy about this election, are you?" the older woman asked.

She'd managed to keep up the pretense for days, but there was something about the way Eugenia looked at her that knocked down her defenses. "I don't think I want to win." Ashamed of herself for admitting it, she quickly glanced away.

"And why not, pray tell?"

Instead of answering the question, Katie whispered, "I should want to. I know I should want to."

Eugenia took hold of Katie's hand. "But you don't."

She shook her head, keeping her eyes averted. They were nearing Homestead. They would leave the river canyon soon and enter Long Bow Valley. They were almost home.

Home. She longed to be home.

"*Why* should you want to be elected, Katie?"

She blinked away sudden tears. "I owe it to all the people who have supported me. I owe it to other women. I owe it to you and Penny and Geoffrey."

Eugenia's grasp tightened. "What do you owe to yourself?"

She met the older woman's gentle gaze once again, not knowing how to answer.

"It's no crime to love your husband, my girl. In fact, it's preferable."

"I never meant to marry. I was going to remain single, like Miss Anthony. I was going to serve the cause with everything in me. I was going to be so devoted, so . . ." She shook her head, unable to continue as another wave of tears overtook her.

"Oh, my dear," Eugenia crooned softly as she cupped Katie's chin in her glove-covered fingers. "I know how much you've admired Miss Anthony. I admired her, too. I was privileged to know her for many years, and she was a remarkable woman. But she was the first to recognize not everyone was meant to be like her. We each have to do our part in our own way."

Katie swallowed the hot lump in her throat. "But I was

always so sure what I was supposed to do. I was so sure I was fulfilling God's will for my life."

Eugenia's hand fell from Katie's chin as she turned her gaze out the window, as Katie had done before, and she sighed softly. "I have long been a supporter of woman's suffrage. I have always believed in the perfect equality of women as a God-given right. So did my dear husband." She looked at Katie. "When Mr. Rudyard was alive, we worked together for the cause of suffrage without ever leaving Massachusetts, and we were no less important than those who traveled far and wide."

Katie felt a flutter of hope, a feeling she hadn't known in weeks. "What about my supporters? They've counted on me. They'll be disappointed."

"Since you respect her so much, Katie, allow me to quote Miss Anthony to you." Eugenia's voice deepened as she continued: " 'Every woman in her own home can be a teacher of this great principle of equality. She can instruct her husband and her children in the ways of justice toward all. But for the good and true woman in all the homes, but for the loyalty of these home women, who never speak in public but who in a quiet way are teaching this gospel in season and out of season, we who stand at the front, could never have stood here. We would have had no constituency but for this silent, magnificent army of women in the homes throughout the nation.' " Eugenia drew a deep breath. "What good is the freedom to choose what is right for ourselves if we fail to exercise that freedom? Isn't it possible your calling is closer to home, my dear? And if it is, that's where you should be."

Katie's heart raced faster than the wheels on the locomotive. It wasn't merely what Eugenia had said. It was what all the people who loved her had been saying in various ways for weeks.

"What greater thing could I have accomplished than you?"

"We could've found a way to make it work, Katie, if you'd only tried to meet me halfway."

"Sometimes life makes us choose betwixt two things. . . . Times like those, kitten, you'll have t' follow your heart or your head, and only you can figure out which is right."

"Maybe that's the problem, Katie. You still think I'm Benjie. Well, I'm not. I haven't been Benjie for a long time."

"Do you love him?"

"I never expected you to be some docile homemaker with nothing more on your mind than what to fix for supper. I only wanted you to love me."

"I only wanted you to love me. . . ."

At last she understood what her heart had been trying to tell her for so long. Eugenia was right. What good was the freedom to choose if she failed to exercise that freedom, if she failed to answer when God called her in a new direction? It *was* possible that her calling was closer to home than she'd thought. She didn't have to model her entire life after Miss Anthony. She could make a difference in her own way.

And her home was with Ben. Ben and their baby. She wanted them both.

Katie stood suddenly. Ben. She had to find Ben.

The train whistle blew. From the back of the passenger car, the conductor shouted, "Comin' into Homestead, folks."

She knew what she wanted, knew what she'd always wanted, if only she hadn't been too stubborn to see. She had to find Ben and tell him she knew what mattered most. She had to tell him she was ready to come home.

She had to tell Ben that she loved him.

TWENTY-FOUR

It looked as if there were few doubters left in Homestead. Even Phillip Carson was at the station to congratulate Katie on her apparent win in the primary. The town band played with enthusiasm as travelers disembarked from the train, and a rousing cheer went up when Katie appeared on the steps of the main passenger car.

From the caboose, Ben watched as his wife was swept into the crowd of celebrants. He knew he should make his way to her, stand beside her, return smiles and handshakes along with her. But he couldn't. Let Mrs. Rudyard and the other committee members help Katie. He couldn't do it anymore. He was through.

Unnoticed, he stepped to the ground and followed the tracks to Barber Street, then walked toward the newspaper office. He'd caught a glimpse of Harvey Trent on the station platform, so he knew he'd have the office to himself, at least for a while.

Homestead was deserted. Signs were up in the shop-windows on Main Street: Closed. The proprietors and their customers were at the depot, welcoming home a triumphant daughter of the town.

Good for Katie. He was glad for her. She would have all their support during the coming weeks. She wouldn't miss him. Geoffrey knew as much as he—probably more—about running a campaign. Penelope and Sophia were tireless workers and full of enthusiasm for the cause. And now Katie would have Eugenia Rudyard, a woman with vast experience in political circles, to help her. No, Katie wouldn't miss Ben.

He fished in his pocket for the key to the office, then unlocked the door and entered. He hung his hat on the rack before walking to his desk, where he riffled through the stacks of paper awaiting his attention. Nothing urgent. Nothing of interest. Nothing to take his mind off Katie.

He sank onto the chair.

A separation from her husband might harm Katie's election chances. That would be one way of keeping her in Homestead, he supposed, but it wasn't the way he wanted to keep her here. She had to *want* to stay—and she didn't.

No, he would have to go on sleeping on the sofa in the parlor of their hotel suite whenever Katie was in Homestead. Her campaign would keep her on the road often over the next nine weeks. Ben could use the *Herald* as his reason for not accompanying her on the trips. The others on the committee would suspect something was amiss between them, if they didn't already, but it would be up to Katie to explain.

He muttered softly to himself as he got up from the chair.

Why didn't he feel better, now that the decision was made? Why couldn't he at least feel angry instead of empty?

He paced to the window and stared into the street. The days had grown shorter as summer ended and fall began, and afternoon shadows were already long. Out in the valley, farmers were busy harvesting their crops. By the end of next month they could conceivably see their first snow. Before Thanksgiving Katie would leave for Washington. Would her pregnancy be showing by then? Would he be able to tell that their child was growing in her womb?

Still muttering to himself, he headed out the door, not bothering to lock up behind him. Long strides carried him toward Pony Creek, then away from town with the unconscious hope that he could walk away from the trouble in his heart, something he'd been trying—and failing—to do for weeks now.

<hr />

It seemed a lifetime before Katie had the opportunity to escape the well-wishers. Protesting weariness, she went first to the hotel, but Ben wasn't in their rooms. So she slipped down the back staircase and out through the kitchen door, wanting to avoid seeing anyone else. She had to talk to Ben. It was too urgent to wait. She had to see him and tell him what she'd discovered on the train.

The door to the newspaper office was ajar. Katie stepped inside, her heart pounding. "Ben?"

He didn't answer, but he had to be here. His hat was hanging on the rack.

She moved toward the back room. "Ben?"

But he wasn't there, either. The windowless room stood silent and empty except for the printing press, a large table, and stacks of newspapers.

She wondered if he might have gone out back to use the privy; then she heard the front door open and close. She turned and hurried toward the front office.

"Ben, I've been looking for—" She stopped when she saw who was standing there. "Blanche." Disappointment was evident in her voice. "It's you."

"You must be proud of yourself, Katie, now that you've won." The schoolmarm sounded shrill, her words echoing in the small office.

"More surprised than anything." Katie glanced out the window, impatient to find Ben. "Have you seen my husband? I was looking for him. We got separated at the station and—"

"They don't know how you betrayed them." Blanche took a step forward, swinging her small black handbag in front of her by its purse strings, her movements agitated, disconnected.

Katie frowned, confused by the comment. "Whom did I betray?"

"You've pulled the wool over their eyes, but not mine. Not mine, I tell you."

Katie stiffened. She'd heard this babble from Blanche Coleson before. She didn't intend to listen to it again. "Perhaps you should leave now."

"How long will you continue to lie to them, pretending to be what you're not?" Blanche moved toward her, shouting now. *Jezebel!* She swung her handbag, striking Katie on the shoulder before she could move. "Liar!"

Katie raised her arms to protect herself. "Blanche, what are you doing? Stop it!"

"I won't let you lie to them. I won't let you. They didn't believe me when I told them you were failing the movement, that you don't truly believe, but they ignored me because you are rich and pretty and educated." She swung her handbag again, this time missing her mark as Katie ducked. "They ignored me because of that man you married, because of what he wrote in his paper. Lies."

A chill gripped Katie as she continued backing away. There was something eerie about the other woman's eyes that struck terror in her heart. She suspected that Blanche wouldn't hear anything she said, but she had to try. With a note of calm she didn't feel, she said, "Why don't we go over to Zoe's and talk about it, Blanche? I'm sure we can straighten this out. It's just a misunderstanding." She tried to move toward the door, but Blanche blocked her way.

"I won't let you do this. And I won't let them ignore me." She raised her handbag again.

Katie was certain she could outrun the schoolmarm if she could make it to the door. She inched her way toward the press room, thinking the back door might be easiest. Blanche followed, continuing to mutter and mumble and sometimes shout words of accusation and complaint. Katie knew she was trapped in that building with a madwoman, and her fear increased with each step she took.

"I'm going to stop you," Blanche threatened darkly. "I'm going to stop you both."

Katie stumbled over a stack of newspapers on the floor.

She fell backward, caught herself, twisted around, and started to rise. But before she could get up, something much harder than a woman's handbag cracked against her skull.

Pain exploded.

Then there was nothing but darkness.

＊—＝◆＝—＊

Ben slowly made his way back toward town, his thoughts no more settled now than when he'd left the newspaper office. The walk had failed to make his decision about ending his marriage any easier to live with.

If only he didn't love Katie so much. If only he didn't continue to want to hold her, to hear her laugh, to see the sparkle in her eyes of brown. If only he didn't believe in the sanctity of marriage, that God had made him and Katie one flesh. If only he could make her see how wrong she was.

He was almost to Main Street when he heard the clanging of the church bell. Startled by the sound, unusual on a weekday, he quickened his pace. Then he saw black smoke billowing out of the roof and windows of the *Homestead Herald* office. He broke into a run. He'd nearly reached the building when Blanche Coleson, coughing and choking, stumbled through the doorway.

He heard sounds of the approaching fire wagon but didn't look to see how close it was. He grabbed Blanche by the arm and pulled her off the sidewalk and into the street.

"What happened?" he shouted at her, his glance darting to the building, where he could see orange flames licking at the walls of the front office.

"You did it. You did it. It should have been me they listened to. It's your fault."

His gaze returned to the woman who was struggling to get loose. She struck him with her free arm. There was a wild, crazed look in her eyes.

"You should be in there with her!" Blanche shrieked. "Why aren't you in there with her?"

Alarm tightened his belly as he gripped both of her arms in his hands, yanking her toward him. "Who? Is someone inside? Who is it?"

Blanche laughed hysterically.

"Oh, dear God. No." He shoved the schoolmarm away and bolted for the burning building. Someone shouted at him to stay back, but he didn't heed the warning. Holding up an arm to protect his face from the heat and smoke, he rushed inside. "Katie!"

Panic made every second agony as he tried to find his wife amid the dense smoke and flickering tongues of fire that filled the front office.

"Katie!"

God, help me. Covering his mouth and nose with his hand, he pushed forward, continuing to pray. *Please, God, don't let me be too late. Help me find her. Help me.*

As if in answer to his prayers, he tripped over Katie's feet. She was lying half hidden beneath the printing press. He knelt beside her inert form. "Katie." *God, please.* "Katie, I'm here."

He scooped her into his arms and carried her toward the back of the building, moving blindly through the thick smoke. When he found the back door, he didn't waste time trying to unlock it. He simply kicked it with every ounce of strength he had. The sounds of splintering wood could be heard above the crackling of the fire, the shouts of men, and the hiss of steam as water from the fire truck hit the flames.

Once in the daylight, Ben looked down at Katie. Her eyes remained closed. Her face was blackened by smoke, and there was an ugly matting of blood and hair on the side of her head. She lay as still as death in his arms.

"Don't leave me, Katie. Please don't leave me." *O God, don't take her from me.*

⊷⊱◈⊰⊷

Her lungs hurt. Her throat hurt. Her head hurt. Everything hurt.

"I think she's waking up again," someone said.

She should know that voice, but she couldn't place it.

"Open your eyes, Katie. Look at us."

Her eyelids felt like sandpaper.

"That's it. Open your eyes."

Everything appeared fuzzy, and the lamplight hurt. She blinked. Once. Then twice more. Her vision began to clear, and she made out Tom McLeod's face hovering above her. Beside him stood his wife, Fanny.

He smiled. "Welcome back. Think you'll stay with us this time?"

"Dr. Tom, what—" She was overtaken by a fit of coughing. Her throat felt raw, as if she'd swallowed lye soap. When she tried to sit up, pain exploded behind her eyes.

The doctor put his hand on her shoulder to keep her down. "Easy now. That's what happened last time. Give yourself a minute or two."

"Last time?" She closed her eyes again, then took a deep breath and let it out.

"You've had a nasty blow to the head, Katie. You woke up once before but passed out again. Do you remember what happened to you?"

Her mind remained blank. She couldn't recall anything beyond a moment ago. It was a terrifying feeling to have no memory.

"Relax, Katie. Give it time."

They'd been in Boise. She remembered that. The election. It looked as though she'd won the election. They'd come back on the train. When? When had they come back? Today? Was it still today? She'd been looking for someone. Ben. She'd been looking for Ben. She'd gone to the newspaper office to talk to Ben.

And then she remembered.

"Blanche." She looked at the doctor. "It was Blanche."

He nodded. "Sheriff's got her over at the jail. She won't hurt anyone again."

"She tried to kill me?" Katie whispered the question, as if doing so would keep the words from being true.

"Looks that way."

She remembered the crazed way the schoolmarm had been talking. She remembered Blanche saying she was going to stop them. Stop them both. Fresh panic ignited as she grabbed the doctor's arm. "Where's Ben?"

"It's all right, Katie. He's the one who saved you. He didn't

327

move from your side until after you came to last time. Sat here for hours."

Her throat tightened as she fought hot tears.

"I finally told him he had to get some air and some rest or I was going to lock him out of my clinic."

"I need to see Ben, Dr. Tom." She tried to rise a second time.

He eased her back on the bed. "He'll return before long, I'm sure. You just rest easy."

"What about the baby?" She covered her stomach with both hands. "Was the baby harmed?"

His expression grew serious. "I can't say for certain, Katie. Your body suffered a serious shock. But you don't show any signs of miscarrying, and I'd say chances are good everything will be all right." He patted her shoulder. "I've done what I can. We'll have to leave the rest in God's hands."

She closed her eyes. *Don't let me lose Ben's baby. Please, Lord. I've been willful and stupid, but please don't let Ben and the baby suffer because of me.*

"You rest now, Katie," Fanny McLeod said. "Someone will be here if you need anything."

"I need Ben," Katie whispered in reply, but neither the doctor nor his wife seemed to hear her.

— ⊱ ❖ ⊰ —

A full moon shed a silvery white illumination over the land. Lamplight twinkled from the windows of houses in town and farmhouses in the valley.

Ben looked down at the picture-perfect setting, then

turned his back on it and stared at the building site. The workmen had already erected the frame. With a little imagination he could see each room of the house he'd planned to build here.

But it meant nothing without Katie. In one horrible moment that afternoon, he'd discovered—almost too late— that what he wanted was meaningless without Katie. He'd discovered that God hadn't called him to be right or to demand his wife meet him halfway. God said Ben was to love Katie so much he would lay down his life for her. God said he was to give all, not half.

Those long hours sitting beside her in Dr. Tom's clinic had been the worst hours of his life. She'd looked so pale, so small and helpless. She hadn't moved, had barely breathed. He guessed the good Lord hadn't heard as much from Ben in all his life as He had in the last few hours. Ben had prayed and pleaded and promised. He'd confessed and asked forgiveness. And finally, he'd trusted Katie and their future to God's sovereign will.

Ben would never forget that wonderful moment when Katie's eyes had fluttered open, when she'd looked at him, her eyes glazed. She'd tried to sit up, then had slumped back on the bed. Dr. Tom had thrown Ben, the Raffertys and the Joneses out of the clinic not long after that, telling them Katie was going to be fine. She wasn't in a coma. She was sleeping.

Ben had started to follow his parents and sister to the hotel but had ended up here instead. And he knew why. He was going to tear it down. This wouldn't be a home if Katie wasn't in it. He'd made God a lot of promises during those hours beside Katie's bed. Now he was going to keep one of them.

He picked up a shovel and placed it over his shoulder. An ax would have done the job faster, but he wasn't going back to town for one. The shovel would have to do. He chose a stud, then readied for his first swing. But he was stopped by the sound of an approaching horse and buggy. He turned around and watched the buggy climb the gentle slope, but he was unable to tell who had sought him here in the middle of the night.

Nothing could have surprised him more than seeing Katie, the white bandage on her head gleaming in the moonlight, step from the buggy. The shovel dropped with a clatter.

Seconds later he cradled her in his arms. "This is crazy," he whispered near her ear. "What are you doing here?"

"I made Sophia bring me."

He tossed another look toward the buggy without relaxing his hold on Katie. His sister was now standing beside it, visible in the moonlight.

"Don't be angry with her," Katie said. "If she hadn't brought me, I'd have come by myself. She knew I meant it."

He tightened his arms, drawing her closer. "I can't believe Dr. Tom let you do this."

"He didn't." She pulled her head back from his chest and looked at him. "He wasn't there. I snuck out."

"Well, I'm taking you right back to the clinic."

Katie shook her head. "Not yet. Please." She touched his forehead with her fingertips. "Soot," she whispered. "Sophia told me about the fire. The newspaper. Everything you've worked for. I'm so sorry."

Funny, he hadn't even thought about the paper. He didn't know if anything had been saved, or if it had all burned to the ground. It hadn't mattered to him while he was sitting beside Katie's bed, praying for her to survive.

"Katie, there's something you need to know. I'm going with you to—"

She placed her index finger over his mouth. "Shh. Don't say anything. Not yet." She glanced toward the skeleton of the house. "Take me over there, Ben."

Gently he lifted her in his arms. She locked her hands behind his neck as he strode toward the house site. He carried her through what would have been the front door and over to the wooden staircase leading to what would have been the second floor. Then he sat down on a step, still holding her in his arms. If he had his way, he would never let go of her again.

━━◆◈◆━━

Katie didn't want him to let go. It was a miracle he still wanted to hold her, a miracle he still loved her. She was the luckiest woman alive, and she knew it.

She drew back slightly so she could see his face, bathed in moonlight. "I was looking for you on the train."

"I was in the caboose."

"I needed to tell you something."

He touched her bandage. "I could've lost you."

"Listen to me, Ben. I've been so wrong. So selfish."

"No, I should have understood."

This time she covered his mouth with the flat of her hand. "Don't interrupt. Please." She frowned, her head aching. It was hard to think, difficult to find the right words to say. "I've realized something over the past week. I've looked at everything idealistically. I've never had to test any of my beliefs. It's all come easily to me."

He kissed the palm of her hand, and she had to fight to ignore the sensations it caused.

"I've never had to risk losing anything, Ben. I've never taken into account any costs. But life is about risks and costs." She moved her hand to his cheek. "I was so busy fighting for freedom for women that I forgot what that freedom meant. I thought the only way to make things happen was to live like someone else."

"Like Susan B. Anthony," he said.

"Yes. Only her life isn't the right one for me. I want my own. I want the life God has given me in His grace and wisdom. I want the Lord in control, not me." She drew a shaky breath. "I want a life with you, Ben. I love you."

Silence seemed to blanket the valley. Crickets and hoot owls hushed. The creek stopped gurgling. The night breeze quieted. All she could hear was the beating of her heart in tempo with Ben's.

"Katie—"

"No, I'm not finished." Her voice softened. "Let me finish." He agreed with a nod.

"You've done all the giving in our marriage." She drew closer to him. "But, Ben, I want to give, too. Remember when you told me marriage was about compromise? I want us to compromise. I want us to find what's best for both of us. I think we can. Don't you?"

His smile was tender, loving. "Yes, I do."

"And, Ben, I want this baby more than anything." She took his right hand and placed it on her belly. "If it's a boy, I want him to grow up like his father. I want him to judge people by who they are on the inside. I want him to have the courage to go after what he wants, no matter how hard it is. I want him to be patient and gentle, just like you. I want him to love, to laugh, and to be strong in his own beliefs. And if it's a girl—" she grinned—"I want her to be like her father, too."

"Are you finished?" he asked after a moment's silence.

She shook her head, ignoring the throbbing it caused. "I want you to know how sorry I am. I hope you can forgive me."

He waited a heartbeat. *"Now* are you finished?"

She nodded.

He drew her closer against him, staring down into her eyes. "That's a lot of thinking for a head that took such a hard blow. Now it's my turn. I came out here to tear down this house. It wouldn't mean anything to me without you. I've been stubborn and angry. I wanted you to want what I want."

"I do, Ben. That's what I've been trying to tell you."

"I tried to take away your dreams and ambitions."

She cradled his head between her hands. "I'm going to withdraw from the race. If the final count shows I've won, I'm going to refuse to continue. Mr. French is the better candidate, and he'll support the amendment. He told me so."

"You don't have to do that, Katie. I'll never make you choose my way again."

Was it possible to love him more with each passing moment?

Katie blinked away sudden tears. "Papa told me we always have to make choices in life, Ben. I want to make the right choice this time."

"Ah, Katie," he whispered, brushing her hair away from her face.

She loved the sound of her name when he said it like that.

He rested his forehead against hers, still holding her gaze. "I think there'll be plenty of time to sort things through, find out what's best for all of us—you, me, and the baby. Right now, there're just two things I want you to do before I take you back to the clinic, where you belong."

Her heart began to hammer in double time.

"First, tell me again that you love me."

She tried to smile, despite the tears. "That's easy. I love you, Benjamin Rafferty. I'll love you the rest of my life and then some." She swallowed the hot lump in her throat. "What's the second thing?"

She could feel the warmth of his breath on her skin. She could smell his wonderfully masculine scent, a hint of sweat and bay rum cologne mixed with smoke and soot. She could see the love in his eyes, blue eyes turned black in the night.

"The second's easy, too," he whispered. "Just kiss me, Katie."

And so she did.

⊷ ≡♦≡ ⊷

The Homestead Triweekly Herald
Homestead, Idaho
Wednesday Morning
November 3, 1926

Katherine Jones Rafferty Wins District Seat in Idaho House of Representatives; Opponent Matthew Jacobs Concedes

The landslide victory of Katherine Jones Rafferty of Homestead was apparent within hours of the polls closing yesterday. An active leader in the Idaho Chapter, National Council of Women Voters, and an advocate of women's rights on state and national levels for more than a decade, Mrs. Rafferty has pledged to fight for better schools for Idaho's children; fairer labor laws, particularly in regard to women; an improved north-south highway to better handle increased automobile traffic; and support for Idaho farming and lumber industries.

When the state legislature is not in session in Boise, Mrs. Rafferty will return to Homestead, where she resides with her husband, Benjamin Rafferty, owner and editor of The Homestead Triweekly Herald, and their three children: Anna Kate (9), Lawrence Michael (7), and Norma Sue (5).

Here to celebrate Mrs. Rafferty's victory are Justice and Mrs. Geoffrey Rudyard of Washington, D.C. Mrs. Rudyard, the former Sophia Rafferty, is well known as the second woman elected to the U.S. House of Representatives and is now completing her third and final term of office. The Rudyards have one son, Benjamin, three months of age.

BIBLIOGRAPHY

American Women's History: An A to Z of People, Organizations, Issues, and Events by Doris Weatherford, Prentice Hall.

Born for Liberty, A History of Women in America by Sara M. Evans, The Free Press.

Failure Is Impossible: Susan B. Anthony in Her Own Words by Lynn Sherr, Times Books.

History of Idaho by Leonard J. Arrington, University of Idaho Press.

Jailed for Freedom, American Women Win the Vote by Doris Stevens, NewSage Press.

Two Paths to Women's Equality by Janet Zollinger Giele, Twayne Publishers.

10 Lies the Church Tells Women by J. Lee Grady, Charisma House.

FROM THE AUTHOR

Dear Friends:

When I wrote my first novel in 1981, I wanted to prove I could write and sell the type of fiction I liked best without including those things I found personally objectionable (coarse language, gratuitous and explicit sex/violence, etc.). I succeeded in doing so, selling my first book and those that followed.

But as time went on, I also began to compromise my ideals, giving in to the demands of the market in the name of success until there was little to nothing about my books that would distinguish them from those written by someone who didn't know Christ. With each compromise I widened the chasm between myself and my Savior, a chasm I created with my own choices. But God is faithful even when we are faithless. He never took His hand off me, and little by little and ever so gently, He drew me back into fellowship with Him.

Catching Katie is a book I first wrote in 1995. When the opportunity arose to take the delightful characters of Katie and Ben and rewrite their love story for HeartQuest, I was thrilled. I love second chances, perhaps because God, in His mercy and grace, has given me so many of them. The book you now hold in your hand is the end result of this particular second chance. May it—and everything I write in the future—be pleasing in His sight.

In His glorious grip,

Robin Lee Hatcher (2003)

POSTSCRIPT

Researching the American woman's suffrage movement during the early part of this century was a fascinating and enlightening experience. When I was in school, women's history was not a part of the general curriculum. I hope that's no longer true, for it's an important part of our past as a nation and especially so to women.

Attempting to be true to historical dates and events while still writing an entertaining novel has its challenges. There were so many admirable and interesting individuals who fought for the enfranchisement of all American women during the second decade of the twentieth century, and there were several interrelated organizations that took different roads to the same end. Christian women played an important role in these organizations and in the ultimate passage of the 19th Amendment ("The right of citizens of the United States to vote shall not be denied or abridged by the United States or by any State on account of sex."). If I have erred in regard to any of these individuals or organizations, I beg the reader's indulgence. The fault is solely my own.

Please note that I have taken creative license in having Katie Jones Rafferty declare her candidacy for the United States House of Representatives. No woman ran for Congress on the Republican ticket in Idaho in 1916 (Burton French won the Republican primary and was then elected to office.). However, a woman was elected to the U.S. House in 1916: Jeanette Rankin from Montana (Montana was one of the twelve enfranchised states at the time.). Also note that my portrayal of Mr. French is entirely from my own imagination.

RLH (1996)

Author Robin Lee Hatcher, winner of the Christy Award for Excellence in Christian Fiction and the RITA Award for Best Inspirational Romance, has written over thirty-five contemporary and historical novels and novellas. There are more than 5 million copies of her novels in print, and she has been published in fourteen countries. Her first hardcover release, *The Forgiving Hour,* was optioned for film in 1999. Robin is a past president/CEO of Romance Writers of America, a professional writers organization with over eight thousand members worldwide. In recognition of her efforts on behalf of literacy, Laubach Literacy International named the Robin Award in her honor.

Robin and her husband, Jerry, live in Boise, Idaho, where they are active in their church and Robin leads a women's Bible study. Thanks to two grown daughters, Robin is now a grandmother of four ("an extremely young grandmother," she hastens to add). She enjoys travel, the theater, golf, and relaxing in the beautiful Idaho mountains. She and Jerry share their home with Delilah the Persian cat, Tiko the Shetland sheepdog, and Misty the Border collie.

Robin welcomes letters written to her at P.O. Box 4722, Boise, ID 83711-4722 or through her Web site at www.robinleehatcher.com.

ROBIN LEE HATCHER
From her heart . . . to yours

RIBBON
OF YEARS
hardcover ISBN 0-8423-4009-2

Standing at the edge of her dreams, Miriam passionately embraces the future. Through tears and joy her ordinary life becomes a remarkable journey as she impacts others in miraculous ways.

"This poignant view of one woman's life is a superb read, and one I am glad I did not miss!"—**Romance Reader's Connection**

"Keep tissues handy. Miriam's life isn't sugarcoated, but a testament to triumph over adversity."—**CBA Marketplace**

*f*IRSTBORN
hardcover ISBN 0-8423-4010-6 · softcover ISBN 0-8423-5557-X

Erika's worst fear is realized when her well-kept secret shows up on her doorstep. As she reaches out to the daughter she gave up for adoption nearly twenty-two years ago, her husband pulls away, leaving Erika with an impossible choice.

"This is a well-written inspirational novel."
—**Publishers Weekly**

"Robin is a gifted writer whose novels unfailingly stir and challenge readers' hearts."—**Francine Rivers**

Turn the page for an
exciting preview from
ROBIN LEE HATCHER'S
BOOK

Speak to me of Love

Upon entering the house, Faith found herself cloaked in a dim, gray light. The windows in each room had been shrouded by heavy draperies, shutting out the sunlight that was so abundant in a Wyoming summer. Faith wondered if someone had recently passed away, then thought not. There was a permanence about it all, a look that said little had changed here in years. An ominous feeling shivered up her spine, and she wanted nothing more than to turn and leave.

Cowards die many times before their deaths.

Parker stopped and rapped on a door.

"Yes?" a deep voice called from the other side.

"Got a minute, Drake?" Parker didn't wait for a reply. He turned the knob and opened the door, drawing Faith with him as he entered the room. "This little lady is Faith Butler. She'd like a word with you." He gave her elbow a squeeze, then stepped back into the hallway and closed the door.

As in the rest of the house, this room was bathed in shades of gray and black, these windows, too, hidden behind heavy draperies. Faith could see she was in a library. The walls were lined with shelves and shelves of books. The only light came from a lamp, turned low, on the desk. Beyond it, she made out the form of a man seated in a chair, out of reach of the lamp's light.

Drake Rutledge rose. His shadow appeared exceedingly tall and threatening. "What is it you want?" He sounded angry.

Her mouth went dry, and she feared her knees would buckle.

"Well?" he demanded.

Don't get stage fright now, Faith. Remember why you came.

"Speak up, madam, or get out."

She drew a quick breath. "Mr. Rutledge, I've come to seek employment as your cook and housekeeper."

"I have no need of either."

"But I have need of a job." She stepped forward, determination driving out fear, if only temporarily. "Mr. Rutledge, my little girl is sick. The doctor says if she travels, she could die. No, he says she will die. I must find work and a place to live until she's well again. Please, sir, I'm desperate. I'm not asking for charity. I'll work as hard as anyone else on your ranch."

A long silence followed. Then Drake Rutledge stepped around the desk, coming toward her with intimidating strides. His sheer height made her want to draw back from him, but she held her ground.

"I don't believe you belong here." His voice was low, resentful.

She tilted her head, staring up at him.

His shoulders were broad. She could see that he wore a suit, as if dressed to go out for an evening. His hair was dark—black, she imagined—and long, reaching his shoulders. His face, bathed in shadow upon shadow, seemed harsh and frightening. In the anemic lamplight, she saw that he wore a patch over his right eye.

Like a pirate. She subdued a shiver.

For a long time, neither spoke, neither moved. Faith's heart pounded a riotous beat in her chest. Never in her life had she felt such rage as that which emanated from this man. It was as palpable as a white-hot fire, singeing her skin.

Finally, he took a step back from her. "I think it's time for you to go, Mrs. Butler."

"But . . . but what about the job? You haven't told me if you'll hire me."

He leaned forward. "Do you want to work for me, madam?"

She managed to hold her ground once again. "No, but I have no other choice. I'll not let my daughter die for lack of a roof over her head or food on the table. And I won't have my children living over a saloon, which seems to be my only other choice of employment in Dead Horse." Suddenly, her courage evaporated, replaced by desperation. Tears flooded her eyes as she extended a hand in supplication, nearly touching his chest. "Please, Mr. Rutledge. Becca's only five years old. Please help us."

There was another lengthy silence; then he cursed softly and stepped around her, heading across the room. "You're only cooking and cleaning until your daughter's healthy. Tell Parker to give you and your children a couple of rooms on the third floor." He yanked open the door. "And stay out of my way, Mrs. Butler, for as long as you're here."

Then he was gone.

Faith drew in a deep breath and let it out slowly, scarcely able to comprehend what had happened. She'd achieved that for which she'd come. She'd found a place to live and a way to support her children until Becca was well again.

Thank You, Lord.

She left the library and walked toward the front of the house.

When her fingers alighted on the doorknob, she paused and glanced behind her, halfway expecting to find Drake Rutledge standing in the shadows, watching her.

He was a man, take him for all in all,
I shall not look upon his like again.

But she would look upon him again, and instinct told her he was not like any man she'd known. She felt another shiver, this one of

apprehension for what the next few weeks might bring.

From the landing on the second floor, Drake listened to the closing of the front door. Then he moved to the window overlooking the yard and surreptitiously pushed the draperies aside so he could peer down.

Faith Butler appeared a moment later, out from beneath the porch awning. She stopped when she reached the buggy and looked back at the house.

Her hair was red, the color of hot coals before they turned white. Red without a hint of orange, bright in the morning sunlight. Her bustled gown was striped in shades of gold and brown. She was small and perfectly shaped.

And she was beautiful.

His fingers tightened on the draperies.

He'd known she was beautiful, even in the dimly lit library. Even her fragrance—soft, tantalizing, womanly—had been exquisite. But he hadn't known the extent of her loveliness until this moment.

What had possessed him to tell her she could stay at the Jagged R? He didn't need a cook or somebody cleaning up after him, and he certainly didn't need a woman in his house causing him grief. Experience had taught him that women, particularly beautiful women, weren't to be trusted.

Yet there'd been something about the way Faith Butler had stood before him—afraid but not fleeing—that had kept him from sending her away. There'd been something courageous in her stance that had given him reason to pause. But it had been the quiet note of discouragement in her voice that had been his downfall.

Just then, Rick Telford, Dead Horse's doctor, strode into view, coming from the direction of the barn. Although they'd never met, Drake recognized Rick from his previous visits to the ranch. With scarcely a word to Faith, the doctor helped her into the buggy, then climbed up beside her, took the reins in his hands, and slapped the leather straps against the horse's rump. The buggy jerked forward, quickly carrying the beautiful woman with the fiery red hair out of sight.

Drake let the draperies fall into place, closing out the light and leaving him in familiar gloom.

She won't stay long. He turned from the window. I'll see that she doesn't.

Coming Soon!

OVER A MILLION BOOKS SOLD!

WILD HEATHER

Olivia Hewes and Randolph Sherbourne are drawn toward a forbidden love that will mean betraying both their families.

DANGEROUS SANCTUARY

Kent Anderson is committed to making Camp Hope a sanctuary for his campers. But when Georgia MacGregor joins his staff, her troubled past threatens to endanger them all.